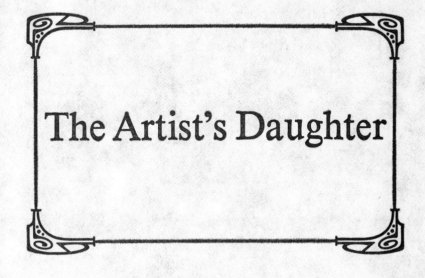

The Artist's Daughter

The Artist's Daughter

by
Leslie O'Grady

St. Martin's Press | New York

To my husband and parents, with thanks.

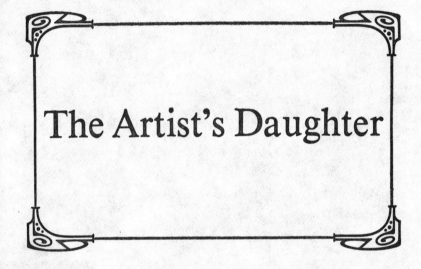

The Artist's Daughter

1

I must have been out of my mind to carry so much money through the streets of London. Yet here I was, coins jangling with every step as I hurried back to my rented rooms at the edge of the St. Giles rookery.

Even the wind, too greedy for April, taunted me for my foolishness by tugging at my skirts as though seeking to pick my pocket. In panic, I thrust my hand down and was relieved to find my purse still there, hard and swollen. Then, I deliberately slowed my pace and resisted the impulse to glance over my shoulder, for I had turned onto New Holborn Street, where every thief could tell what your pockets held just by looking at you.

I should have hired a cab, I scolded myself nervously, but cabs were expensive, and walking was free. Besides, I didn't have far to go now.

As I wove my way between a crush of carriages and pedestrians to reach the terraced house I called home, the familiar cry of "Flowers! Fresh flowers!" rose high above the street's din. Looking up, I saw the gaunt form of Posies, the flower vendor, beseeching an indifferent throng to buy the bright flowers crowded into the large shallow basket she balanced on one hip.

Posies. What a fresh and fanciful name for someone who looked as though she'd been born old.

"Hello," I called. "How's business this morning?"

She brushed a strand of hair off her face with a dirty hand, then set her basket down on the curb. "Good morning to you, Mrs. Nora. Business ain't bad. Care to buy some of me pretties?"

I hesitated, then decided the coin would be well spent if it kept the flower vendor on my side. Posies had the sharpest eyes and ears in the whole rookery. She could tell you who was new to St. Giles, where they came from, and the nature of their game.

"I'll take two bunches. I think Mrs. James would like flowers today."

She looked startled. "Why, that's right nice of you, it is, Mrs. Nora."

Suddenly, as I bent down to choose my flowers, a blur came out of nowhere and rammed into me, so that I nearly fell into the street.

"Oh, no, you don't!" I heard Posies snarl. When I had regained my balance and looked up, she had her hand clamped around a child's wrist, like a hawk with a pigeon in its claw.

"Thought you'd go buzzing Mrs. Nora, did you?"

At the sight of my purse in the boy's hand, I blanched. Even Posies' eyes widened when she grabbed the purse and felt its weight. She returned it to me somewhat reluctantly, and I stuffed it into my pocket before anyone else could notice it.

Posies then turned on the boy, a tiny ragged child who must have been new to his trade, for he stood there and trembled when anyone else would have tried to escape. She shook him. "Didn't your kidsman tell you not to go buzzing Mrs. Nora? You try your lay on her once more, and so help me, Gentleman Harry will eat your ears for breakfast!"

The boy started violently at the mention of Harry's name. "I'm sorry, missus. I won't go buzzin' you no more. I'm sorry. I truly am."

"See that you don't." Posies gave him one last shake, then flung him away.

"He must be all of six years old," I murmured, as the retreating figure narrowly missed being crushed under the wheels of a lumbering dray. "He could use a bath and some hot food, too."

"He can take care of hisself. It's you I worry about, Mrs. Nora." Her face was inches from mine as she hissed, "You shouldn't go walkin' around St. Giles with so much gold. Some as soon slit your throat for a shilling, never mind what you got in there."

I licked my lips nervously.

"Harry's got the word out no one is to touch you," she continued, "but there are some who'd even risk tanglin' with him to get what you got."

"Next time I'll take a cab," I promised.

She stood back. "See that you do. Speakin' of Harry, he's waitin' for you."

I picked up my flowers and paid her. "Thank you. See you tomorrow. And thank you for saving my purse."

"'Bye, Mrs. Nora." Posies gave me a broad wink and moved down the street with the basket balanced on her hip, her cry of, "Flowers! Fresh flowers!" lingering in the air.

As I made my way toward the house, I could see "Gentleman" Harry Leeds leaning against the spiked fence that guarded these respectable houses from the rookery beyond. The cut of his clothes was impeccable, and you could easily mistake him for a gentleman from a distance. But when you moved closer and saw his battered face, his left cheek puckered by vitriol, you knew Harry Leeds was no gentleman.

He was a man who lived by his wits. Although small, like most of his kind, Harry was as light on his feet as a cat, and probably could see in the dark as well. He was the most powerful and feared criminal in St. Giles. I also owed my safety to him.

Harry and I were friends of sorts. We spoke if we happened to meet on the street. We occasionally walked together through the park. He bought me hot potatoes from the street vendor stationed on the corner of New Holborn Street, and I had once gone to a noisy, steamy chophouse with him. But he kept his distance, for there was the unspoken understanding between us that this was all our relationship would ever be. I never even gave a thought to what I would do if Harry demanded more than I was willing to give.

"Good morning, Mrs. Nora," he greeted me, looking me over as if I concealed a weapon. "What did the lad want?"

He missed nothing. "Good morning, Harry. The boy picked my pocket, but Posies caught him, so there's no harm done."

His mouth hardened. "He looked like one of the Shepherd's dippers. I'll have to have a talk with him. The Shepherd knows better than to set his sheep on you, Mrs. Nora."

"Please don't harm the boy."

Harry looked at me thoughtfully for a moment. "You can't save them all, Mrs. Nora."

"I'd try. Their faces haunt me so. Children with old faces."

Harry gave a derisive snort. "Don't waste your sympathy. They look like little angels, but they'd rob their mothers for a crust of bread." When I made no comment, he abruptly changed the subject.

"Flowers from Posies, I see," he said with a smile. Harry Leeds was almost handsome when he smiled.

I smiled back. "One for Mrs. James and one for me."

He rubbed his jaw and looked up at the house, as though assessing its strengths and weaknesses. "You could live in a better drum than this, Mrs. Nora."

"As your mistress, Harry?"

He looked down at me and glowered. "As my *wife!*"

"I am one man's wife already," I reminded him gently, to cool his anger.

"You need a man, Mrs. Nora. You're just a slip of a thing that needs protecting." He eyed me up and down so that his meaning was clear. "What have you got against me? It ain't like I'm a resurrection man like Posies' old man."

I shuddered, wondering what it would be like to be married to a man who dug up corpses and sold them. "I have nothing against you. I value you as a friend."

He grinned slowly, savoring our exchange. "Someday, Mrs. Nora . . ."

"We shall see." I started up the steps, and when I reached the door, I turned. Harry bowed with a flourish, then disappeared. I unlocked the door and went inside.

The dark, narrow foyer always had a stale smell of yesterday's cooking. No matter how hard Mrs. James scrubbed, she could not eradicate the odor. It was as though that smell deliberately clung to remind Mrs. James of her altered circumstances since her husband, the Sergeant, had passed on.

"Miss Fowler, is that you?" a small, wispy voice called from the parlor.

"No, Mrs. James. It's Mrs. Woburn." We always addressed each other formally because Mrs. James thought it added a dignity sorely lacking in our sorrowful situations.

My proprietress, a worried-looking woman in her early forties, suddenly materialized at the parlor door to glare at me.

"I don't know why you bother with the likes of that footpad, Mrs. Woburn." She shuddered delicately. "Miss Fowler says he trains little children to steal, and Madame Leclerc claims he's wanted by the police. Aren't you afraid of him? I am."

"Harry Leeds is no kidsman, Mrs. James," I contradicted her gently, while thinking to myself that Madame Leclerc was so right. "Harry saved me from being beaten and robbed when I first came to live here, and he probably keeps this house safe for Miss Fowler and

Madame Leclerc as well as you and I." I placed the flowers in her hands. "I thought you'd like these."

"Why, Mrs. Woburn. How thoughtful of you." She drifted off toward the kitchen, then suddenly turned and said, "I almost forgot. There's a gentleman upstairs to see you. He didn't leave his name, but he's well-spoken and genteel. As the Sergeant always said, you can judge a man by the way he speaks. I allowed him to wait in your parlor, since Madame Leclerc isn't here to complain."

"A gentleman to see me?" I drew my shawl off and hurried upstairs.

"Who can be calling on me?" I muttered to myself as I hurried down the hall to my rooms. Perhaps it was Dante Rossetti or William Morris or one of my father's many artist friends, so adept at disappearing, then resurfacing. Or perhaps it was even my father himself. My hand trembled in anticipation as I turned the knob.

I burst in, unable to restrain myself any longer. "Father?"

The man seated on the sofa slowly rose and turned to face me.

"Oliver!" The blood drained from my face, and for a moment, the parlor wavered and dissolved.

He smiled. "Hello, Nora. How are you?"

"What are you doing here?"

"Is that any way to greet your husband? And after how many years?"

"Three," I said, eying him warily. He hadn't changed. A pale mustache drooped across his upper lip, and his clothes were of an expensive cut, but his eyes still held the glint of an opportunist.

He sank back down onto the sofa and smiled.

I repeated, "What are you doing here, Oliver? What do you want?"

"I just want to talk to you. You needn't look as though you'd run through that wall, Nora. I won't devour you. I promise."

I stood where I was. "Tell me what you want."

"If you'll sit down."

"I prefer to stand."

Anger flashed across his face, then was gone in an instant. "Stand then." When the silence stretched between us, he broke it with, "Well, so my wife has become a famous writer. All of London is talking about *The Green Tree,* you know."

"I'm hardly famous," I retorted.

Oliver put his hands behind his head and looked around the room. "I should think you could afford better lodgings than this."

I used my shawl to conceal my purse—filled with royalties my publisher had given to me just this morning—as I removed it from my pocket. "They suit my purpose," I replied.

"Oh, come now, Nora. Three miserable rooms on the edge of a thieves' den? That's not your style at all."

I lay my purse on the desk. "They're the best I can afford."

"And where are all your grand friends?" There was no mistaking the mockery in his voice. "The Rossettis, the Morrises . . ."

"Many drawing rooms are closed to me since I left you," I admitted quite frankly. "My father's friends have always welcomed me, but I don't wish to make them choose between us, so I live alone. And Georgina Burne-Jones—you remember her; the one who never liked you—comes to visit me sometimes."

More silence. Then he said, "You're still very beautiful, Nora. A bit thin, perhaps . . ."

"And you look . . . prosperous," I replied, taking in his expensive suit and the gold ring winking on his hand. "You have generous friends."

He startled me by jumping up, but he made no move toward me. "Come back to me, Nora."

I recoiled before I could stop myself. "I will never go back to you. Never."

"We can settle our differences. I love you, Nora."

My laugh sounded bitter to my own ears. "Have you forgotten the arguments, the beatings? Have you forgotten how you made me lose our baby? I haven't."

"There will be other children."

I looked at him in disgust. "Oliver, I must ask you to leave."

An angry flush mottled his pale skin. "I could force you to come back to me."

I laughed. "What will you do? Kidnap me and lock me away? This is 1863, not 1800."

Rage burned in his eyes now. "Stop mocking me! All you've ever done is belittle me with that viper's tongue of yours, making me feel like half a man compared to your father. I might have known you'd reject me. But you'll be begging me to take you back." He stopped just long enough to reach into his pocket and draw out a small sack. "Do you know what this is, my high and mighty wife?"

"Oliver, I—"

"This is the contents of your bank account. One hundred pounds, to be precise."

Slowly, like rain dripping into a barrel, his words penetrated my brain. "You took my money?"

He smiled and nodded.

"Who gave you the right!" I lunged for him, but he sidestepped me neatly.

"It's my right," he said gleefully. "As your husband, I'm entitled to anything you earn, my dear Nora. My solicitors have already informed your solicitors—Burke and Burke, isn't it?—that I fully intend to claim every single shilling you earn. Your bank has already, however reluctantly, given me what you had in your account, and your publishers will be instructed to deal with my solicitors."

I felt sick, and steadied myself with the aid of a nearby chair.

Oliver said, plainly amused, "I never thought I'd see the day when you'd be at a loss for words."

I bit my lip. I mustn't fly at Oliver again. I must not anger him. "You can't mean to do this, Oliver."

"Oh, but I most certainly do."

I gestured helplessly. "What will I do? Where will I go?"

"Take heart, my dear. The solution is quite simple. You can come back to me. I would take very good care of you."

Suddenly, his scheme became very clear to me. "Go back to you, Oliver?" I plunged on recklessly, as contempt overrode caution. "You started out as a surgeon's apprentice, but that was too taxing and required too much ambition. So you thought that by marrying a famous artist's naive daughter, some of his talent would wear off on you. You never really dreamed Ivor Stokes would disown me, did you?

"And now you have a scheme to cut yourself in on my small talents. My father was right. You display a singular lack of originality. Or is it because your women will no longer buy you suits and jewelry?"

Oliver went rigid, his blue eyes dark and furious. "You have a filthy mind, Nora. I am weary of your insults and your vile tongue." He walked over to the parlor door and closed it. "I think it's time I taught you a lesson, my dear wife." He began to remove his coat. "I know you would like another child to replace the one you lost. What? Recoiling in horror at the advances of your husband?" Oliver flung his frock coat atop my shawl. Then he walked toward me, very, very slowly. "You used to crave my advances once. Have you forgotten how you would often *seek* them, wanton that you are? Behavior that would revolt a decent wife! So why so shy, my dear Nora?"

I bolted for the bedroom, but Oliver reached me first. The bruising grip of his fingers on my shoulders brought my danger home to me. I screamed as he whirled me around to face him. He tried to slap me, but I kicked him. When he doubled over in agony, I broke his hold and started for the door.

Just as my fingers gripped the knob, Oliver jerked me away from safety and flung me back into the room, where I collapsed onto the floor. "Get up!" He pulled me to my feet. "I've dreamed of doing this for years."

Before I could draw another breath, the door to the parlor opened and crashed against the wall. Gentleman Harry crossed the room in three strides, grabbed Oliver by his collar, and wrenched him off me. Before Oliver could recover, Harry hit him on the jaw and sent him staggering.

"You all right, Mrs. Nora?" I had never seen murder in Harry's eyes before. "That *trasseno* didn't hurt you, did he?"

"No," I murmured, shaking uncontrollably as I stared at Oliver's form sprawled on the floor. "You shouldn't have hit him so hard, Harry. He'll have the police on you in no time."

"Don't worry about the coppers. I can smell them coming a mile off." He led me over to the sofa and sat down next to me, holding my hands. When I finally stopped shaking, he asked me once again if I was all right. I nodded.

A rustle followed by groaning caused us to turn around. Oliver was struggling to his feet with the assistance of a chair. When he finally stood swaying before us, a thread of blood trickling down his chin, and his wonderful golden hair disordered, I couldn't help pitying him. But not for long.

"Well, Nora," he began with great difficulty, "you've got yourself a protector, I see. What sewer did you drag that out of?"

"Why, you—" Harry started forward, but I restrained him.

"No, Harry. He's not worth bruising."

There was enough hatred in Oliver's eyes to kill me, as he took his coat and limped away. But nothing had changed. My insults had not dissuaded him from his purpose. If anything, they had instilled in him a greater desire to strike back.

"Who was that dimmick?" Harry asked when the halting footsteps ceased. "He looks like the sort who'd steal from children."

"That was my husband."

I was spared Harry's comment by the appearance of a bewildered Mrs. James. "Is everything all right, Mrs. Woburn?" She regarded Harry dubiously. "I heard you scream, and the next thing I knew, this gentleman was tearing up the stairs. And what happened to the other nice young man? I saw him leave, and his mouth was bleeding."

"Everything is all right, Mrs. James."

After casting one last suspicious glance at Harry, my proprietress murmured, "If you say so, Mrs. Woburn," and left.

"You look like you need a drink." Harry's voice and eyes were tender with concern. "Do you have any gin?"

I laughed as I put my hand to my forehead. "No, I can't afford even that." Especially now, I added to myself.

"What did your husband want?"

I thought it best for Oliver's sake not to tell Harry the truth. "He just wanted to . . . renew our relationship."

Harry's dark brows knotted together in anger. "The swine! I should cut out his tongue for that. Lucky for you I was passing beneath your window when you screamed."

"Very lucky. And . . . thank you, Harry."

"I wish you'd let me do more for you, Mrs. Nora," he said, almost wistfully.

"There is one more thing you could do for me, if you would." I rose and reached for my shawl. "Would you mind calling me a cab? I must attend to a personal matter immediately."

Harry rose, and once again the penetrating gaze was lightly mocking as he bowed and said, "Anything for you, Mrs. Nora."

Fifteen minutes later, I had given the driver the address of my solicitors, Burke and Burke, and clattered off. As I sat twisting my fingers together in the well-sprung vehicle, the initial shock of Oliver's visit was replaced by utter hopelessness. I felt like a numb limb suddenly coming back to life, making its presence known by prickling and tingling.

What was I to do? I had paid Mrs. James my rent for the upcoming month of May, and I had enough money hidden away to keep myself fed. But what would happen to me when that had disappeared? I could still write—even Oliver could never take my skill away from me—but what purpose would it serve if he received the income my literary efforts brought me? Perhaps others could write for fame rather than profit, but I could not afford that luxury.

There was an alternative. I could become a governess. I was well-educated, and even if Oliver did claim the few pounds a year I'd earn, at least I'd have a roof over my head and food in my mouth. But the thought of trying to drill long-forgotten Latin verbs into some newly rich tradesman's heirs, to live in neither the servants' world nor the family's . . . No, I couldn't, not after having been my own mistress for so long.

I sighed dismally as I stared out the window, seeking distraction. Neat houses presented their well-kept faces to me, then slid by, as did a straight-backed soldier flirting with a blushing maid, and two mischievous boys screaming after a terrified mongrel.

Of course, there was always Gentleman Harry's offer. I shuddered at the thought of disappearing in St. Giles' Holy Land, never to be seen again. What would it be like, I wondered, to live with thieves and murderers?

Like living in hell, I thought. Even Oliver's hell would be preferable to that. At least it would appear respectable. Shiny on the outside, rotten inside.

Pressing my fingertips to my throbbing temples, I prayed my solicitor would have the answer.

John Burke was the well-fed younger member of the firm. As I sat before him in his office, recounting Oliver's visit, I got the distinct impression his mind was elsewhere. Finally, my irritation got the best of me, and I snapped, "Well, Mr. Burke, can you stop shuffling those papers long enough to tell me just what I can do to stop my husband from stealing my money?"

John Burke cleared his throat and said, "Nothing, Mrs. Woburn."

"Nothing?" The room became unbearably hot and stuffy.

He shuffled his papers and finally set them in a precise pile off to one side. "Mrs. Woburn, your husband's solicitor informed us this morning of his client's intention to exercise his legal claim to your earnings. There is nothing you can do to stop him."

I was dumbfounded.

"You see, Mrs. Woburn," Mr. Burke continued, rising and striking a lecturing pose, "the law puts women in the same category as children—and rightly so, because they, too, need guidance and protection from themselves."

"Mr. Burke, may I remind you that I have not been under my husband's protection and guidance for the past three years? We live apart, and I support myself by working, just as you do."

He looked at me as though I were a child or a simpleton. "But that makes no difference, Mrs. Woburn. You are still legally married to Oliver Woburn. You could get a divorce. But," he wrinkled his nose distastefully, "they are tedious, expensive, and scandalous."

"And just what am I supposed to do in the meantime?"

"As I've said, Mrs. Woburn, I'm afraid you can do nothing."

My temper skyrocketed. "Nothing!" I sprang to my feet. "Do you mean to tell me that I must stand by helplessly while a man I haven't seen in years robs me?"

"You could go back to your husband," he suggested.

"Never. I'd starve first."

"Madam, you're being overly melodramatic. Please try to calm yourself. The law is the law, after all. What would happen if there were exceptions made?"

"The world would be vastly improved!" I headed for the door, opened it, then whirled on the hapless Mr. Burke. "While I pay my shiftless husband's rent, who is going to put a roof over my head and feed *me*? You? Or perhaps I could go to our neighborhood workhouse. Or perhaps I could even become a prostitute and ply my trade in the Haymarket!"

"Mrs. Woburn!" I had scandalized the righteous Mr. Burke at last.

"Just think of the income I could bring my husband then!" I turned on my heel and stormed out, barely noticing the man seated in the waiting room, who rose as I sped by. Hot tears of anger blurred everything, and I barely managed to stumble down the steps and back into the street.

I started walking. I walked past dozens of houses and down as many streets, but went nowhere and noticed nothing. My throbbing head was the only part of me that did not feel beaten and bruised as I wandered about in a mindless daze, tears of frustration pricking my eyes.

An hour—two hours?—later, the river sliced across my path, forcing me to stop. The whistle of a boat gliding majestically downriver shook my numb brain, while the stench of dead fish and garbage revived me quicker than any smelling salts. I sighed as I looked down into the dark elusive waters of the Thames. My reflection bobbed and rippled, as if it would be torn into fragments and swept away, but it was tenacious, this reflection of mine, and refused to be destroyed.

Suddenly, the will to survive coursed through me. If my reflection would not be torn apart by the river, why should I let Oliver do the same to me? Hope straightened my shoulders and put some spring into my step as I hailed an empty cab clopping by, and started for home.

I sank back in my seat and crossed my arms. A plan began to take shape in my mind. I would swallow my pride and go to my father. He would have to take me back. There was a wall of bitterness separating us, but he didn't hate me. What father would abandon his only daughter to a man like Oliver Woburn?

I would throw myself at his feet. I would plead and be penitent.

I pictured my father. Ivor Stokes possessed the body of a bear topped by the round solemn face of a monk constantly beset by temptation. He also had the disconcerting habit of giggling, which was at odds with his distinguished appearance and sharp intellect.

I hoped he would laugh and take me into his arms. But, I reminded myself brutally, he could remain adamant in his decision to have nothing whatsoever to do with me. Ivor Stokes was as proud and stubborn as I, and I had hurt him deeply.

"You made your bed, Nora, girl," I could hear his voice boom at me. "Now lie in it. I'll not help you."

Yes, Ivor Stokes could go either way. But I had to try. At least I had to try! My only problem was finding my wandering father. He could be anywhere—Paris, Rome, even New York. Certainly Dante Rossetti would know, and if he had been sworn to silence, perhaps William Morris could be persuaded to tell of my father's whereabouts. As I began formulating my plan to call at Rossetti's house in Chelsea, the cab rolled to a stop in front of Mrs. James' house. I stepped down, paid the driver and went inside.

"Mrs. Woburn, is that you?" came a familiar voice.

"Yes, Mrs. James."

I had climbed halfway up the stairs when my proprietress stopped me. She was distressed, as usual.

"There's a gentleman waiting upstairs in your drawing room."

"Not Oliver again!" I directed my irritation at the befuddled Mrs. James. "Why did you let him in again? After that scene a few hours ago—"

"Oh, but it's not Mr. Woburn. And it's not"—she wrinkled her nose—"that man from the streets. No, this is a very proper, well-spoken gentleman who said he had a business matter to discuss with you, and that he's from your solicitor's office." She patted a stray hair into place as a bit of color stained her cheeks at some remembered flattery. "He's very good-looking and tall. He's clean shaven though, and I always like a beard on a man. So much more distinguished, don't you think, Mrs. Woburn?"

I frowned. "That doesn't sound like John Burke. Did he give his name, or leave a card?"

"I never asked," she replied in alarm and confusion. "Oh, Mrs. Woburn. You don't suppose—?"

"Don't worry. It's probably just one of their clerks," I replied, and climbed the rest of the stairs.

As I opened the door to my rooms, a man I had never seen before rose and said, "Mrs. Woburn? Please forgive the intrusion. My name is Mark Gerrick."

I stopped and stared. This was no clerk. "Mr. Gerrick? Have we ever met, sir?" I was as bewildered as poor Mrs. James.

Mark Gerrick smiled. It was not the white, even teeth that held my attention, but his eyes, clear and gray like rainwater. "Only briefly, Mrs. Woburn. In the offices of Burke and Burke a few hours ago."

Now I recalled Mr. Gerrick, a shapeless mass through watery tears. "I see. You were waiting to go in as I was leaving."

"Yes, Mrs. Woburn."

"You must forgive me if I seem obtuse, Mr. Gerrick, but, why are you here? My proprietress said you had business to discuss with me, however," I shrugged apologetically, "I cannot fathom what business we have to discuss."

He was blunt. "I understand that you are in financial difficulties, Mrs. Woburn."

I colored furiously. "Mr. Gerrick!"

"I did not mean to offend you with my bluntness. I must confess I overheard the latter part of your conversation with Mr. Burke." When I made an exasperated sound, he smiled disarmingly. "After all, you *did* leave the door ajar."

I tried to suppress a smile. "Why, so I did."

"Mr. Burke said nothing to me about your visit. The man is a discreet solicitor in any case."

I removed my shawl. "Do sit down, Mr. Gerrick. I'll make some tea and then we'll talk."

After fending off Mrs. James' questions while I made tea downstairs in her kitchen, I carried a tray back upstairs to where my visitor waited. As I poured and passed him a cup, I had a better opportunity to study the man.

Superficially, he was good-looking. But what intrigued me was his quiet air of authority. Here was a man accustomed to giving orders and having them carried out. It was a power that went beyond wealth and class. Whether Mark Gerrick was a king or a potato vendor, he would always have it.

"I am in financial difficulties, Mr. Gerrick." I hesitated to tell him why, for he was a stranger.

"Can you tell me about it?"

My eyes met his, and before I knew it, I had told him about Oliver's visit. Smiling wryly, I said, "So I will soon be unable to support myself, thanks to Oliver Woburn."

Mark Gerrick's eyes grew cold. "There's a word for men who live off women. I believe I may have a solution to your dilemma, Mrs.

Woburn. To come to the point, I would like to offer you a position as companion to my younger sister."

I smiled. "Old women usually require companions, Mr. Gerrick, not young ones."

"I know what you must be thinking, but please, let me explain." His eyes took on a dreamy, faraway look. "My family home is in Devonshire, right on the edge of Dartmoor. I recently returned to it after spending some time abroad. In my absence, my sister Amabel had been, shall we say, wayward. Last year, she gave birth to a child, and refused to name the father." He shrugged. "I'm a realist, Mrs. Woburn. These things happen. But I'm afraid others are not as tolerant. The friends she once had among the gentry of the neighborhood have closed their doors to her."

"But what could I possibly do?"

The gray eyes held mine. "Talk of London to her. Play croquet. Go riding. Be her friend. Amabel needs a friend desperately."

"This is a most unusual offer, Mr. Gerrick." I eyed him suspiciously. "You don't even know me."

He smiled. "Devon is hardly London—it can be quite desolate and lonely. And, I must admit, I myself am not the most congenial company in the world. But you would be fed, housed and paid twenty pounds a year for the inconvenience. And," he added with that persuasive smile, "you would be free to write for the pleasure of it."

I felt like a starving dog confronted with a side of beef, but I kept myself in check, and said, softly, "Why, Mr. Gerrick? Why are you doing this for me?"

"You are Ivor Stokes' daughter?"

"Why, yes."

"I met him in Rome two years ago. He saved my life. I owe him a debt of gratitude."

I leaned forward, and, in my excitement, almost dropped my teacup. "You met my father? Is he well?"

"When I saw him, he looked very well."

"Had he been painting?"

"He said he had done several new canvases."

"Did he ask after me at all?" When Mark Gerrick hesitated, I added, "Please don't be afraid of hurting my feelings, Mr. Gerrick."

"He did mention that he had a daughter, but that she had disappointed him."

"Oh, I did indeed do that," I admitted, trying to smile. "My father disowned me the day I ran away with Oliver Woburn. He never forgave me, even when I left my husband. But, I won't bore you with past family scandals, Mr. Gerrick. In any case, I'm afraid I must decline your generous offer."

"I'm not offering you charity, if that's what you're thinking," he said. "If you won't accept the position, I shall find another suitable young woman who will. And, I assure you, you would earn your room and board. Amabel is beautiful, willful and spoiled. She will try your patience until you want to strike her." His eyes flashed a challenge to me. "Will you accept such a challenge?"

Something in me bristled at being regarded as a cog in a machine. Mark Gerrick had worked out his plan, and assigned me my place in its efficient execution. But if I refused, he would assign my role to someone else without a second thought, and I would be the loser. I really had no other choice but to accept.

I heard myself say, "All right. I will be Amabel's companion."

"Splendid!" he said, rising and consulting his pocket watch. "I must leave for Devon tonight, unfortunately, and I trust you have matters to settle here." He reached into his coat pocket and removed an envelope. "I've taken the liberty of booking passage on a train for you. You'll find your instructions in here. Can I expect you at Raven's Chase on Thursday, then?"

I nodded and rose, a little overcome by what I had just done, and resentful that he had assumed all along I would accept. Mark Gerrick smiled and placed the envelope discreetly on the table, then picked up the hat he had left there.

As I started toward the door to show him out, I noticed that he walked with a slight limp. Whether temporary or permanent, this handicap seemed of little importance to him, for he moved quickly and with erratic grace.

"I regret not being able to accompany you on the train down, Mrs. Woburn," he said, putting on his hat.

I remember thinking that he didn't look like the type of man who wore hats. "Lack of an escort won't deter me, Mr. Gerrick," I said.

"I didn't think it would," he replied with a dazzling smile. He offered me his hand, and as I felt its hard, calloused palm and strong fingers grasp mine, something like a shock went through me, sending the blood rushing to my cheeks. "Good day, Mrs. Woburn. We shall be expecting you Thursday then."

2

Thursday found me situated luxuriously in the first-class carriage of a train rattling its way across the south of England to Devonshire. I was left with nothing to do but sit back in my seat, appreciate the sheen of spring on the countryside, and reflect on the days preceding my departure.

After Sir Mark Gerrick—I was to learn he had a title—left my rooms, and the clatter of his departing cab faded away, I stared at the packet he had left and thought about what I had agreed to do. My knowledge of the man would barely fill a pea's pod. But he had said he knew my father, and somehow, that reassured me, for Ivor Stokes set high standards for his friends.

After pleading a headache to avoid Madame Leclerc's inquisition at the supper table, I spent the rest of the evening agonizing over my decision. The next morning, I quickly downed my breakfast, put on my shawl, and walked to John Burke's office. Oddly enough, he was the one who convinced me I had been right to accept Mark Gerrick's offer.

The solicitor listened with exaggerated patience as I told him what had happened. To my amazement, John Burke, Esquire, did not even shuffle his papers once.

But he did clear his throat before saying, "Yes, Mrs. Woburn, Lord Raven—he just came into the title, you know—did come in after you left, and he did make inquiries. And I can assure you, Mrs.

Woburn, all I told him was your name, and"—he had the grace to smile uncomfortably—"your address when he became persistent. He is, after all, a highly valued client."

I had no wish to hear his explanations, so I raised my hand and said, "I am considering his offer, Mr. Burke."

He sprang to his feet, jammed his hands into his pockets and grimaced. "You cannot be serious, madam."

"Oh, but I am, Mr. Burke."

"You, a married woman, would go down to Devon with a man of unsavory reputation, under the guise of being a 'companion' to his sister? Oh, come now, Mrs. Woburn."

The smirk on his face annoyed me. "Is Sir Mark Gerrick's reputation unsavory? Then perhaps you would care to enlighten me, and perhaps save me from my folly."

My sarcastic tone eluded the man, and he lectured me as if he were addressing a jury. "Sir Mark made a fortune in trade—India, China, and so on. But there's something very mysterious about his personal life. Sir Charles Gerrick, his father and a valued client of this firm, died under unexplained circumstances. Suddenly his eldest son, whom no one had seen for *years*, appeared on our doorstep, claiming the title and taking over, if you will. Evidently, his partner now handles the shipping business, and Lord Raven has taken over the management of the estates, which are vast." He paused for a breath. "And there's some tragic business about the younger son of the family. Sir Charles, God rest him, wasn't an open sort, so we never did hear all the details. But the boy's in some sort of asylum."

"Just what are you implying, Mr. Burke?"

"Nothing, madam, nothing. I'm merely trying to inform you of the situation. What concerns me most is your reputation. True, you haven't much of one left, after leaving your husband as you did," he said, "but to wantonly flaunt convention . . . beware, Mrs. Woburn!"

The sharp retort on my tongue would have been wasted on Mr. Burke. To his narrow, respectable way of thinking, it was preferable for me to end my days by going blind in a dress factory or enduring Oliver's refined tortures rather than by risking my reputation. Mark Gerrick offered me my freedom, which was something the John Burkes of this world would never understand.

So I just rose and said, "I've decided to accept Lord Raven's offer."

"Mrs. Woburn!"

"No, let me finish. I assume you have the address of Raven's Chase, since the Gerricks are such valued clients? Good. If my publishers, or anyone else wishes to contact me, feel free to tell them my whereabouts. Since my husband will be receiving my earnings, you won't have those to forward to me. Good day." And I left Mr. Burke sputtering behind me.

Once my decision had been made, I set about putting my few affairs in order. After notifying my publishers of my plans, I told Mrs. James, who smiled and wept at the same time. Next, I sat down and wrote a long letter to Georgina Burne-Jones, in which I apologized for not visiting her before I left, and gave her my address, in case she wished to contact me. She was older than I, but a dear friend and my last tenuous link with the bohemian life of my father. Georgina's husband, Edward, was one of the Pre-Raphaelite faithful, whose paintings took their inspiration from Arthurian legend. "His paintings are flawless pieces of craftsmanship, but they lack soul," was my father's pronouncement on their artistic merit. However, Georgina was devoted to Edward and knew what to look for in a husband. She had warned me about Oliver. Now I wished I had listened.

That evening at supper, Mrs. James' two other tenants wished me well. Madame Leclerc claimed to be descended from French royalty, but I suspected her name was a fabrication to give her small dress shop status. Madame insisted that Mrs. James treat us all equally, right down to the last spoonful at mealtimes, and I knew she begrudged me my three rooms to her one, even though I paid extra for them. Miss Fowler, her niece, was a north-country girl who had come to London to find her fortune and found consumption instead. She also wished me well, in between the coughs that wracked her body.

As we four women sat around the table, I marvelled at us. Many were not as lucky as we. The hounds of poverty were snapping at our skirts, but we had managed to elude them. Soon, I would be far out of poverty's reach, but what of the others?

Strangely enough, I found it more difficult than I could imagine to tell Gentleman Harry I was leaving.

He sat on the edge of my sagging sofa and stared at me with soulful eyes that never left my face. I told him of my new position. A muscle twitched in his scarred jaw. "You don't need to take any position, Mrs. Nora. You could let me . . . take care of you."

"I can't, Harry." I shook my head as I knotted my fingers together. "We're different, you and I."

His lip curled, and his voice became bitter. "It's beneath you to take up with the likes of me, is it?"

Giving him a reproachful look, I said quietly, "That isn't true. It doesn't matter to me." I rose and walked over to the window and looked out on nothing in particular. "I'm afraid of your world, Harry. Afraid it will break me into little pieces. Every time I look at the children . . ."

"You needn't be afraid, Mrs. Nora." He came up behind me and put his hands lightly on my shoulders. The scent of his hair oil was cloyingly sweet. "I'm not denying life in St. Giles ain't brutal. We family people have to be if we're going to survive. But I'd take care of you. I'd see nothing happens to you, like I done all along."

I shook my head, and felt his hands drop. When I heard him walk away, I turned around.

He was standing by the door, staring at me as if memorizing my features. Then he smiled ruefully, and said, "If you ever need a friend, Mrs. Nora . . ." And he was gone.

"I know, Harry, I know." Foolish tears pricked at the back of my eyes as I went to pack the one straw bag I owned.

In two more days, that bag, which was all I needed to carry my scant wardrobe, some sketches of Father's, a delicate miniature of my mother, and the beginning of a new novel I was writing, stood on a platform in Paddington Station. I watched with last-minute misgivings as it disappeared into the train, but I followed it, and soon had settled myself comfortably in the compartment reserved for me.

As the train shuddered, moaned, and began to inch forward in a hiss of steam and grinding of gears, I waved frantically at Mrs. James, now sobbing into her handkerchief and waving back. A figure in the background caught my eye as the train pulled away; his eyes met mine for a split second, then Harry blended in with the crowds. Five minutes later, a policeman sauntered by. So he could smell them a mile away after all, I told myself as the train lunged for Devonshire.

Devonshire! What awaited me there, I wondered as the green velvet Somerset countryside slid past my window. Mr. Burke's sinister insinuations left me undaunted. I was never one to place faith in rumors. I would soon learn for myself.

My employer occupied much of my thoughts as I sat with nothing so much as needlework to occupy my fingers or a book my mind. Oliver had made me doubt my ability to judge men, but I was impressed with Mark Gerrick. He was forthright, yet vaguely disturbing.

Years of seafaring had calloused those powerful hands. I wondered how much those pale eyes had seen. Brother fighting brother in America's Civil War? Chinese courtesans with dainty bound feet? The hot stinging sands of the Sahara?

There was a commanding presence about him despite his lame leg —"like he owns the whole world," as my father would say. I trembled a little as I realized that I was now part of the world he owned. I had escaped Oliver Woburn, but to what was I fleeing?

I yawned, stretched, and turned my attention back to the scenery. Soon I tired of spotted cows and church steeples piercing the blue sky, and found my gaze focusing on the window glass. Staring back at me were great tawny eyes that seemed to overwhelm my thin sharp face.

"It's a good thing you take after your mother, Nora, girl," my father often said to me. "It wouldn't do to have a gal who looked like a monk."

Now, for the first time in years, I recalled the only portrait Ivor Stokes had ever painted of his own daughter. I had been so jealous of all the women in Rossetti's august circle, for they were always posing for their husbands or lovers. William Morris painted Rossetti's wife, Lizzy—called "The Sid" because her maiden name had been Siddal— and Rossetti painted Morris's wife, Jane. My father painted both Jane and Lizzy, and so it went, like a game of mathematical combinations.

Of course, sometimes it bordered on the ridiculous. I was only ten years old at the time, but I remembered staring wide-eyed at Lizzy shivering as she floated in a tub of water to pose as Ophelia for Ruskin. One had to suffer for one's art.

But no one ever painted me, for I was not tall and was more skinny than willowy, and far from ethereal. With the passion of an outsider desperately seeking admittance, I badgered my father to paint my portrait, my ticket to acceptance. Finally, Ivor Stokes surrendered.

"Are you satisfied, Nora, girl," he said to me the day the painting was completed, "now that I have immortalized you?"

It was called *The Edge of Experience*, but we called it *Amber Eyes*. I was delighted with it. Ruskin couldn't praise the picture enough when it had its London showing. Two years later, at eighteen, I ran away with Oliver, and later I heard my father had sold my portrait not long afterward. Where it hung now was anyone's guess.

The sun passed behind a cloud, turning me melancholy. Where were we all now? Lizzy was in her grave, and—so I had heard—Rossetti's poetry tucked between her cheek and hair. My father was on the Continent, and I was embarking on an adventure of my own.

I sighed and rested my head against the seat. When I next opened my eyes, the conductor was announcing my stop, where I would board a connector for Sheepstor.

"Sheepstor! Next stop, Sheepstor!"

As Sir Mark had instructed, in Sheepstor I found a hired chaise waiting at the station to take me to the Headless Horseman Inn, where one of the servants would meet me. Sure enough, there was a one-horse trap waiting as the chaise clattered into the inn's cobbled courtyard. My hopes for stepping inside for a quick lunch vanished when a white-haired man with a chinful of stubble and a pungent stable odor about him shuffled up to the chaise.

He peered up at me. "You Mrs. Woburn from London?"

"Yes, I am. And you are—?"

"Old Corman," he replied in a voice that sounded like carriage wheels on gravel. After helping me down, he collected my bag and threw it into the trap. "I'm to take you to Raven's Chase."

I found myself seated next to Old Corman (was there a Young Corman, I wondered?), who clicked his tongue and sent the bay mare into a brisk trot.

My introduction to Devonshire was literally in a fog, for that's what engulfed us as the mare trotted along. Any hopes I had of seeing the countryside were quickly blotted out.

I felt as though I were wrapped in cotton, unable to see, and floating helplessly through a cold, damp void. Sometimes a tree or wall would materialize, like a wraith, then disappear behind us into the mist. I pulled up the collar of my old pelisse, grateful for even this small comfort.

"How do you know where we're going?" I asked Old Corman as I squinted, trying to pierce the mist.

"Bonnet here could find her way back to the Chase blindfolded," he replied with more confidence than I felt. "The mist comes up on ye real quick hereabouts. One minute ye see the road in front of ye, the next minute"—he snapped his fingers—"nothing."

Somewhere off to my right, a cow lowed mournfully, causing me to start and grip the edge of my seat.

"You ever been here before?" he asked.

"No. I've lived in London all my life."

London. I could see smoky skies, hear Posies' cry of "Flowers! Fresh flowers!" and smell yesterday's cooking in Mrs. James' dark hallway. No. London seemed as far away as the moon. To hide the sudden rush of homesickness that engulfed me, I said, "What is Raven's Chase like? Is it a castle, with turrets and towers and dungeons?"

His laugh crackled like burning paper, and he was amused by my girlish enthusiasm. "No, missus. 'Tis just a house. Oh, a grand enough house to be sure, but no castle, like Ashcroft, a ways down the road. Gerricks have lived at the Chase since time began and before that. And Cormans have always been there to serve them." Then he passed a hand over his bristly jaw and said, "But not a happy house, since the master died."

I started in panic, until I realized he must be speaking of Sir Charles, and not Mark Gerrick. "Oh?" I said, hoping it was all the prodding the old servant needed. It was.

"Life at the Chase was good before *he* came back. True, Lady Katherine was gone—God rest 'er—but Sir Charles was a kind master, and he loved Miss Amabel and Master Damon so." The old man's face darkened, and his voice became bitter. "He should have stayed away, that one. Starting up trouble with the Standish witch. Sir Charles never would have died, and Master Damon . . ." He shook his head sadly.

My head was spinning with so many names I felt as though I was reading a theater program. "What happened to Master Damon?"

Old Corman stared straight ahead at the road he couldn't see. "Found him out at the abbey one morning. Lost his mind, he had. I don't know what horror he saw there, but whatever it was, 'twas enough for Doctor Price to lock 'im in Goodehouse. Poor lad'll never be right in the head now."

An eerie cry split through the mists, causing me to start.

"Only a crow," my companion said. "We'll be comin' to the Chase any minute now."

The oppressive mists cheated me out of my first glimpse of Raven's Chase. All I saw was a massive, spectral shape looming out of the fog. Old Corman halted the trap, handed me and my bag down, then left me facing a giant door. I heard the slap of leather on Bonnet's flanks, followed by the creaking of the trap as it rolled off. Finally, that sound too was devoured by the soft, swirling mists, leaving only the clopping sound of the mare's hooves growing faint in the distance.

Deserted, I stared at the ferocious-looking brass lion with a ring clamped in its jaws, and felt an unmistakable chill of dread come over me. Suddenly, I wished I had never met Mark Gerrick, and had never agreed to come to this cold, fog-shrouded land.

"Coward," I scolded myself.

I grabbed the brass ring and brought it down hard, once, then twice. And I waited, while the sound reverberated throughout the house, announcing my presence.

At first, there was no sound beyond the door, as though the crashes had not been heard. Then, suddenly, the door swung open, seemingly of its own volition, and a woman dressed all in black stood before me.

"Yes?"

"My name is Nora Woburn. Sir Mark is expecting me."

The woman smiled. While not exactly pretty, she had very strong, exotic features that were attractive. She said, "Oh, yes. Amabel's new companion. Please come in. I am Marianne Meadows, the Gerricks' housekeeper."

As I reached for my bag, she gave me an odd look and said, "You needn't bother. One of the footmen will take it later."

I followed her into a large, cool foyer, our heels tapping against the hard slate flagstone. Huge, burnished copper pots filled with fresh flowers gleamed in the corners, adding color and scent. At either end, staircases of rich old woods met in a balcony that overlooked the hallway and led to the second floor. I caught a glimpse of myself in a gold-framed mirror, and except for the unruly curls springing from beneath my hat, I was pleased to see I wasn't too travel-worn.

Suddenly, Miss Meadows turned around and smiled. "I'm afraid Lord Raven is out at the moment. But perhaps you'd like to go to your room and freshen up after such a long journey."

"Thank you. That would be most welcome."

"And I'll have Flanna bring you a tray."

The very efficient housekeeper, I thought to myself as I followed her up the staircase to our left. Raven's Chase must run like a well-oiled clock with her in charge. Her black dress had not one wrinkle, and not a single dark hair escaped from the heavy knot that rested on the nape of her neck. I thought of my own curls springing every which way, and felt as gauche as a schoolgirl.

When we reached the top of the stairs and started down a corridor, we surprised a young, red-haired maid staring dreamily into space. She took one look at me and started, nearly dropping all the scented linens she carried.

"Flanna!" the housekeeper rebuked her. "Flanna O'Brien."

The girl stopped. "Yes, Mrs. Meadows, ma'am?"

So the efficient creature had a husband.

"After you put those where they belong, have Mrs. Baker make up a tray for Mrs. Woburn and you bring it to the Ming Room."

"Yes, ma'am." The girl curtsied, gave me a swift glance, and disappeared down another corridor.

"That girl," Mrs. Meadows said with a shake of her head. "Always daydreaming of handsome knights and pots of gold. I suppose it's because she's Irish."

We continued on our way past closed doors, turned a corner, and kept walking toward the back of the house. Finally, she stopped before yet another closed door, opened it, and went inside. I followed her into the Ming Room.

A gasp of astonishment escaped my lips as I entered an Oriental paradise. My feet seemed to sink into the richly-hued Oriental carpet, while my eyes drank in a canopied pagoda bed with a brass-bound trunk squatting at its foot; a lacquered coromandel screen; and what I knew to be rare paintings on the walls. Two huge blue-and-white china vases that Rossetti would have coveted for his collection stood guard on either side of the fireplace. All I needed was to smell the heady scent of incense and hear the tinkle of temple bells and I would be in China.

"It's . . . it's beautiful!" I was overwhelmed.

A smile touched the housekeeper's mouth, and her dark eyes seemed to fill with laughter at some unshared joke. "Sir Mark recently had this room redone with treasures he brought back from the Orient. Of course, some pieces, such as the bed and the desk, are chinoiserie and were acquired by the Regency Gerricks." She stopped, then said, "Your bag will be here shortly. If you need anything, the bellpull is by the bed." And she left me to the splendor of the Ming Room.

I walked over to the windows, but the persistent fog pressed against them, as though to restrain my sight. Sighing, I turned back to the elegant room. That was the cause of my bewilderment and uneasiness, for the Ming Room was too elegant for a hired companion, more suitable for a guest. I had expected a cramped box in the attic, not Kublai Khan's pleasure dome.

A knock interrupted my thoughts.

"Come in."

A footman brought my bag in and set it by the bed. He was followed by Flanna, who was holding a tray.

"Your lunch, madam." She set it on the desk. "Would you like me to unpack for you? I'll bring you hot water, if you'd like to wash."

I smiled. "I think I'd like some hot water, but I'll unpack for myself, thank you, Flanna."

"Very good, madam." She curtsied and left.

I sat down and proceeded to devour a delicious lunch of cold roast beef, eggs, pickled onions, rolls, and a slab of cake that tasted of almonds and strawberries. As I poured myself a cup of steaming tea, Flanna returned with hot water.

When I had washed myself, I resumed my reflections about Raven's Chase. Perhaps Mrs. Meadows had made a mistake and put me in the wrong room, but I doubted that. Marianne Meadows wore efficiency like a cloak. She had probably never made a mistake in her life.

Why had I, a paid servant, been given such a luxurious room?

I stretched, unpacked my belongings, and hung my few dresses in one corner of the cavernous closet, which smelled of fresh verbena or vetiver. There was no room on the walls for my father's sketches, so I put them in the brassbound trunk for safekeeping. I slipped my manuscript into an empty drawer in the desk. Then weariness overcame me, so I went to lie down on the pagoda bed. No sooner had I closed my eyes than sleep enslaved me.

"Mrs. Woburn, wake up!"

I opened my eyes to find Flanna anxiously shaking me.

"Flanna. I must have dozed off. What time is it?"

"Four o'clock, madam. And Lord Raven wants to see you in his study."

This news slapped me into wakefulness. I swung my legs over the edge of the bed. "My dress is all wrinkles. I must change it."

"If I may be so bold, you look fine. And the master gets in a temper when he's kept waiting."

"Very well, then. Just let me brush my hair."

When I turned around, Flanna gasped as though she had met her dead mother on a dark night, and, quite frankly, the girl's stares and starts were beginning to prey on my nerves. But there was no time to express my irritation. I said, "Please take me to Sir Mark."

We went back the way I had first come, and, finally, the red-haired maid stopped. She rapped on a door with her knuckles and waited.

A voice from inside bade us come in. Flanna opened the door, smiled hesitantly at me, then left. I took a deep breath to calm my quaking insides, and entered.

"Mrs. Woburn." Mark Gerrick greeted me with a wide white

smile. He crossed the room effortlessly in spite of his limp. He was dressed in riding clothes, and I saw that his tall, spare frame was well-suited to rough tweeds and top boots. The clear gray eyes held mine as he took my hand. "I'm pleased you decided to accept my offer."

"I . . ." The words died in my throat as I spied the painting that hung in his study.

The Edge of Experience—the missing *Amber Eyes*—stared at me from over the cold, unlit fireplace. Ignoring my employer, I walked over to the portrait and stood before it. I saw myself at sixteen, the blush of innocence on my face matching that of the lilies I was arranging in a vase. I wore a white, loose-fitting dress. My head was half turned, and a sweet smile of anticipation lit my mouth, as though someone—a lover, perhaps—had just entered the room. In the lower left-hand corner was my father's sprawling signature. No wonder Flanna and Mrs. Meadows stared at me. They had seen this portrait often enough.

I whispered, "Where did you get this?"

"I have always admired Ivor Stokes' work," he said, "and when I happened upon this portrait in the home of an old friend, I had to have it. I think it's your father's best piece." He leveled those eyes at me, and suddenly I felt as much one of his possessions as the portrait. "Please sit down, Mrs. Woburn. You look as though you might faint."

A mixture of emotions ranging from rage to despair was coursing through me. I eased myself into a soft leather chair opposite his desk. "You have a great deal of explaining to do, Sir Mark."

He cocked an amused brow at me. "Do I?"

"Yes!" My temper flared. "I find it most strange that you offered me this position in the first place, without even knowing me. Then I arrive here in Devonshire, am put in a room fit for an empress rather than a paid companion, and discover my employer has my portrait hanging in his study. Does it amuse you, Sir Mark, to also own the model of your portrait? Am I to be displayed at dinner parties, for the delight of your guests?"

A scowl appeared momentarily between his brows, then vanished. "That was not my intention," he said quietly. "You are in my employ, but I own no one. I have no wish to embarrass you, Mrs. Woburn. As I told you in London, I knew your father briefly in Rome a few years ago. He saved my life. This is my way of repaying that debt."

I suddenly felt very foolish. "I am sorry, Lord Raven. My waspish tongue gets the best of me at times. But you should repay my father, not me."

He walked over to a leaded crystal decanter and poured an amber liquid into two glasses. "Knowing Ivor Stokes as I do, helping his daughter is tantamount to repaying him."

"But I don't want anyone's charity!"

A corner of his mouth jerked into a sardonic grin. "Charity? Once you meet my sister—and you will at dinner, in two hours—you'll know it would have been more charitable of me to have never offered you the position. You shall earn your keep, and more."

As he handed me a glass of sherry, I wondered why men always felt spirits fortified one.

He continued. "But I won't keep you here against your will. If you still feel you must leave the Chase, I'll put you on a train back to London tomorrow."

London. I sipped my sherry as I solemnly regarded the portrait. No matter in what direction I moved, there was a man waiting to control me, like a puppeteer pulling strings. Oliver, Harry, and now Mark Gerrick. But of all of them, Mark Gerrick offered me some semblance of freedom. No, I told myself, as I took another sip of sherry (men were right, it did fortify one) this was no time to let stiff-necked Stokes pride stand in my way.

"What's it to be?" he asked, but I had a feeling he knew my answer.

"I'll stay."

"Splendid." Again the white smile. "Is the Ming Room satisfactory?"

I felt my neck and cheeks grow warm. "It's—it's splendid. But I had been expecting something less grand, in the servants' quarters."

For the first time, I saw those gray eyes grow cold, like the relentless mist pressing against the glass. His voice was edged with impatience when he spoke. "There is no question of your staying in the servants' quarters. You may be Amabel's companion, but you are also my guest."

"Thank you," I murmured, humbled.

Again the smile, and with it, a softening of his harsh features. "What do you think of Devon, Mrs. Woburn?"

"I saw so little of it because of the fog."

He limped over to the window and stared into the gray wall beyond. "I had almost forgotten it," he admitted with a scowl. "I used to hate it when I was a boy. It was so silent, so secretive. Before you realized what was happening, you were engulfed against your will."

He laughed sharply and said, "Good preparation for the intrigues of adulthood, one might say."

I said nothing, but sipped the last of my sherry in silence. His vague speech reminded me even more forcefully that there was little I knew about this man.

"Well," he said, "I hope the mists don't keep our dinner guest away. Now, if you'll allow me to show you back to your room, someone will show you down to dinner at six. You'll dine with us, of course."

I put on a fresh dress, a serviceable dark-green taffeta I had had no cause to wear in years, and pinned up my hair so as not to be mistaken for the girl in the portrait again. It had been so long since I had dressed for dinner that I couldn't resist primping and posturing, delighted with the elegant creature before me.

A knock on my door sent me scurrying to answer it. The implacable Mrs. Meadows smiled briefly and said, "Are you ready for dinner, Mrs. Woburn?" as her cool gaze passed over my dress, exposing every darn and mend.

I lifted my head a notch higher. "I am ready."

She turned and I followed, hoping my glare bored a hole in her straight back. I found myself wondering about her as we walked down hallways and stairs. How long had she been housekeeper here, and did her husband work somewhere else on the estate? Perhaps he was a gamekeeper. I was sure I'd find out all in due time.

"This is the library," she said, as we stopped before large double doors. "Sir Mark wishes you to meet his guest."

Without waiting for so much as a polite comment from me, she opened the doors and glided in. "Mrs. Woburn," she announced. I followed her in like an obedient puppy, hesitant and somewhat unsure of myself. Then Mrs. Meadows left me, and I heard the doors close softly.

I loved the library immediately. What reader wouldn't appreciate this lofty, hushed room with ceiling-high windows on the opposite wall? The room smelled faintly of stale tobacco, fine leather bindings and the books themselves, which lined row upon row of shelves. Several tufted, red leather chairs I longed to curl up in were scattered here and there.

It was from such chairs in front of the fireplace that Sir Mark and his guest rose as I entered.

Mark Gerrick, looking as at ease in evening clothes as in his country tweeds of a few hours ago, bowed over my hand. "Mrs. Woburn, may I introduce you to our family physician and friend, Dr. Samuel Price. Sam, this is Nora Woburn."

Dr. Price, a wiry man no taller than myself, grasped my hand and murmured, "My pleasure. It's not often one meets a painting come to life."

I quelled my annoyance, smiled at the rusty-haired man, and said, "The pleasure is mine, Dr. Price. Are you familiar with my father's works?"

"Oh, no. I'm afraid I'm not the connoisseur of fine art that my friend Mark is," he admitted. "I appreciate a good engraving or two though."

I envisioned cheap reproductions of *The Royal Family at Balmoral* or *The Monarch of the Glen* gracing his walls. Not everyone appreciated beautiful paintings, I reminded myself.

"Mrs. Woburn, Sam, please sit down." Sir Mark indicated two chairs. "We have fifteen minutes before dinner is served, and I'm sure Amabel will be late." When we were all seated, Sir Mark turned to his friend and said, "Mrs. Woburn has consented to be Amabel's companion."

"Oh?" Dr. Price wore spectacles so thick they hid his eyes, but I was sure I did not imagine the faint look of disapproval in them.

"And what did you think of Mrs. Woburn's books, Sam?" our host said suddenly.

I stared at him in surprise. He had never once mentioned he had read my books.

"Come, Sam. Let's have your opinion."

The doctor turned white, while the freckles on his forehead stood out angrily. He seemed disconcerted and embarrassed as he looked everywhere but at me, all the while mumbling something. Then he blurted out, "I thought they were quite scandalous, actually!"

I was not taken aback or offended, for, in fact, my books had been regarded as such by certain London critics who had righteously warned all mothers to hide them from their daughters. Why, even Mudie's Circulating Library had refused to stock them until Mr. Mudie could no longer ignore their popularity.

"Nora," my father always said, "not everyone will like everything you do. And would you want them to, anyway?"

Smiling demurely, I said, "And what did you find so scandalous about them?"

The doctor stirred in his seat, obviously ill at ease. Finally, he said, "What I objected to in *Leomandre* was that the heroine—Cecily,

I think her name was—went to London to escape her brutal guardian and became a . . . a . . . I cannot bear to say such a word."

"I've heard worse," I said, bringing a faint smile to Sir Mark's mouth. Then I leaned forward in my chair and continued. "My books speak the truth, Dr. Price. Many serving girls or shop girls in London are forced to sell their bodies in order to survive, like Cecily. Why should they go blind in some factory when they can earn more money working the streets?"

"But she's never punished for her sins," the doctor protested. "Why, she even marries the man she loves, in the end!"

"Fancy women often do, and become quite respectable."

Although concealed by thick glass, I was sure Dr. Price's eyes were furious. "Having practiced medicine in London at one time, Mrs. Woburn, I know what you say is true. I have numbered such women among my patients. I'm not disputing the truth of what you say, I'm just questioning its moral value. Where will the gentle daughters of the English family find an example of righteousness in your books? The wicked are not punished but actually triumph. A woman like Cecily should pay for her sins, not be rewarded for committing them. She must serve as an example."

Sir Mark, who had been observing all this with a bemused expression, suddenly spoke. "Well, Sam, am I to assume you think me too lenient with my wanton sister?" He caught my eye, and tried to keep from smiling.

The doctor shifted in his chair. "It's not for me to judge. Amabel certainly cannot be compared to . . . to those other women. She was taken advantage of by some scoundrel, and now she's paying for her folly. Which proves my point. The reading matter of young girls should warn them of the consequences of such behavior."

"There are many such books that do," I said, "such as Charlotte Yonge's. But I must write the truth as I see it."

He stared at me. "Do you have children, Mrs. Woburn?"

"No, Dr. Price."

A brief look of triumph flickered across his face. "I'm sure you'd feel quite differently if you had a daughter to protect from outside influences."

"Perhaps," I conceded calmly, while thoughts of an unborn child churned within me.

The tense moment passed when Sir Mark asked the doctor about one of his patients, a nearby farmer who had been gored in the leg by a bull. I took the opportunity to ask him about his practice, and learned that Dr. Price had a thriving, but poor one. Most of his patients were farmers and millworkers, but he did attend to the health of the gentry as well.

Suddenly, a knock sounded at the door, and Mrs. Meadows announced dinner as gravely as one would someone's death. The three of us rose and followed her to the Garden Room.

I was enchanted with it as soon as I entered. Somehow, I had envisioned a room akin to my mother's solarium, filled with sunlight and deep green shadow and the strong scent of earth. But upon seeing a row of French doors buttressed by the thick, misty darkness, I realized at once that the room took its name from what surely must be a garden beyond. The family, Sir Mark informed me as we entered, preferred to take its meals here rather than in the formal dining room down the hall. I could see why, for it was small and intimate.

Silver, crystal, and old china gleamed against snow-white linen, and the dark buffet set against one wall stood up admirably against more silver dishes crowded on its top. Two servants stood at attention on either side, and Mrs. Meadows deftly began giving them orders as we were seated.

By the grim set of his jaw, I could see that Dr. Price's annoyance with me had not worn off. A twinge of guilt caught at me. Perhaps I shouldn't have been so outspoken at our first acquaintance, but something in me rebelled against being a complaisant female, one who agrees with everything a man says.

As Sir Mark held my chair, he said, "Mrs. Meadows, would you be so kind as to see what's keeping Miss Amabel?"

She nodded and departed.

He then seated himself at the head of the table and said, "My sister should be making her grand entrance at any moment now."

We didn't have long to wait. The Garden Room's doors were flung open, and Amabel Gerrick arrived in a rustle of taffeta.

"How dare you send Mrs. Meadows for me as if I were a child!" She seated herself at his left, totally ignoring the doctor, who held her chair, and barely glancing at me. "I know when dinner is served and I shall come down when I'm ready."

I glanced at Sir Mark, expecting an outburst to match Amabel's, but except for his eyes, which had become a storm-tossed sea, his features were composed. "We'll have no scenes tonight, Amabel," he said. "Say good evening to Dr. Price and then to Nora Woburn, whom I've engaged to be your companion."

Amabel said nothing to the doctor, and merely raked me over with her fierce blue eyes. "I don't need a companion."

"Nevertheless, you shall have one," was her brother's benign reply as a bowl of steaming soup was set before him.

"What if I refuse to have one?"

"Will you please repeat that, Amabel?"

I kept my eyes on my plate and inwardly cringed, waiting for the explosion.

Amabel tossed her golden hair back over her shoulder, sending an overpowering geranium scent my way. She had pushed him too far and she knew it. In bored tones, she murmured, "Well, if I *must* have a companion. . . ."

"You must," he replied.

Dr. Price said, "I'm sure you'll find Mrs. Woburn to be a delightful companion. Why, she's an authoress, you know"—he made it sound as though I had two heads—"and her father is a famous artist."

Amabel stared at me with more interest this time. "Are you really a writer?"

I smiled. "Yes."

"What have you written?"

"Ghost stories under the nom de plume of Mrs. Burns," I replied. "They are the most profitable. But I am proudest of my two novels, *Leomandre* and *The Green Tree*."

She replied, "I've never even heard of them. I don't read anyway. Only bluestockings read."

I bit back the retort on my tongue, for I realized this spoiled child took delight in contradicting everyone.

"If you're a writer," she continued between spoonfuls of soup, "why has Mark hired you to be my companion? And where is your husband? Or are you a widow?"

There was no point in deceiving Amabel if I was to gain her trust. "My husband and I have been separated for three years. Until recently, I was able to support myself, but certain . . . circumstances have forced me to seek a position. Your brother offered me this one."

I was conscious of the approving look on Sir Mark's face and the incredulous one on Amabel's.

"You supported yourself?" She made a face, as though the word tasted bitter on her tongue.

It amused me to see that Amabel found my supporting myself more reprehensible than being separated from my husband. "Yes. I took rooms near the St. Giles rookery, and—"

"Rookery?" The pert nose wrinkled. "What's that?"

"London's slums," Dr. Price's baleful voice replied.

Amabel was horror-stricken. "You lived in slums? With poor people and criminals? How ghastly!"

I shrugged. "It wasn't Belgravia, but my rooms were cheap and clean. And as for my neighbors . . . they were an education. I did survive." But barely, I added silently to myself.

As Amabel shuddered delicately, Sir Mark said, in a bemused voice, "I wonder what you would do, my fair sister, if you were in Mrs. Woburn's place?"

Did I imagine a shadow of fear in those great eyes? I must have, for suddenly Amabel was all gold and blue defiance. "I would fare quite well, dear brother, for there would always be a man to protect me."

Before anyone could comment, a joint of ham was set before Sir Mark. He proceeded to carve and serve it, while Dr. Price and Amabel lapsed into quiet conversation about a neighbor of theirs. I had ample opportunity to study the Garden Room's occupants as I enjoyed the ham, sweet potatoes, and mashed carrots, which I washed down with a mild white wine.

I fancied I could feel Mrs. Meadows' dark veiled eyes boring into my back as she supervised the removal of endless dishes. I couldn't fathom whether she was hostile to me or just taciturn by nature. Indeed, it was difficult for me to imagine her in the arms of her husband or loving children.

Dr. Price had forgiven me, judging by the polite questions he asked about London. But I wished he'd remove his thick spectacles so I could see his eyes, for then I would know what he really thought of me. There was a distinct guarded air about him, a wall he was quick to throw up around him to hide behind.

Amabel reminded me of the beautiful thoroughbred women who came to buy my father's paintings when he finally began to make a name for himself. They radiated a well-kept air and the confidence that they would always be well-kept, first by their fathers, then their husbands, and perhaps even by a lover or two. I could believe Amabel when she said there would always be a man to take care of her.

But as I watched Sir Mark, a vague uneasiness began stirring within me. He and Amabel rarely looked at each other, and when they did, it was with hostility or impatience. Their words were always barbed and taunting. What had turned them into implacable enemies, I wondered? I soon found out.

It all began innocently enough. Amabel turned to me and said, "You must meet Peter."

"Peter?"

"Peter Gerrick, my son," she explained, beaming with maternal pride. "He's the most beautiful child, and bright, as well. Why, just the other day . . ." And she launched into an anecdote that only she, as Peter's mother, could fully appreciate.

But we all listened attentively, and when Amabel finished, I turned to Sir Mark and said, "I've been told you have another brother. Am I to meet him soon?"

There was a stunned silence, followed by a sharp intake of breath. I felt as though I were watching a crack slowly starting in a mirror, then racing across its surface, shattering it just as this perfect mood was being shattered.

Sir Mark finally broke the silence. He looked grim, and his voice was tight and controlled as he said, "You must mean my younger brother, Damon. I'm afraid he's very ill, and doesn't live with us."

"I'm sorry."

"Why don't you tell her the truth, Mark?" Amabel broke in. She was a cat again, ready to spit and scratch. "Ill? My brother is mad, Mrs. Woburn. Insane, and locked up in an asylum called Goodehouse. Isn't that an amusing name for an asylum?" A hysterical sound burst from her throat. "Goodehouse. And you drove him there, didn't you, Mark? You and LaBelle Standish. Why don't you marry her, Mark? You've got the title, Raven's Chase, and Damon's safely locked up, out of your way."

"Amabel," Dr. Price began softly, laying a gentle hand on her arm, "that will be enough."

The girl's face crumpled as she threw off his hand. "Oh, what good does it do to fight? Mark always wins, in the end, and you help him, don't you, Sam?" With a sob, she rose and fled from the room.

I felt as though the cold, damp mists had finally forced their way into the room and were swirling triumphantly about me.

"You must excuse my sister," Sir Mark said, his voice expressionless. "She has an active imagination."

We finished the meal in embarrassed silence. I could see that both the doctor and Sir Mark were shaken by Amabel's outburst, and each seemed to retreat into their own thoughts. Before I went up to my room, Sir Mark informed me that Mrs. Meadows would take me on a tour of the house in the morning. All mornings were my own, he said, but afternoons and evenings were to be devoted to Amabel.

Later, in the darkness of the Ming Room, thoughts of this strange household intruded on my sleep. Amabel's sharp accusations spun around in my head. "And you drove him there, didn't you, Mark?"

And who was LaBelle Standish? John Burke, between shuffles, had intimated there was something dreadfully wrong with the whole Gerrick family.

Were Amabel's words the accusations of a high-strung girl, or words of warning from someone who knew the truth?

3

Upon rising the next morning, I pulled back the curtains to see if the sun had rolled back that depressing mist. A day as crystalline as white wine awaited me, and it was as though the mist had never existed.

So this is what Devon is like, I said to myself as I gazed out over slumbering lawns that gave way to sharp hillsides in the distance. After squinting at what looked like ruins half hidden by the crest of a hill, I turned and went downstairs.

I smiled in pleasure as I entered the Garden Room, delighted that I had been correct to assume that a garden existed beyond the French doors. There was no one else here, so I went out onto the spacious fieldstone terrace. Beyond the low balustrade were hedges that crisscrossed neatly laid-out gardens. I could envision it in the summer, warmed with a profusion of yellows, reds, and pinks. At the far end of the garden stood a folly, which guarded the entrance to a small grove of oaks. My mind conjured picnics there, and endless gentle games of croquet on the long green carpet.

A rueful thought intruded on my summer fancies. Perhaps by summer I wouldn't be here at all.

Then I walked back, took a plate, and helped myself to toast and hot chocolate. As I seated myself, the sound of the door opening caused me to start. It wasn't Sir Mark or Amabel, but Marianne Meadows.

I tried to hide my disappointment by saying, "Good morning, Mrs. Meadows. Have Sir Mark and Amabel had their breakfast already?"

The dark eyes regarded me without expression. "Sir Mark always breakfasts at seven, and as for Miss Amabel, she never rises before ten." The woman then checked plates and platters at the sideboard and made no further attempts at conversation.

Just as I downed the last drop of hot chocolate, she said, "Are you finished, madam? Sir Mark has instructed me to show you the house."

We began our tour down in the kitchens, where I met the cook, a woman with the improbable name of Mrs. Baker, so thin she probably never sampled her own cooking. I also met Nellie, baby Peter's nurse, a rosy, expansive woman with huge, soft arms and an infectious laugh.

Mrs. Meadows then proceeded to the schoolroom, where countless Gerricks had memorized mathematical tables under the stern eye of their tutor.

"Do you live nearby?" I asked, as we silently threaded our way through the Blue Room, the Red Room, and the Green Room.

"I live here. My rooms are near the attics, with the other servants."

"And your husband?"

"He died at Balaklava."

I stopped to express my sympathies.

"Why should you be sorry? You didn't know him."

Well, she certainly stilled your tongue, Nora, girl, I said to myself as we entered the gallery. I stopped to stare at all the Gerricks parading before me on the walls. I peered at Gerricks framed in Elizabethan ruffs and those resembling spaniels in their Stuart curls. Not all were golden and beautiful. I passed Hanoverians stuffed into satin breeches like sausages, but stopped when I came to the portrait of an ethereal creature in a high-waisted dress of the Regency.

I asked Mrs. Meadows who she was.

"Lady Katherine Gerrick," she replied.

So this was Sir Mark's mother. She was like all the women I envied, confident of adoration and claiming it as her due. Life was so easy for the Amabels and Lady Katherines of the world.

"She was killed in a railway disaster years ago," Mrs. Meadows went on, in a rare burst of chattiness. "But that was long before I came to Raven's Chase."

"How tragic," I murmured as we moved on to the next painting, which was of Lady Katherine's husband, Sir Charles, Mr. Burke's highly valued customer who had died under mysterious circumstances. He had a stern, intelligent face, but there was an air of impatience about him, as though no matter where he was, there was always somewhere else he'd rather be.

The final portrait, a group portrait of the Gerrick children, fascinated me. In the foreground was Damon at perhaps ten years old, happy, glowing, golden. He and baby Amabel shared a furry kitten. Despite the differences in their ages, one could see the great bond between them. And in the background stood a stiff and black-browed Mark, staring off into the distance. He looked both remote and rebellious.

"Sir Mark was fifteen when this was painted," the housekeeper told me. "Four years later, I'm told, he ran away to sea. He never even knew his mother died until he came home two years ago."

So he hadn't seen his family for almost ten years. "How sad," I murmured.

She shrugged and mechanically wiped a speck of dust off the carved frame. "From what I've heard, they shed no tears when he left. Look at him, black as night with the devil's own look on his face."

"He is your employer," I reminded her stiffly.

A dark flush rose and receded across her face. "Shall we go on?"

Well, Nora, you've done it now. Enemies you don't need here.

Once back in the Ming Room, I seated myself at the desk and began to finish a ghost story I had started for *Everywoman's Magazine*. Since mornings were mine, I would make good use of them. I wrote, crossed out, and rewrote, until the desk top was covered with paper. Finally, I titled it "The Spectral Sailor" by Mrs. Burns, collected the pages together, and prepared it for posting. *Everywoman's* readership adored everything I wrote, so I was sure it would be accepted for publication.

A knock at the door put an end to my literary efforts. I opened it to find Amabel there, holding the most beautiful baby I had ever seen.

"Good morning, Nora," she greeted me pleasantly, last night's rebelliousness forgotten. "This is Peter. Would you like to hold him?"

"Miss Amabel, he's adorable. He looks like one of Botticelli's cherubs." As I took him from her, his chubby face broke into a wide, winning grin. "Da!" he cried.

Amabel gave him an affectionately exasperated look. "He calls everyone 'Da,' don't you, my sweet?"

"How old is he?" I asked.

"Nine months," she replied as she swept into my room. "I'm sure Mark has told you I'm not married to Peter's father."

"He did mention it," I replied, as if this information was of no consequence.

"Peter is a love child and I'm in disgrace. I'm a fallen woman and no respectable person will have anything to do with me."

I set Peter on my bed and began rolling him from side to side while he giggled in abandon.

Amabel spoke without a trace of shame, as though having an illegitimate child were no more bothersome than a blister on her finger. But then, why shouldn't she take her situation lightly? She was the pampered darling of a doting family, with an army of servants to buffer her from the intolerances of the outside world. I trembled to think what life would have held for Amabel and her bright, happy child had she been Miss Fowler.

"Are you writing something?" she inquired, flitting over to the desk.

"A story for *Everywoman's.*"

"*Everywoman's.* Why I save every issue. You mean your story will appear in its pages?"

I smiled. So she did read after all. "In two or three months, you shall read 'The Spectral Sailor' by Mrs. Burns, and be able to say, 'Why, I know her!' "

Amabel laughed. "That's commendable. But what I really came to find out is, are you good at archery or croquet?"

"Passable," was my response.

She clasped her hands together. "Splendid! We can go for picnics up to the Eyrie—that's my very special secret place—or riding. Yes, Nora Woburn, I think I'm going to enjoy having you for a companion."

"I hope so." Or it's back to London for me, I thought to myself.

"I used to have lots of friends," she said wistfully, as she seated herself on the bed. "The Ashford sisters down at Ashcroft, Sarah Siddons, Agnes Folkes. . . . We went to the same schools, and would go to balls and house parties together. But when I had Peter, they stopped coming to see me. I called on Sarah one day, but her mother said she had gone to London to visit her cousin. I saw Sarah at her window, before she backed away. Her mother lied."

I could think of nothing to say.

Her mood changed abruptly, for she suddenly scooped up Peter and kissed him all over his face, causing him to squeal in delight. "But I don't mind being snubbed. I wouldn't give up my Peter for all the friends in the world, would I, precious? And now that you're here, Nora, I'll have someone to talk to besides Nellie." Amabel gently removed Peter's fingers from his mouth. "I did have a French maid, Odile, but Mark sent her away after Father died."

Suddenly, the girl snapped out of her reverie. "I think we shall go riding after lunch. You *do* ride?"

It was a hesitant question that expected an affirmative answer.

"I do, but badly."

She laughed, a rich, tinkly sound. "I'll find you a mount Peter could ride." She rose to leave. "I'll see you at lunch then."

As her light footsteps faded away, I sighed. I had been given my first command, and despite the fact that horses terrified me, I would have to surmount that fear if I was to retain her trust.

When I went down to the Garden Room promptly at noon, I found Amabel nibbling delicately on a wedge of cheese. Her fair brow held a trace of a scowl, as did her expressive mouth, and I felt I had imagined the vivacious creature of a few hours ago.

"Nora," she began ominously, raking me over from hair to hem, "is that the only dress you own? You wore it yesterday, and even our servants look more presentable. And why do you keep your hair pinned up? You look forty, and you can't be a day over twenty."

"Twenty-three," I corrected her, ignoring her rudeness as I took a plate and helped myself to the cold meat. "I find that one dress suffices for all my needs. After all, I'm not trying to impress anyone."

"That's quite obvious."

"And," I continued, "I wear my hair pinned up because I don't wish to be compared to *Amber Eyes*."

Amabel wrinkled her nose. "Who?"

"The painting that hangs in your brother's study. It's a portrait my father painted of me years ago. You mean you haven't seen it? I'm amazed. Everyone else has."

"I go nowhere near Mark's rooms."

Now I was alerted to danger. I glanced sharply at the girl. All the light had gone out of her face, and she was staring at me through narrowed eyes.

"Is something the matter?"

"Did Mark hire you to spy on me, like Mrs. Meadows and Young Corman? Is that why you're here, to ingratiate yourself with me? Or are you his mistress? Has he finally thrown over LaBelle Standish then?" She laughed hysterically. "By God, I'd love to see her face when she learns she's been thrown over by a dowdy little wren with only one dress to her name!"

I set down my fork very deliberately, fighting to retain my self-control. When I spoke, my voice sounded surprisingly calm. "I am neither your brother's spy nor his mistress. I had never heard of Mark Gerrick until the day he offered me employment to save me from an embarrassing situation. If it hadn't been for your brother, I'd be starving now—or worse."

Amabel snorted in derision. "Mark never did a kindness for anyone in his life without having an ulterior motive."

"Regardless. What's it to be, Amabel? Are we going to get along with one another, or are we to be enemies? The choice is yours."

We sat in silence, gazes locked for what seemed an eternity. Finally, she spoke. "All right, Nora. I'll believe what you say. But be warned. You are in his debt now, and my brother will expect to be repaid. He's the type of man who takes advantage of people and uses them for his own ends. Look at me. He knows I have nowhere to go because I have an illegitimate child. Not even my aunts will receive me. So I must stay here, and he knows it. Oh, he threatens to cast me out periodically—you heard him last night—but that's to remind me of the power he holds over me." The blue eyes were grim as she added, "You'll see, Nora."

I felt as though a cold hand was clamped around my heart. "What do you mean?"

"You'll see," she repeated. Suddenly she rose, flung down her napkin, and said in a peeved tone, "I'm tired of this conversation. I don't want to talk about Mark anymore. I do want to go riding, and you will accompany me. But not," she added disdainfully, "until you're attired in a proper habit. I think I have one that may fit you."

Later, clad in a modish black habit Amabel had pulled out of an attic trunk, I followed her down a tree-lined path to the stables. She looked elegant in a costume of deep blue, her favorite color, with a full skirt and saucy matching plumed hat.

I looked back over my shoulder for my first glimpse of Raven's Chase, the glimpse the mist had cheated me out of yesterday. It was as black as the bird it had been named for, and seemed to measure me up as it stood there, so wary and watchful. A chill flitted over my shoulders as I turned away, strangely disturbed.

While Amabel chatted on about how many horses they owned, I was recalling our mealtime conversation. So Old Corman's "Standish witch" and Amabel's "LaBelle Standish" were one and the same: Mark's mistress. I don't know why I had been surprised to discover he had one. He was, after all, young, handsome in a dark and brooding way, and virile. "A man's got needs, Nora, girl," was always my father's reply whenever I dared question him about his affairs. And LaBelle Standish took care of Sir Mark's needs.

"Nora, are you listening to me?" Amabel's voice broke into my thoughts.

"Yes, you were saying . . . ?"

"I said you shall have Guinevere. She's old and sweet-tempered."

When we reached the stables, Old Corman led out Amabel's mount, a dancing red monster I expected to breathe fire. Guinevere sounded quite appealing in comparison.

"This is Flame," Amabel said, with as much pride as she had exhibiting Peter. "She goes like the wind and will jump over anything. Would you like to ride her?"

I replied, "No, thank you. I want to live to a ripe old age."

She laughed as a serious-looking groom who was the spitting image of Old Corman thirty years ago came up to help her mount. I watched in horror as the animal reared and pawed the air, but Amabel stuck to Flame, and soon had her docile with a few soothing words.

"You have to let me follow you, Miss Amabel," Young Corman said earnestly. "The master, he gets fearful mad at me if you ride alone."

Amabel sighed, then said, "All right," somewhat reluctantly. When Young Corman went back into the stables, Amabel said to me, "I usually lose him on the moors and ride alone."

"Isn't that dangerous?"

She tossed her head. "I ride well, so there's no danger. And besides, it gives me some time to myself without Mark's spies."

Next Guinevere was led out. The gray mare looked for all the world like Old Corman himself. She even had a chinful of stubble. She nuzzled my hand thoughtfully as a gesture of friendship. Following Amabel's example, I climbed up on her and gathered in the reins.

"I'll never remember all this," I protested, as I nudged Guinevere into a walk and followed Amabel. Young Corman made up our trio by following behind me at a discreet distance.

As we walked our horses down by the garden, I stole covert glances at Amabel. Her brow was peaceful, and her mouth no longer sullen. The outburst had been erased from her face as footprints on the shore were erased by relentless waves. She seemed untroubled and almost cheerful.

I decided to take advantage of her amenable mood and also satisfy my curiosity about the people I lived with.

"Have you always lived here, Amabel?"

She seemed surprised. "Where else? There have always been Gerricks at Raven's Chase. Oh, I visited Aunt Augusta in Yorkshire once, and I've been to Italy and Ireland with Papa. Then, of course, I went away to school—Miss Firthwright's, near London—and I was going to have a season. But," she shrugged, "then Peter came along and I was in disgrace. All my friends had contracted eligible marriages. Except me," she added a trifle wistfully, I thought. Then she said, "A London season was no great loss. I'm happy here. *Was* happy here until Mark came back and Papa died."

The sullen expression was creeping back, so I said, "Mrs. Meadows showed me the portrait gallery this morning. I especially liked the one of your mother. She was very beautiful."

The shadows receded instantly. "Yes, she was. She was killed when I was only ten. But I remember how beautiful she was, and how I loved her.

"She was so happy, always singing while she sewed or arranged flowers. My mother had a beautiful voice and would accompany herself on the piano. And she rode like a centaur. She'd often ride out to visit the poor and sick. Everyone loved her, especially Papa. They were always dressing up to visit all the neighbors. Before they left, Mama would come up to the nursery to kiss me good-night. She called Damon and me her 'Golden Gerricks.' " Amabel stared off in the distance, deep in thought.

And yet, Mark, the Black Gerrick, had run away from this paragon.

We rode in silence, and I was content to concentrate on staying on the swaying Guinevere as we walked our horses down a grassy knoll. Suddenly, the ruins I had seen from my window came into full view.

"What are those ruins?" I asked.

Amabel reined in Flame so we could catch up to her. "It used to be St. Barnabas' Abbey. It was destroyed by Henry's soldiers during the Dissolution of the Monasteries. From what I understand, the monks who lived there were a rich and powerful order. Papa told me about the chapel's three statues. Each wore a crown of gold and gemstones."

"So much for vows of poverty," I murmured dryly.

"When the soldiers came, they found no crowns and no abbot, just frightened monks, who were promptly slaughtered."

"What happened to the abbot?"

Amabel sighed. "Oh, he supposedly fled through some secret passage with the treasure. Your typical romantic nonsense, of course."

"Of course."

She was quiet and thoughtful for a moment, then said, "My brother, Damon, saw something in those ruins that drove him mad."

I stared at her.

She urged her mount on, and I had no recourse but to follow at a bone-rattling trot. As we made our way to the ruins, I puzzled over the girl's behavior. If her brother's affliction was so painful to her, why was she willing to show me the ruins?

At the same time, I wanted to know about Damon Gerrick and the mystery that surrounded him. I burned to know why Amabel hated Mark so. My father called my interest in others healthy; Oliver had considered me interfering and bold. I was probably all of that, and right now there was much about these people I wanted to know.

Amabel stopped Flame at the top of a steep hill, and I brought Guinevere to a halt alongside her. Together we stared down at what had once been St. Barnabas' Abbey.

It must have been magnificent in its day, all those hundreds of years ago. Even now, it had a haunted grandeur that seemed to shroud it in melancholy. Some parts of the cloister and outer buildings had collapsed into piles of gray stone, leaving other parts as silent skeletons.

"I'll wager that, forty or fifty years ago, artists flocked here to paint these ruins by moonlight."

Amabel nodded. "My mother had one of those paintings somewhere. I must warn you, it's dangerous to go in there. One never knows when a beam or wall will collapse. I think it would have been better if that had happened to Damon, but he had the misfortune to live."

"What did happen to him?" I whispered, but the breeze ruffling the horses' manes snatched the words from my mouth, and she heard me.

"Mark is to blame," she replied. "If he hadn't come back Papa wouldn't have died, and Damon would be sane. It's been almost twelve years since Mark went away. I was six at the time, and Damon fourteen. We were glad when he left, Mama, Damon and I, because he never fit in, and was forever embarrassing us with his scrapes. Once he rode Damon's favorite horse to death, and another time he tore up one of Mama's favorite dresses just before a party. We were glad when he ran away.

"Papa felt very badly that Mark left, and he even hired people to look for him. But as the years passed, even Papa accepted the fact that Mark had gone. He told us that if Mark never came back, Papa would assume him dead and Damon would inherit." Amabel's face glowed. "Sir Damon Gerrick! How I wanted that title for him.

"Then Mama was killed, and Damon went to Oxford. I remember the day he came home, sent down in disgrace. I'd never seen Papa so angry. He summoned Damon to his study and they stayed there all morning. I tried to listen at the door, but Nellie caught me. Later, when I did see Damon, he was white-faced and furious. I begged him to tell me what was wrong, but he just called me a baby, and said I'd never understand. A week later, he had joined the Army and was off to India."

Suddenly her voice changed, making me shiver with its coldness. "I was packed off to Miss Firthwright's. One day, we received a letter from Damon, saying he had met the most wonderful girl there—Lucy Middlebury, her name was—and they were to be married. Nora," she said, turning in the saddle to face me, "have you ever heard of the massacre at Cawnpore?"

Startled by her sudden change of subject, I blurted out, "Why, yes. I was only seventeen at the time, but I remember reading about it in all the papers. In the mutiny, all those women were herded away and butchered."

Amabel nodded. "Lucy Middlebury was one of those women."

I felt sickness rising in my throat.

"And Damon was in the regiment that found the bodies."

"Oh, Amabel . . ."

She sighed deeply. "It unhinged him, of course. They sent home a shell of a man, not Damon. You wouldn't believe the change in him." Amabel shuddered. "Oh, I think he would have recovered eventually here at the Chase, given time. But then Mark came back.

"He was very wealthy, he told us, because he was a partner in a shipping company, and he traded all over the world. And now he was home where he wasn't wanted, disturbing our world. Papa was pleased at first, but then he began to change, becoming melancholy and always arguing with Mark. Six months after Mark came back, Papa was dead. With him out of the way, Mark started on Damon, picking away at him, bit by bit. Mark taunted Damon, telling him he'd throw him out and force him to make his way in the world like any other younger son. Damon was so sensitive. He couldn't take that badgering."

Flame pawed the ground restlessly, and Amabel soothed her in a gentle, crooning voice. Then she continued. "I could see him getting worse and worse. He began to forget things and fly into rages. Dr. Price despaired of him." The girl put a gloved hand to her head as if to keep it from aching. "One morning, Young Corman found Damon wandering in the ruins. All he did was babble, 'Lucy! Lucy!' endlessly. He didn't recognize any of us. So Dr. Price committed him to Goodehouse six months ago, with Mark's consent." She paused to pluck at her horse's mane. "I begged, I pleaded with Mark to let Damon stay. We could watch him, take care of him, love him. Both Dr. Price and Mark were against me. They said Damon would get better care at Goodehouse."

Her tragic story cut through me like the sudden chilling wind that rose behind us. There was nothing I could say.

She gave me an appraising look. "They won't let me see him, either. No one will let me see my poor, mad brother." Her mood changed abruptly once more. "I'm tired of staring at these ruins. Follow me." She sent her skittish mare bolting forward.

I gave Guinevere her head, letting her canter lazily after the other horse. We rounded the ruins and started up a bare path riddled with stones and hoofprints. I was beginning to enjoy the horse's rocking gait as we sped through trees and kept climbing, while Young Corman followed.

At one point, we passed a small cottage of black stone that looked out of place sitting on the hill, away from the mainstream of life below. I shouted, "What is that building?"

Amabel turned in the saddle and shouted back, "Our old playhouse."

Finally, when the wild ride had pulled my hair from its pins and my breath was coming in ragged gasps, Amabel slowed her horse and waited for me. She, of course, had not a hair out of place, and looked as fresh as when she had first mounted Flame.

"Still with me?" she inquired sweetly.

I nodded, still trying to catch my breath.

"The moors start once we leave the trees," she informed me.

Our horses were climbing again, and I was astounded at the way the terrain suddenly changed. All this time, while I had been wondering where the moors were, they were hiding behind the trees. Rocks, not trees, were all that could grow here.

We rode onto the moor and stopped our horses abreast of each other.

Dartmoor took my breath away with its harsh, lonely majesty. The barren land, studded with mountains of rock ("tors," Amabel called them) and shot with strips of water, swept before me and seemed to stop at the edge of the sky. It was not soft and green and beguiling like its eastern neighbors, but hard and stripped down to the essentials. It was not seductive. You met it on its own terms or you turned away.

As we rode down the hill, my eye became aware of colors and textures I hadn't noticed before. What had seemed like a brown wasteland from far away came suddenly to life. Dry grasses were streaked with new green growth, while golden gorse burst alongside dark purple heather. Here and there, tiny flowers of pink and yellow dotted the landscape.

We finally came to a road, and Amabel informed me that such roads crisscrossed the moors, connecting houses such as Raven's Chase, Ashcroft, and Kent House.

"Here comes a carriage now," she exclaimed, as we heard and saw the vehicle rumbling in the distance. We moved our horses off to the side and stood there, waiting for the carriage, drawn by four high-stepping bays, to pass.

Amabel, standing up in her stirrups and squinting, said excitedly, "It looks like Angel and Jennifer Ashford. They were a few years behind me at Miss Firthwright's. They must be home for the summer. I'll have to call on them at Ashcroft. Perhaps we can all go on a picnic."

As the vehicle drew nearer, Amabel smiled and waved frantically, obviously hoping it would stop. It didn't. The carriage sailed by as though Amabel and I were invisible. Its occupants, two rather plain girls and a long-faced older woman, didn't even glance at us. My heart went out to Amabel as I saw her eager expression freeze.

"What gives them the right to turn up their noses at me?" she demanded, more stung than she wanted to admit. "New money, that's all they are. Ashcroft! Built ten years ago to look like a Gothic castle. They probably imported moss for the walls. Who wants them for friends anyway."

Gone was the invincible young woman, replaced in an instant by a vulnerable child.

Amabel kicked her horse, sending the animal shooting forward. I had no recourse but to do the same. We kept on riding. It was all I could do to retain my seat aboard the plunging Guinevere and keep Amabel in my sights. Fortunately, Young Corman still followed us, keeping a discreet distance behind.

We seemed to be riding farther onto the moor, and I was beginning to feel a little uneasy. Although there were no trees to speak of,

I felt as lost as if I had wandered into Sherwood Forest. Finally, just as I contemplated falling off Guinevere to attract Amabel's attention, she stopped.

Both Guinevere and I were puffing as we drew alongside Flame, who was barely winded and ready for more. Suddenly, Amabel turned her mount around, ready to ride again.

"Please. Do you mind if we rest?" There was more than a hint of asperity in my voice. "Both Guinevere and I will drop if we have to take another step."

She eyed me coldly. "I don't want to stop here." She jerked her head to the valley below. "That's Kent House, the Standish home."

I saw an Elizabethan-looking dwelling, impressive, but without comparison to the Chase. Kent House was surrounded by a stark expanse of lawn, broken only by a circular drive.

Amabel said, "I have no desire to meet any of the Standishes."

"You may be too late," I said, looking over her shoulder at a rapidly approaching horsewoman.

"Damn!" she hissed as she turned to look.

"Who is it?"

"Jane LaBelle Standish, Mark's mistress."

I stared at the woman riding toward us, but all I could discern was the flashy horse she rode.

"I hate her," Amabel muttered. "She has an invalid husband and a son my age. But she is Mark's whore, with her eye on becoming Lady Raven someday."

Flame snorted and pawed the ground, sending a clot of earth flying. Amabel placed a soothing hand on the mare's neck and murmured, "She and Mark used to be quite flagrant about their relationship until poor Dennis, her son, threatened to kill Mark. He even came to blows with my brother, but only got pummeled into the ground for his pains. Ever since then, they've been most discreet."

Amabel stopped as the woman came within earshot, and smiled, jerking her mount onto its haunches.

"Hello, Amabel," she said in a voice that conjured images of dimly lit rooms with heavy red velvet drapes.

As a name, Jane did her scant justice. She was as beautiful and vibrant as some tropical flower, and it was no mystery why Mark Gerrick had come under her spell.

Amabel merely acknowledged her with a brief nod, and made no attempt to hide her frank dislike.

This seemed to amuse the older woman, who ignored Amabel's

rudeness and said, "Dennis is down from Oxford for the summer. Perhaps he could call on you."

"I think not," she replied, studying a burr on Flame's mane. "I'm sure we would find each other quite tedious."

"I doubt that. Well, my dear, aren't you going to introduce me to your friend?" When Amabel said nothing, anger flashed in Jane Standish's eyes and her lip curled.

"I'm Nora Woburn, Mrs. Standish," I said. I was suddenly very conscious of my curls springing every which way, and of my ill-fitting habit.

"Oh, yes. Raven told me he had hired a companion for Amabel." She had put me in my place with one sentence.

"Nora is also a guest at Raven's Chase," Amabel snapped. "She happens to be a writer."

The black eyes twinkled. "A bluestocking. How droll."

"Mrs. Woburn's father is a well-known artist," Amabel added. "As a matter of fact, Mark owns one of his paintings. Perhaps you have seen it in his study? It's of Nora."

That's a shabby trick, Amabel, I said to myself as Jane's eyes narrowed menacingly.

"Ah, yes. I knew I had seen you somewhere before." She regained her composure beautifully. "It really is a handsome portrait."

I thanked her for the compliment.

"I can't understand why Raven bought it, though," Jane Standish said. "Portraits aren't to his liking at all."

I could visualize this woman sizing up the portrait, not evaluating it for its artistic merits, but shrewdly assessing me as another woman. And the thought that she had no doubt turned away with a tiny smile of dismissal made me inexplicably angry.

"How is your husband?" Amabel asked.

"As well as can be expected," the other woman replied.

"I'm sure you could care less," Amabel said. "After all, you have . . . other diversions."

I could see what was coming, and was powerless to stop it.

"You'll never become Lady Raven, you know," Amabel continued lightly, as though she were discussing the weather.

A slow smile crossed her adversary's face. "Who is going to stop me? You?" And she laughed.

To give Amabel credit, she didn't lose her temper. She replied, "Oh, yes. Most certainly."

"Amabel, don't threaten me."

The girl smiled. "Or you'll go running to Mark?"

"I'm capable of fighting my own battles, my dear, and with weapons you've never even heard of."

Amabel turned suddenly to me and said, "Nora, let's go home."

"I must also take my leave," Jane Standish said. No one left her standing in the middle of the moor. "My husband becomes frantic when I'm late."

"Then you should spend more time with him," was Amabel's comment.

The black eyes hardened. "Good day, Mrs. Woburn. It has been a pleasure meeting you. Do call on us at Kent House." With a curt nod, Mark Gerrick's mistress and her flashy horse left us.

Our meeting with the woman must have infuriated Amabel, for, without a word, she wheeled Flame around. Soon we were racing back toward Raven's Chase. We didn't stop until we reached a high hill overlooking the house.

"What's that?" I asked her above the rush of the wind, as I pointed to another stone house. Devonshire seemed to be filled with them.

"Shepherd's hut," she replied.

As if on cue, a man emerged from the dwelling and stopped when he saw us. Then he raised an arm and shouted, "Amabel!"

Instead of acknowledging him, she kicked Flame and snapped, "Let's get back to the house."

By the time my astonishment wore off and I got Guinevere going, Amabel was halfway down the hill. As I followed, I glanced back over my shoulder to see the man still watching my departure. Then I focused all my energies on staying aboard my mount. By the time I caught up with Amabel, the man had disappeared behind the crest of a hill.

Why, I wondered, had she been so rude to a man who seemed to know her? Servants never called their masters by their first names. No, this man knew Amabel, and I was willing to wager she knew him.

My thoughts went no further, for suddenly I felt Guinevere's back arch and found myself flying over her shoulder, my arms outstretched to break my fall. The ground, I discovered, was not as soft as it looked.

"Nora, are you all right?" A concerned Amabel was bending over me, swimming before my eyes.

"I . . . I think so," I said shakily, as Young Corman rode up, dismounted and helped me to my feet. "I think I just had the wind knocked out of me."

"You're sure nothing's broken?"

"I'm sure. But I daresay I'll be very sore tomorrow." I managed a weak smile as a sheepish Guinevere poked at my shoulder in apology with her whiskered muzzle.

Amabel's verdict was that Guinevere had shied at a rabbit. "Here. We'll help you mount," she said.

I hesitated. "Must I?"

"Of course," she snapped, holding the stirrup for me.

"It's best, miss," Young Corman agreed. "If you don't get back on now, you may be too afraid to ride again."

Privately, that suited me just fine, but as my tutor was implacable, there was nothing for me to do but swing up on Guinevere and follow Amabel back to the house. She seemed quiet, almost sullen, so I said nothing.

Once the horses were led away and we were back inside the Chase, Amabel sighed as one who has reached safety from a pursuer. Then she flashed me a smile and said, "I won't require you for the rest of the day, Nora."

Before I could comment, Mark Gerrick's angry voice rang through the foyer. "Improved, you say? Sam, I see no improvement in his condition whatsoever. He just stares right through me without saying a word."

Amabel went gray as her grim-faced brother and a solicitous Dr. Price appeared on the balcony above us and started to descend the stairs. Amabel ran to meet them halfway, and clutched at Sir Mark's arm.

"You went to Goodehouse without me!" she accused. "Why? Why won't you let me see him? What are you afraid of?"

He stopped and looked down into her anguished face. "What good would it serve? He'd only stare at you, as he stares at me, without a trace of recognition in his eyes. And it would only upset you to see him, Amabel." Then he removed her from his arm and continued down the stairs.

"You could at least let me see him," she pleaded, following him. "Why can't you allow me that?"

"Because Damon is not well."

Ever the peacemaker, Dr. Price said, "Mark is right, Amabel."

"You're all in it together, aren't you? Monsters! All of you!" She whirled on her heel and fled up the stairs, her choked sobs filtering down to where I stood.

"Mrs. Woburn." Sir Mark noticed me for the first time. "I see you have been out riding. Did you enjoy it?"

"Why, yes," I replied, "but I'm afraid I wasn't very successful at it."

The black brows shot up. "Oh?"

"I'll never be a horsewoman until I learn to stay on my horse."

"You were thrown?" he demanded.

"Actually, it was more my fault than poor Guinevere's."

He did not return my smile. "Falls are not to be taken lightly, madam. Sam, have you got a moment to examine Mrs. Woburn?"

"Certainly."

I began to protest, but Sir Mark cut me off with a curt, "You are a member of my household, Mrs. Woburn, and your safety is my concern. No arguments. Sam?"

"After you, Mrs. Woburn," Dr. Price said with a flourish, indicating the stairs. I had no choice but to give in.

The animosity the doctor had displayed toward me last night had vanished. He examined me quickly and competently and pronounced me bruised, but fit otherwise. As he prepared to leave, I steeled myself and blurted out, "Dr. Price, why does Amabel hate Sir Mark so?"

He stopped to face me, his eyes hidden by those spectacles. "Why, Mrs. Woburn, I thought that was quite obvious."

"Forgive me. I can be obtuse at times."

"Amabel believes her brother and his—his—"

"Mistress?"

Dr. Price reddened, looked away, and said, "So Amabel's told you about Jane Standish, has she?"

I nodded. "We met her while we were out riding. Amabel was not very kind to her."

"I'm not surprised. Amabel has delusions that we've all conspired to keep the poor boy locked away. Nothing could be further from the truth." He prepared to depart, then turned to me. "Ah, well. I suppose we all have our own delusions to live with."

"Yes," I agreed, "we do."

4

Dawn found me already awake. I even forgot the stiffness in my arms and legs in my eagerness to continue work on my novel. During the past months, ideas had flowed into my mind in odd, disconnected pieces, like a puzzle. Characters assumed life, and their world became as real to me as my own. Whole scenes flashed through my mind in rapid succession, and I hurried to my desk to put them all on paper before they eluded me.

When I finally raised my head, the clock on the mantle said half past eight. I stopped, pleased at the quantity of work that covered my desk, but chagrined that I would have to breakfast alone again.

But to my surprise, Sir Mark rose to greet me as I entered the Garden Room. "Good morning, Mrs. Woburn. And how are you feeling after your tumble yesterday?"

I smiled. "Sore."

"The best cure for that," he said, as I went to the sideboard for toast, "is to go riding again today."

"So Young Corman advised." I seated myself in the chair he held for me.

"What do you think of the moors?"

"They're beautiful, like a wild, untamed beast crouching at the gates of civilized eastern England. One can easily imagine witches and elves living there."

His gray eyes seemed to dance, and he was far removed from

Amabel's monster. "I'm pleased you've taken to our moors and country ways." He was silent as he poured himself another cup of coffee. Then he asked, "How did you ever become a writer, with Ivor Stokes for a father? I would've thought your father would have encouraged you to paint."

"He did put a brush into my hand as soon as I was old enough to hold one," I replied, "but I'm afraid I lacked his talent. My mother, though, always encouraged me to write, for she had once had literary aspirations. So I kept journals and wrote verse, most of it silly and melodramatic. One day Algernon Swinburne happened to pick up my journal and read a decidedly unflattering sketch of himself. He seemed to think my talent was worth developing. By the time I married, I had written reams of unpublished material, but during the first year of my marriage, I wrote *Leomandre,* and it was accepted for publication."

He smiled. "Judging from your novels, I would say you are very knowledgeable about life."

I found myself blushing. "Not really. Most of the time, I feel I know so little about life."

"So do I," he confessed with a broad grin. His smile vanished as he suddenly said, "How has my sister been toward you?"

I glanced up to find those eyes watching me warily. "As you know, she is of an up-and-down temperament. Sometimes she's sweetness itself, and other times . . ." Because it was in my nature to be blunt and inquisitive, I added, "Amabel has accused me of being your spy, Sir Mark. Is that why you hired me?"

"No." His face revealed nothing, but I believed he told me the truth. "Contrary to what my sister thinks, I did not hire you for that."

"Why does she hate you?"

He stiffened and frowned, and, for a minute, I thought I'd feel the lash of his tongue. But Mark Gerrick just sighed somewhat sadly. "To this day she won't admit that Father was an aging and enfeebled man, grieving too long for his wife, and ripe for what befell him. Damon had also suffered a great loss in India." He looked at me. "She has told you of his fiancée?"

I nodded. "Very, very sad."

He agreed. "So Amabel must look elsewhere for causes of all our tragedies, and her suspicions fell on me."

And your lovely mistress, I added to myself.

He rubbed his eyes, as if he'd been reading for a long time. "Perhaps I was responsible for all of it. If it weren't for this useless leg, I would have stayed on the seas where I belonged, and never come back." He rose, bowed stiffly, and said, "Please excuse me." I watched him limp away.

Sir Mark's confession disturbed and confused me as I went back to my room. Was Amabel right? Had her brother inflicted so much pain on his family? But not without great cost to himself, I decided, recalling his tormented face etched with sadness.

Pity he doesn't need and wouldn't want, I reminded myself, as I opened the door to my room. I immediately noticed the clean desk top.

My manuscript was gone.

I rushed inside quickly and scanned the floor, then frantically pulled one drawer open, then another and another. Nothing.

What would anyone want with my manuscript, I wondered? Sir Mark would have to be told immediately. As I marched out of the Ming Room and down the corridor, I saw Flanna emptying a small basket of papers into a larger one, and I instantly knew my manuscript's fate.

"Good morning, Flanna," I greeted her.

"Morning, ma'am," she replied, bobbing me a perfunctory curtsy.

"Flanna, did you take some papers from the desk in the Ming Room?"

She bristled and retorted, "I just picked up those on the floor. It's my duty to collect them for burning."

"There's been some mistake," I said, and explained about my manuscript. "May I look through your basket and sort them out?"

"Suit yourself."

"May I take this to my room?"

A second sullen shrug. "Don't bother me none. Just ring for me when you're through."

I took the basket, hurried back to my room, and began smoothing out the tightly wrapped balls of paper. I had to unwrap several to find two sheets of my manuscript. They would have to be recopied, for they were badly wrinkled. Then I turned the basket over to find the other sheets. The next wad of paper sent me reeling.

"CHILD WANTED FOR ADOPTION," the headline screamed. In shock, I read the rest:

Anyone seeking a permanent home for a male or female child under one year should contact the advertiser. All guaranteed a

*mother's loving care. Terms, fifteen shillings a month, but will
adopt for flat rate of ten pounds. All replies in confidence.*

I scanned the rest of the other advertisements in revulsion. I had
lived near the rookery long enough to recognize a "baby-farm" letter
when I saw one, and after finding the rest of the manuscript, I set out
at once to show my discovery to my employer.

I found him in his study, papers spread out before him and a pen
in hand. "Yes, Mrs. Woburn?"

With *Amber Eyes* watching me, I apologized for the interruption
and explained how my manuscript had been discarded, then re-
trieved. "I came upon this among the papers," I said, thrusting the
letter at him.

As he read it, I asked, "Do you know what it is?"

"Advertisements for adoptions."

"It's more than that. It's a baby-farm letter circulated among
maids, shop girls, actresses—anyone likely to have an illegitimate
child." I knotted my fingers together. "Ostensibly, they advertise
homes for these children, but in reality, they're slaughterhouses, Sir
Mark. Babies, tiny, helpless infants, are neglected, or have 'accidents'
while in the care of these monsters. And the law can—or will—do
nothing."

His harsh features softened, and his voice was kind as he said,
"This has obviously upset you. But what would you like me to do?
There are no baby farms in Devon."

"But don't you see? Someone from Raven's Chase must have had
this letter. Perhaps one of your own servants is in trouble and plans
to use the services of a 'farmer.'"

The man leaned back in his chair. "I can hardly prevent them
from doing so."

I unknotted my fingers. "Isn't there something you could do?"

Sir Mark regarded me in silence for the longest time, a strange expression on his face. "And it really matters to you, what my servants
do?"

"A child is a child," I said.

Reaching across his desk, he tugged at the bellpull. "We'll see
what Mrs. Meadows has to say about this."

I thanked him.

Marianne Meadows was knocking at the door before I had a
chance to think another thought, or so it seemed.

"Yes, sir?" Obsidian eyes flicked over me.

Sir Mark handed her the paper. "What do you know about this, Mrs. Meadows?"

As the housekeeper read it, I fancied she grew a trifle pale. But otherwise, she was as serene and collected as ever.

"Why, I don't know what this means, sir." She glanced in my direction. "Should I?"

I quickly explained the nature of the letter, adding, "I thought perhaps one of the maids in your charge might need the services advertised here."

Mrs. Meadows became indignant. "None of my girls would do such a thing! And if they did, they'd be sent packing at once."

I looked away as my cheeks burned. I was saved by my employer's smooth intervention. "That may be true, Mrs. Meadows. But the letter *was* found here, so someone is obviously intending to use it. See that they don't, if it comes to your attention."

"Yes, sir," was all she said.

When the door closed behind her, I smiled, thanked Sir Mark, and left, my mind at ease.

I went back to the Ming Room, where I wrote until my fingers rebelled. Before going down to luncheon, I took the precaution of shutting my precious manuscript away in a drawer.

Only Mrs. Meadows was in the Garden Room, and I ate my lunch hastily to free myself of her presence. Her hostility toward me was a tangible thing now. I suppose I deserved it, taking her housekeeping to task. She was proud of her work, and by complaining to Sir Mark I had unwittingly made an enemy of her. What could I say to make up for what I had done? Nothing.

Afterward, I searched for Amabel to find out what she would require of me. She wasn't in her room, so I tried the nursery.

"Come in, madam, come in," urged Nellie when she answered my knock. "His lordship is just awakening from his nap."

As if to confirm this, Peter gave a joyous, "Da!" when he saw me.

"He calls everyone that," Nellie said with a chuckle.

"Is Miss Amabel here?" I tiptoed over to the crib and made faces at the baby, who laughed heartily as he tried to snatch at my nose.

"Miss Amabel went out riding a while ago," Nellie informed me, as she rolled up her sleeves over huge, soft arms. "I saw her myself, riding off on that comet's tail."

"Perhaps I should wait for her."

"Why not go after her yourself?" the nurse suggested, expertly folding tiny garments and stacking them neatly on shelves.

Picking up the baby, I replied, "That's a thought." I rocked him gently, patting his back and listening to his babbling sounds while I walked over to the window. "Doesn't he ever cry?"

"Not my precious," she crooned from the depths of the cupboard.

As I gently stroked the downy head and rested it against my shoulder, a terrible yearning to hold my own child like this stung the backs of my eyes. Silly, silly Nora. What good did it do to dredge up the old bitterness?

"Too bad the little one don't have a father," the nurse said.

I looked at her. "Do you know who Peter's father is?"

Nellie's infectious laugh filled the nursery like sunshine. "I know many secrets of this house, miss, but only Miss Amabel and God know that one."

Now was my chance. "If you know so many secrets, who was Odile?"

"Hmph. Little Frenchie tart, if you ask me."

"Why was she sent away?"

The nurse stopped and eyed me warily. "Asking a lot of questions, aren't you, miss, for being here only two days?"

"I just want to help Miss Amabel," was my response.

Nellie, guileless by nature, suddenly brightened. "I didn't mean no offense. No, Odile saw Sir Charles fall down the stairs and the master —Sir Mark—staring down at his father. Well, old Doc Bright said Sir Charles was dead before he fell, but the little Frenchie started rumors that Sir Mark pushed his father."

Peter tangled my hair in his tiny, chubby fingers and yanked, but I hardly felt it.

"Oh, Nellie, how terrible!"

"See now why she was sent packing? Lying little baggage."

A figure on horseback coming from the stables caught my eye. I leaned forward to see Sir Mark astride a mettlesome black horse, the likes of which I'd never seen before. Without any visible signal, the animal broke into a canter, but one could see Sir Mark was in control, for he was a superb horseman in spite of his leg. Although it was April and warm, Sir Mark wore a black cloak that rippled out behind him, giving him the look of a highwayman from another century. Two black devils, I murmured to myself, as they bounded across the yard in half a dozen strides, then disappeared from view.

"That be the master?" Nellie was suddenly peering over my shoulder. Then she nodded to herself. "Only he rides that daughter of Satan."

"What kind of horse is that, Nellie? I've never seen one like it before."

She shrugged. "Isn't a good solid English horse, that's for sure. I heard the master got it from some heathen chief for saving the man's life, or something like that."

I imagined Mark Gerrick, muffled in the loose robes of a desert chieftain, his face bronzed by the sun as he and his black whirlwind raced a sandstorm. The picture sent a tingle down my back, and I silently chided myself for such romantic nonsense.

"He's probably riding off somewhere to meet Jane Standish," Nellie said with a disapproving sniff.

"I met her yesterday," I said.

Nellie began changing the baby's crib linen. "Standish—her husband I'm talking about now—was a fool to be taken in by her beauty. He becomes sick and what does she do? Chase after Sir Mark instead of tending her own. The whole countryside knows about it, too." She shook her head. "Sir Mark and Jane Standish. All she's after is—" Nellie caught herself, then grumbled, "My heart goes out to the boy. Nice lad, is Dennis."

"I heard Dennis tried to kill Sir Mark once." Would Nellie rise to my bait?

"No, he only threatened," she corrected me. "Oh, they came to blows once, with Dennis getting the worst of it in spite of the master's bad leg. Finally, they sent Dennis off to Oxford. A fine excuse for getting the lad out of the way, if I do say so myself."

"Convenient," I agreed.

"Everyone is supposed to think it's over between them, but I've seen her carriage here often enough." Nellie tucked the sheet corners in and smoothed them. "Sir Mark is a man, and Jane Standish quite a parcel of goods, I'll say that for her." Suddenly the plump face became somber. "Mark my words, girl, no good is going to come of any of this.

"But I shouldn't begrudge the master his pleasures," she said. "He's done more than his father did for the people around here."

"How's that?"

She looked at me. "The Gerrick family owns mills and mines. Sir Mark has seen that the workers get a decent wage and working conditions. I should know. My sister works in one of them."

I thought of the poor people of London, and how lucky those were who worked for the Gerricks.

"Peter's wet," I announced.

Nellie made a clucking noise as she crossed the room and took him from me. "You'd best be on your way if you're ever to find Miss Amabel."

After putting on the riding habit Amabel had given me, I went to the stables and had one of the grooms saddle Guinevere. When the mare and I ambled off, followed by the groom, I wondered about the wisdom of my decision, since every muscle screamed in agony. But as we climbed the hill toward the moors beyond, the aches gradually worked themselves out as Sir Mark had predicted.

The longer I rode, the more I enjoyed it, marveling at the power I had over the lumbering animal beneath me. A pressure of my hand or a touch of my heel, and Guinevere would do anything I asked.

As we followed the path around the tor, I scanned the moors for any sign of Amabel and her half-wild mount, but silent rocks and noisy birds were its only inhabitants. However, as much as I wanted to find Amabel, I enjoyed being alone with only Guinevere and a silent groom for company.

Now I could think about what Nellie had told me. I put myself in the long-gone Odile's place, staring at the broken body of Sir Charles at the foot of the stairs, while above, his brooding prodigal son stared down at him.

My father's voice ran through my head. "And what would you think, Nora, girl, if you were in her position?"

"Nothing!" I cried aloud, causing Guinevere to throw up her head in surprise.

Could Sir Mark have pushed his own father? A tremor shook my shoulders at the horror of it.

My thoughts were jerked back to the present as Guinevere scuffled up a hill and stopped without my permission. I could now see the little stone shepherd's hut, and what looked like Amabel astride Flame. She must have evaded Young Corman again, for he could not be seen.

I was just close enough to be heard if I shouted at the top of my lungs, but when the impatient red mare moved and revealed who Amabel was talking to, I kept silent.

The same man who had called to Amabel yesterday, and who she had claimed not to know, was holding the mare's bridle and talking to Amabel. Her conversation was animated, for she shook her head vigorously several times, and even raised her crop to Flame. The mare danced in place, not knowing whether to obey her rider and lunge forward, or stay, restrained by the man at her head.

Finally, the girl's whole body shook violently, the man stepped back, and the horse gratefully bolted free, charging down the hill at a dangerous speed. Moved to action, I stood in my stirrups and waved and shouted, but Amabel chose not to hear me as she sped on. By the time Guinevere picked her way down the rocky path, Amabel would be back at Raven's Chase, cosseting her son.

As I turned to go, I glanced back at the stone hut. The man just stood there, staring at me, with his hands in his pockets. Even though we were separated by an expanse of moorland, I could almost feel his eyes blazing out at me. With the embarrassment of an eavesdropper caught, I kicked Guinevere a bit too sharply, causing her to groan in astonishment and bolt for home, the groom not far behind.

Once back at the Chase, I changed into my brown merino dress and sought Amabel. It was Flanna who told me the mistress had a headache and would not leave her room until supper.

The afternoon was mine, and I was going to use it well. I went down to the library, which I longed to explore.

When I walked in, I inhaled deeply, savoring the rich smell of fine leather bindings as I scanned their titles. Homer, Ovid, Dante, French and Italian originals were here, as well as Shakespeare and more slim volumes of verse than I cared to count. But the book I chose to read that afternoon was the intriguingly titled *Haunted Devon,* by some local squire with literary aspirations.

Instead of availing myself of the reading table, I discovered a bench that someone had thoughtfully tucked away in a far corner. I proceeded to read my fill of reappearing bloodstains, ghostly hounds, and an assortment of both gray and white ladies. My interest in *Haunted Devon* had begun to wane long before I came to the fourth white lady tale that caused me to clap the book shut in consternation. Amabel haunted me, not white ladies.

Yesterday, when the shepherd had waved and called her by name, she had ignored him, claiming not to know the man. Yet just minutes ago I saw them together, talking as if they knew each other well. Why had she denied it?

"Actually, little Miss Amber Eyes," I could almost hear my father say, "it's none of your affair."

And in my own stubborn way I thought, "But it is my concern. I am living here now. What affects the Gerricks affects me."

So intent was I in thought that I failed to hear the telltale creak of the library door, and I nearly jumped out of my skin when I heard someone speak.

"Did Amabel tell you I met her on the moor yesterday?" It was

Jane Standish. "Her companion was with her, riding Guinevere, of all things."

I heard Sir Mark reply, "Neither Nora nor Amabel mentioned meeting you."

"No, I don't suppose they would." The woman's voice bubbled with laughter. "Your sister hates me, little witch that she is. You should have heard the vile things she said to me."

Both of us waited for him to pursue the matter, but he didn't, so Jane Standish continued. "I must confess I'm quite disappointed in your portrait's subject. She's rather a colorless little thing, isn't she? Oh, those tawny eyes are decidedly her best feature, and her skin is quite good. But that hair! Frizzing went out of style with the farthingale, for goodness' sake. Raven, I would have expected better of you, connoisseur of beautiful things that you are."

The hackles on the nape of my neck rose as I listened to my faults and virtues being discussed as though I were a heifer being entered in a country fair.

"Beauty, as they say, is in the eyes of the beholder," was Sir Mark's ambiguous response.

"Do you find her more beautiful than I?" I could picture her upturned face, eyes smoldering provocatively at him.

He laughed, a low, intimate sound. "You are physical perfection, my dear."

There was an interval of silence. Were they in each other's arms, I wondered? I felt my cheeks grow warm as I heard a little sigh of satisfaction escape from Jane.

"You still haven't told me why you invited her here," the petulant voice demanded.

"Jealous?"

"Me? Jealous of a dowdy little mouse? Raven, you surely have taken leave of your senses. Don't tease me, darling. Tell me why she's here."

"I have plans for Mrs. Woburn," was his reply, "very definite plans. But, isn't it time you were getting back home?"

She sighed audibly. "Yes, I suppose. By the way, darling, Dennis is down from school for the summer, so we must be especially discreet. He thinks it is over between us, you know."

"Thank you for warning me. I'll carry loaded pistols with me wherever I go."

"He is so very loyal to his father, poor dear." Suddenly her voice grew ragged. "If Dennis ever harmed you, I think I'd kill him myself."

"Your own son?" Sir Mark's incredulity matched my own.

"I'd do anything to keep you."

I groaned inwardly at such theatrics and was grateful that I was spared Sir Mark's reply, for they left the library, closing the door with an audible click. The silence was deafening.

The breath I had been holding escaped with a hiss as I emerged from my hiding place. "Mouse, indeed!" I muttered to no one in particular.

Sir Mark's words kept running through my mind like mice in an attic. "I have other plans for Mrs. Woburn, very definite plans."

What sort of plans, I wondered?

Fear trickled down my back. A man of unsavory reputation, John Burke had said. Amabel called him a monster. They had warned me about Mark Gerrick and I had refused to listen.

As I left the library for my room to write until supper, I asked myself, what if they are right?

When Amabel made her entrance into the Garden Room, one could almost see the storm clouds amassing around her. One look at her scowling face warned me to tread carefully tonight. Her brother, however, used to her flashes of temper, merely cocked a sardonic brow in her direction and ordered Mrs. Meadows to begin serving the meal.

"Did you have a pleasant day, Mrs. Woburn?" he asked.

Yes, I eavesdropped on you and your mistress, I would have liked to have said. But I replied, "Yes, very. I hope you don't mind, but I took Guinevere out myself this morning. It seemed like such a lovely day for a ride."

I felt, rather than saw, Amabel's lightning glance.

"Of course I don't mind," he replied. "My stables are at your disposal."

"*Your* stables?" Amabel's voice was almost hysterical. "Those stables should be Damon's by right. This house should be his, by right. It's not fair! You've always envied Damon and me because we were Mama's favorites, and now you want to destroy us."

Sir Mark listened patiently to his sister's tirade, his face expressionless. "Are you through, Amabel? Mrs. Woburn and I would like to enjoy our meal in peace, for once."

I smiled tentatively at her as I sought to keep the conversation neutral. "Who was the man I saw you talking to on the moor today? Does he live close by?"

"What man?" she snapped. "I met no man today."

"But I'm almost certain—"

Her body went rigid as she said between clenched teeth, "I said I spoke to no man today."

I knew better than to press the issue, so I apologized and said, "I must have been mistaken." Mark Gerrick gave me a quizzical look, but I refused to meet his probing stare. As we ate, the silence seemed to widen, relieved only occasionally by the tinkle of silver on china.

Finally, I hit upon what I thought was an innocent topic of conversation. I asked Sir Mark about the horse I had seen him ride.

"Odalisque was given to me by a desert chieftain as a reward for performing him a service."

This surprised me. "Wouldn't a stallion be a more valuable gift?"

"Arabs value their mares more highly than we English. To give your precious mare to an infidel is not only a great sacrifice, but against the law."

His sister snapped, "You care more for that mare than for your own family."

Sir Mark just smiled, raised his glass, and said, "In the best Arab tradition."

We spent the next few moments eating in silence. Finally, Sir Mark said, "I think it's time we had a ball here at the Chase."

I suspect he was attempting to placate his sister, but instead of perking up, she sank further into the sullens. "No one would come, and you know it."

"I'm sure that's not true," I protested.

"Have you so quickly forgotten how the Ashford sisters snubbed me? No one will receive me, even people who have known me all my life."

Sir Mark looked thoughtful, then said, "If you'll just tell me who Peter's father is . . ."

"No!"

"Amabel—"

Her eyes flashed like lightning in a blue sky. "I don't want to marry Peter's father. Never! And you can't force me."

"As you wish," her brother said.

We ate Mrs. Baker's delicious pheasant in silence, the animosity growing between brother and sister. Just as dessert was about to be served, Amabel became agitated once more.

"Let me visit Goodehouse," she begged.

"Amabel, this is no time to discuss Goodehouse."

"I'll go there myself then."

Sir Mark seemed to explode. "You'll do no such thing. I'll not tolerate your temper tantrums any longer, do you hear me? One more, and I'll put you on the train for Aunt Augusta's myself."

Amabel's lower lip began to tremble, and her eyes filled with tears. "I hope Dennis Standish kills you!" She sprang out of her chair and bolted away.

I quietly rose to follow her, but was stopped by Sir Mark's command of, "You stay here."

"But she's upset."

"She'll soon calm down if you don't fuel her fire with sympathy." His voice grew almost gentle. "And you needn't look at me that way."

As I sank back down into my chair, he turned to Marianne Meadows and said, "Have one of the maids bring the coffee to my study. Mrs. Woburn will be joining me there."

Once inside his sanctuary, Mark Gerrick seemed to unwind, like a racehorse after a meet. I realized why this man was so at ease here: this room held no traces of Damon or Amabel or their mother. From the jade dragon crouching on the desk to the primitive Greek icons arranged side by side on a shelf, this room was Mark Gerrick's creation, and reflected his life since leaving home.

And where does *Amber Eyes* fit in, I wondered.

Just as the maid left and closed the door behind her, Mark's face turned white and contorted in a spasm of pain.

I rushed to him. "Are you all right?"

"My accursed leg pains me upon occasion."

"Shall I have them send for Dr. Price?"

"And disturb his supper? No need. I shall be all right. Would you be so kind as to pour?"

As I poured the rich, aromatic brew into twin cups of paper-thin porcelain, I could feel his hypnotic eyes watching me.

"You think my treatment of Amabel too harsh, don't you?"

I handed him his cup. "I must confess I do."

"How would you handle her, then?"

"I think she needs sympathy. Amabel is very lonely, and tries to hide it with outbursts. She is cut off from friends her own age because she has 'sinned.' Her parents are dead, and her brother is in an asylum. When she turns to you, you're as unyielding as a stone wall." I blushed furiously as I heard myself. "I'm sorry for being so blunt, but you did ask my opinion."

He smiled grimly. "When I was growing up, I faced stone walls everywhere. My mother was besotted with her beautiful golden children, and my father with his beautiful wife. Everything was Damon-this or Damon-that. Later it was Damon and Amabel. With no room for Mark, the changeling. There was never any warmth or sympathy offered to me. And now you expect me to show some to Amabel?" He sipped his coffee, never taking his eyes off me.

"Yes," I insisted stubbornly. "That all happened so long ago, when you were children."

He shrugged. "Bitterness takes a long time to die."

"You could try to lay it to rest."

"Do you often champion lost causes?"

"If I'm sure I can win."

"The Gerricks are all lost causes no one can ever hope to win," he said.

"Amabel needs to be cosseted. She's been badly abused, too."

Sir Mark continued to stare at me in silence. Finally, he said softly, "And where do you turn when you hurt, Mrs. Woburn? Who cossets you?"

If he sought to reduce me to stammers and blushes, he would not succeed, for I was no prim and proper miss.

"No one, Sir Mark," I said flatly. "I am quite adept at taking care of myself."

He leaned back in his chair and smiled slightly in a bemused way. "Such a heavy burden for one so delicate."

"I'm stronger than I look." I was being forward and I knew it, but something in me thrilled to this verbal sparring.

"Did he hurt you so badly then?"

"Who?"

"Your husband."

I took a deep breath to steady my shaking insides. "He hurt me so badly I'll never trust another man again," I blurted out. Before Sir Mark could comment, I set down my cup and hastily rose. I had to get out of this room, away from this man who eroded all my self-sufficiency, leaving me vulnerable and alone.

"You must excuse me, Sir Mark. I—I have a headache and must retire."

"As you wish," was all he said, but he knew why I was running.

Now that conversation haunted me, keeping sleep away. His questions had caught me off guard, and in my folly I had exposed my vulnerability to him. Why had I let my tongue run away with me again? Sir Mark was extremely clever. I had exposed the source of his bitterness, and he had exposed mine.

Quite irrationally, I wondered if his relationship with Jane Standish ever went beyond the fireworks of physical passion. Did they ever talk about how they felt? Did Jane, I wondered, know about her lover's bitterness toward his family?

Overcome by restlessness, I rose, lit a candle, and sat in the chair near the cold fireplace. There was so much about this tormented family that puzzled me.

Foremost was Sir Mark himself. So many accused him of so much. What was truth and what was rumor?

I thought of Damon's portrait in the gallery. Oliver had cured me of my passion for men with fair good looks, so Damon's golden handsomeness did not make me swoon. I knew his type well.

But if Damon had been such a gentle person, why had his father shipped him off to India? And to find the woman you loved butchered . . . I shuddered. No wonder he was unhinged.

And there was Amabel, erratic, explosive Amabel. I was convinced she knew that man on the moor, and yet she denied it.

Yawning, I snuffed out the candle and let the black velvet darkness envelop me. I rose and went to the window, where night leaned against the glass. Everything was so quiet, so at peace in the moonlight, even the abbey's shell. But there was something alive and expectant about it tonight, as though the building were waiting for its monks to return.

Out of the corner of my eye, an abrupt movement caught my attention. I gasped as a cloaked figure scurried furtively through the garden. It was headed for the abbey.

I strained my eyes to discern who it was, but the hood was drawn, so I could not tell who ran to keep a clandestine meeting in the ruins. I shivered. Those ruins were not my idea of a trysting place.

Who could it be? Mrs. Meadows, perhaps, leading a wild double life?

That, I reminded myself with a smile as I turned toward my bed, is none of your affair.

Later, I was to look back on this night and wish I had taken more notice of the mysterious cloaked figure.

5

I was seated at my desk at sunrise, but was unable to put one phrase on paper. All writers and artists experience these periods when ideas fail to materialize, and I knew the best cure was a change of scene. So I draped my shawl around my shoulders and went outside for a walk.

When I left the house, my first intention had been to stroll down the footpaths through the garden, admire the spring buds, and perhaps sit quietly in the folly, alone with my thoughts. But as I rounded the building, the ruins of the abbey, dismally etched against the flat, leaden sky, beckoned irresistibly. I hesitated, recalling Amabel's warning. I had no desire to disappear under a wall of rubble.

Oh, well, I told myself as I started for them, I'll just be careful.

A breeze, fierce and authoritative, pushed at my back, as though trying to propel me toward the abbey. I felt my hair being wrested from its pins again, and wished I had worn a bonnet. But I hurried on, and soon the ruins took form. Finally, nearly out of breath, I reached the abbey's north side. There I stared up at window frames that must have once been filled with magnificent stained glass. Now they stared sightlessly toward the moors.

Picking up my skirts, I tiptoed around to the eastern side, where most of the wall had caved in and demolished some of the floorboards, leaving a cavernous hole filled with stones. On the other side, I could see that some of the second level was still intact, and wondered if there was any way to get up there. I entered cautiously, picking my way around shattered rocks.

Suddenly I froze. A sound, high and hymnlike, floated on the wind above me. My eyes darted back and forth as my heart leaped into my throat.

"What do you expect to see." I could almost hear Ivor Stokes' mocking voice, "the good abbot and his doomed monks?"

I laughed uneasily as I shrugged off the eerie feeling. It had only been that same breeze, whistling through stone teeth, making noises to frighten silly women who went where they didn't belong.

My curiosity got the better of me as I surveyed my surroundings. All that was left was the stones . . . stones steeped in sadness that had lingered through the centuries. Oh, if only these stones could speak. . . .

"Nora!"

I squeaked in alarm and spun around to face Mark Gerrick. Today he was not the impeccably dressed country gentleman, but more the buccaneer he resembled. Coatless, he wore trousers streaked with dust and a waistcoat, which accentuated his lean, hard body. His shirtsleeves were rolled up to just below the elbow, exposing muscular forearms, and his dark hair was wind-tossed.

"Sir Mark. You startled me."

He glowered as he came toward me, moving smoothly in spite of his limp. "What are you doing here? Don't you know these ruins are dangerous?"

I flushed. "I was curious."

His face softened, and as he looked around, he smiled and said, "They are fascinating, aren't they? I often used to play here as a boy, trying to find the old abbot's secret passage. I'm lucky I wasn't buried alive for my pains."

"Amabel told me about the abbot, and about Damon, too."

"I suspected she would," he said without looking at me. He bent down, picked up a stone, and sent it skipping along the rocks. "Damon was obsessed with this place. He thought his fiancée was here."

A soft cry escaped my lips.

"It was after our father died last year," he continued, a faraway look in his eyes. "Up until then, Damon was docile. He'd just sit in his room, day after day, staring out into space. Sometimes he'd carry on perfectly normal conversations with us, and"—this he said with wry amusement—"he even seemed to accept me.

"Amabel, expecting her child at the time, took care of him. They were like two lost souls clinging to each other, my mother's favored ones. Damon appeared to be getting over the India business. I began to press him to assume some responsibility for the management of Raven's Chase." Sir Mark rubbed his jaw. "I don't know. Perhaps I did push him too hard, did ask the impossible of him.

"Then he claimed he saw lights coming from the abbey, and that his Lucy was out there. Where he got that idea, I'll never know. Soon, he became excitable and began wandering out here in the middle of the night. The maid would find his room empty in the morning, and when we searched for him, we'd find Damon out here, either sleeping against a rock or staring out into space like a baby. He claimed he saw Lucy and that he talked to her." Sir Mark shook his head. "After one of these wanderings, Damon just refused to speak or move. It was as though he had locked his mind away and refused to give us the key."

I made some sympathetic noise.

He picked up a second stone and sent it spinning. "My father never would tell me what Damon had done at Oxford to merit him being sent to India." He laughed, a bitter, unamused sound. "Spineless, beautiful Damon in the Army. He must have done something unforgivable to deserve that."

"Spineless?"

"My brother was an emotional coward. He was very handsome—you've seen his portrait?—and, like many gifted with physical beauty, Damon felt we all owed him allegiance and adoration, no matter what he did. When I went away, Damon was fourteen. He'd get involved in all sorts of scrapes, and I was expected to bail him out. Later, without me around to protect him, Father had to rescue Damon from gambling, wenching, whatever. I'm glad I wasn't here to have to do it. Damon destroyed wherever he went, and other people had to pick up the pieces."

"Surely you're being too harsh on him."

He looked at me with an intensity that made my heart stop. "You think me a beast, don't you?"

"No," I replied, and looked away.

"You will, in time."

I stared at him, but said nothing.

The persistent breeze swerved and came at us again, tugging at my hair and pulling it from its pins. With a small sound of consternation, I tried to pin it back into place. Finally I gave up, and yanked out the pins one by one.

"That's better," Sir Mark said, smiling.

I felt my cheeks and neck grow warm. "Is it? Frizzy hair hasn't been fashionable since women wore farthingales," I retorted spitefully.

His eyes danced with suppressed laughter, but he said gravely, "Nevertheless, it suits you." He held out his hand and said, "Would you like a tour?"

I nodded and placed my hand unselfconsciously in his. As his fingers tightened on mine, I resisted the impulse to pull away.

He led me over rocks and down stairs, and I listened attentively as he pointed out what used to be the chapel, and showed me the monks' rooms, no bigger than closets. Still, I found myself concentrating on the man by my side. I really didn't know what to think of Sir Mark. Perhaps he could not warm to Amabel because the years of neglect had scarred him too deeply. I could envision him as a boy, bearing the burden of being the eldest, neglected by his beautiful mother because he was not one of her golden children, and as he grew older, having to rescue his hated brother and never being rewarded for it. Then, after ten years away from all this, to return and find them still allied against him.

But then again, they had all given him ample cause to hate them. I shivered: a father dead, a brother mad, and a sister helpless.

"Are you cold?" Sir Mark's words suddenly brought me back to the present.

I smiled. "No."

"You trembled just then."

"It must be this place."

He accepted my answer, and we continued our walk.

The floor stopped, and I found myself looking across a chasm.

"The floor partially caved in here," Sir Mark explained. "No one is allowed down there, for one never knows when the ceiling might fall in, but we can go down the stairs and get a glimpse of the interior if you like."

I hesitated. I felt as though someone was spying on us.

"What's wrong?" he demanded.

I laughed. "Too many stories of haunted abbeys."

He smiled and led me down the stairs, which had somehow managed to remain intact. Once we reached the bottom, I peered down into the cellars, a maze of tunnels leading God only knew where. All around, gray walls towered and closed in on us, while the wind-tossed sky floated farther above.

"What an eerie place," I murmured, pulling my shawl closer about me.

"Isn't it? As a matter of fact, this is where we'd find Damon."

I trembled. "Why would anyone come down here at night?"

"To find their lost love," was his reply.

I marveled at how well the huge blocks of stone, as thick as I was tall, had withstood centuries of wind, rain, and man.

Suddenly Sir Mark looked up and went rigid. Before I had time to think, he lunged at me and pinned me to the wall.

"Sir Mark!"

Even before the words were past my lips, thunder roared behind us and the earth rocked, sending up a cloud of dust that choked me and stung my eyes.

Slowly, almost reluctantly, Sir Mark moved away from me. "Are you all right?" The dark face was inches from my own and soft with concern.

Coughing, I replied, "I think so."

"Good. Stay here and don't move. I'll be right back." He went limping off, taking the steps two at a time, and disappeared from view high above me.

Suddenly I saw what had caused the earth to shake, what Sir Mark had saved me from. A stone, about my height, had plummeted from the wall above. All I could do was stare at it in horror.

"Oh, God." I sagged against the wall, my trembling knees refusing to hold my weight. This was the state Sir Mark found me in moments later, as he limped back down the stone steps.

"Nora?"

"That rock—" I babbled. "That rock—"

He was at my side in an instant, his arm around me. I sagged against him gratefully. "You're safe," he murmured, "safe now."

"If you hadn't pushed me out of the way . . ." Gradually, the hysteria began to recede. "Thank you, Sir Mark."

He smiled and patted my hand. "Now you can see why it's dangerous to explore these ruins alone. Some of the stones have been loosened by farmers seeking them for their own cottages. Let's get back to the Chase. I think you've had enough excitement for one day."

I nodded and allowed myself to be led out of the cellars. When Sir Mark saw that I had regained the use of my legs, he took his arm from my shoulders. To my surprise, I found I missed his support.

"What exactly did happen?" I asked, as we continued down the path.

"Just as I looked up, I saw the rock teeter and begin to fall."

"I owe you my life, Sir Mark."

"You owe me nothing, Nora," he said, then squinted at someone coming down the path. "It looks as though we have a visitor."

I looked up to see Dr. Price walking briskly toward us.

"Mark! Mrs. Woburn!"

Sir Mark raised his hand in response. "Sam. How are you?"

Dr. Price looked from one of us to the other, and his smile vanished. "Mark, is something wrong? Mrs. Woburn looks like she's seen a ghost, and your leg seems to be bothering you."

I looked up at Sir Mark, whose mouth was drawn in a thin line of pain. "One of the abbey's stones almost fell on us," he said.

"Why, that's horrible!" The doctor's face sobered instantly. "Are you all right?"

I nodded. "Sir Mark pushed me out of the way in time."

"You're lucky you weren't killed."

"Very," I replied.

"Mark, I'm surprised you didn't warn Mrs. Woburn about those ruins."

I spoke up. "I was warned, but my curiosity got the better of me."

"What brings you out to the Chase, Sam?" Sir Mark asked.

The doctor's face was grim. "I've just come from Kent House. Standish is dying."

I made a sympathetic comment, while Sir Mark said, "That bad, Sam?"

"He won't last the summer."

The doctor was watching Sir Mark intently for some reaction to the news. But the man's face told us nothing. He should be elated, I thought, for then he will be free to marry his mistress. Jane Standish would be Lady Raven, and Amabel would not be able to stop her.

"It looks like rain," was all Sir Mark said.

We reached the Chase just as the first drop fell. Mrs. Meadows, as reticent as ever, was there to greet us. Her sharp eyes took in my disheveled hair and the white powder clinging to my clothes, but she restrained herself from dusting me like a piece of furniture.

On my way back to my room, Amabel pounced on me as I passed the nursery.

"There you are, Nora. Where have you been?" she berated me in a peeved voice. "I've been looking for you all morning."

I quickly explained what had happened at the abbey.

"Why, Nora, you could have been killed!"

"I might have, if it hadn't been for your brother."

The astonishment was replaced by a look of cold cynicism. "Mark was there? Are you sure he didn't assist the rock a little?"

"Amabel!"

"Don't 'Amabel!' me. He's capable of anything."

I was becoming exasperated with the girl's willingness to blame her brother for anything, whether logical or not. "Sir Mark was right next to me at all times. Besides, why would he want to kill me when he hired me to be your companion? It doesn't make sense, Amabel."

Her face lit up like a candle. "It must have been Dennis," she said with gleeful conviction. "That stone wasn't meant for you, Nora, it was meant for Mark. Don't you see? Dennis always swore he'd like to kill Mark for cuckolding his father. And now that he's down from Oxford, he'll have every opportunity."

"You actually seem pleased that your brother could have been killed."

She tossed her golden head. "He deserves it."

"No one deserves to die, Amabel."

"He does," she insisted. "Did you see anyone up there?"

I shook my head. "We saw no one. Your brother even went up to investigate, but no one was there."

"There are plenty of places where one could hide," she said. "It would be fairly simple. All Dennis would have to do is wait for Mark to come by—he prowls around there often enough—push the stone, and hide."

"And possibly kill someone," I added.

Amabel didn't even hear me. "At last he's going to get what he deserves," she murmured, and flounced off.

I watched her disappear around a corner, and my head began spinning with thoughts. How could a house hold so much hatred, I wondered as I proceeded to the Ming Room. I thought of my own family. When I was growing up, my mother and father encircled me with their love. How sad that Mark Gerrick had never known such love.

As I reached my room, a bolt of lightning cracked the sky open like an egg, and the wind flung rain at my windows.

The rain put all of us, myself included, on edge. Amabel lashed out at her brother at every opportunity, and Sir Mark gave her measure for measure. Peter whined incessantly so that even Nellie lost patience with him. I even heard the implacable Mrs. Meadows snap at the maids on more than one occasion.

Sunday saw no letup in the foul weather, and I wondered if the rain would impede the family from attending church services in

Sheepstor. When I approached Sir Mark about this, he gave me his most sardonic smile and replied, "I am not a churchgoer, Nora. A carriage takes my servants, and you're welcome to join them, if you're of a religious bent. I'm afraid the Gerrick pew has been woefully empty. Amabel cannot abide self-righteous stares and I"—he spread his hands apologetically—"am past redemption."

"No one is past redemption," I retorted.

Since I myself was not of a religious bent—Ivor Stokes did not believe in organized religion, although my mother did, and attended church faithfully—I declined to join Mrs. Baker and Nellie in the carriage, and instead busied myself with my writing.

Monday promised to be a clear and warm day, and began with a summons to Sir Mark's study.

"Yes, Sir Mark?" I inquired.

He nodded briefly at an envelope propped up against the inkwell. "Your wages for the first quarter. Five pounds."

"Thank you, sir," I said, taking the envelope and turning to leave. I hadn't gotten more than three steps away from him when he called my name.

"Yes?"

The gray eyes were lightly mocking. "That's for you, not your husband. Do you understand?"

I looked down at the envelope in my hand. "Oliver will never see it."

"Good."

"I thought I'd have Old Corman drive me to Sheepstor to buy dress material."

He looked my faithful brown merino up and down and commented, "Good idea," before turning back to his work.

Before leaving, I asked Amabel to come with me. She declined, saying she had a headache. But she did give me the name of the shop where she purchased her dress material, and also asked me to stop at Dr. Price's office for some medicine for Nellie, who complained of a stomachache. I left Amabel lying on her bed, peering into a kaleidoscope.

My ride to Sheepstor was a silent one, for Old Corman wasn't in a talkative mood. So I concentrated on the beauty of the Devonshire countryside, and soon the trap had pulled up before Dr. Price's door.

The doctor's house was tucked away in a grove of trees at the end of a quiet, narrow street. There were a few houses nearby, but by and large, it was secluded and separate from the rest of the village. I thought this an odd choice for a doctor, who should want to be near his patients, not separated from them.

"You'll find me at the Headless Horseman," Old Corman announced, and with a nod of his head, he and Bonnet went trotting off.

A little bell tinkled as I opened the door to Dr. Price's office. I hesitated in the neat foyer, listening for any signs of habitation, and thought it strange that the only doctor in the neighborhood had no patients waiting to see him. Perhaps, I reflected as I peered up a flight of stairs, it was too early for calls.

"Dr. Price?" I called out. My voice sounded too loud in the hushed hallway. "It's Nora Woburn."

I opened one of the closed doors to my right, revealing an examining room that reeked of medicine. I closed that quickly. The other door led to a study of some sort, for I could see a desk strewn with papers, and heavy, worn medical tomes piled haphazardly on the shelves. Just as I turned to go, an ornately framed picture shining like a beacon from the desk caught my eye.

Curiosity is one of my many faults. Perhaps it is my writer's need to examine everything for details, or for an inherent story. But whatever drove me, I stepped inside to examine that picture.

A bright girlish face—she couldn't have been more than seventeen—smiled shyly out of the photograph. She was well-dressed, and a stray blond curl lingered on her shoulder. The girl had Amabel's fair beauty without its coolness or haughtiness. One instantly warmed to this person. There seemed to be writing in one corner, and so intent was I on reading it that I barely heard the warning tinkle of the bell over the door.

"To Father," it read. "From your loving Lucy."

"Do you always make it a habit of snooping, Mrs. Woburn?"

I whirled around, coloring furiously, the photograph still in my hand. Dr. Price filled the doorway, and the freckles on his forehead stood out in angry rusty spots. He regarded me mercilessly from behind his spectacles.

"Dr. Price! You startled me."

"Mrs. Woburn, I'll have you know this is my private office." He was furious as he snatched the photograph from my hand and set it reverentially on the desk. "I do not like people prying about my private office."

"I certainly didn't come here to rummage through your things." Now my temper was rising dangerously. I resented being treated as a thief. "Amabel asked me to come here for some stomach medicine.

Your door *was* open, and I called out several times, but no one answered. So I opened these doors, which were not locked," I reminded him, "to see if you were here. I was attracted to the photograph because the girl is lovely."

"Well, I hope you've satisfied your curiosity," he snapped.

I tried to placate him. "Is she your daughter?"

But my efforts fell flat. His mouth hardened into a thin, uncompromising line, and he said curtly, "She *was* my daughter. She's dead, drowned in a boating accident because of some young careless fool. Her mother died soon after." Before I could make any appropriate remarks of sympathy, he said, "Stomach medicine, did you say? I'll write you a prescription and the apothecary will fill it for you." He rushed into his outer office.

As I followed him out, I groped for something to say, words to soothe him. "Lucy is such a pretty name. That was the name of Damon Gerrick's fiancée, wasn't it?"

"I imagine there are hundreds of Lucys in Sheepstor alone," he replied, scratching out the prescription. "It's a common name."

He thrust the paper at me. "Once again, I apologize for entering your chambers," I said, then left.

I began walking in the direction in which I had seen Old Corman last, and fifteen minutes later reached the apothecary. Once I had procured the medicine, I decided to purge my thoughts of Dr. Price.

The kind proprietor of Fleetwoods was most attentive when I mentioned I was from Raven's Chase. For the next hour, I was treated like a Gerrick as bolts of sprigged muslins, taffetas, merinos and velvets were carried out one by one for my inspection.

When I finally walked out of the shop, I had parted with almost all of my first wages, and needed a boy to carry my parcels. I had bought both a dark blue and brown merino, as befitted a hired companion, but I had also bought fabrics that appealed to my frivolous side. One was a light sprigged muslin shot through with knots of green floss, another a crisp taffeta in a Nile-green shade, and a third of rich, elegant gold damask that complemented my amber eyes.

I had nowhere to wear them, but I was starved for their luxurious look and texture. Even if they never saw a ballroom, I was glad I had purchased them.

6

I am always amazed by how life's devastating revelations are often accompanied by warm spring days, with the sun ripening like cheese for summer and the air calm and languid. When I was seven, my father told me my beloved hound Toby had been crushed under the wheels of a carriage. Six years later, he told me of my mother's death of a lung ailment. And three years ago, kind-voiced Dr. Hickok told me I had lost the child nestled within me. On each of these occasions, the weather had been perfect, when it should have been filled with winter's wind and ice.

Even on this day at Raven's Chase, when I first learned my life was in danger, the weather held no warning of the terror I would come to know.

As soon as I rose, I went to the sewing room to lay down the light green muslin and cut out a pattern I had found in one of Amabel's fashion magazines. By the time Amabel walked in many hours later, with Peter in tow, I had the dress all cut out and pinned together.

"What, Mrs. Woburn?" she teased as she seated herself at the window to watch me work, "neglecting your precious writing to make a new dress, are you?"

"Oh, it's a very modest dress that won't waste material by using hoops," I said.

Amabel snorted disdainfully as she opened the window and set Peter's toys on the sill. "You don't fool me. Though you'd never admit it, you're as much a woman as I am and get just as excited about a new dress as I."

"No one," I retorted in mock severity, "gets as excited about a new dress as you do, Amabel Gerrick."

She laughed, a rich, honeyed sound so seldom heard. "You're quite right. But that is such lovely material. I look quite ghastly in that shade of green, but it suits you. Do let my dressmaker put it together before you ruin it."

"I can manage. Sewing is one of my few feminine accomplishments."

Amabel shook her head in wonderment as Peter mouthed one of his toys contentedly. "You don't play the piano or sing. You scorn needlework. And you don't know how to flirt or be demure, I daresay. Whatever did your husband see in you?" she demanded, half in jest.

"My father's influence as an artist," I told her, equally seriously.

All of a sudden, Amabel gave a little shriek of dismay, slapped Peter's backside, and chided, "Naughty boy!" As the baby wailed, his mother leaned out the window. Then she turned to me and said, "Peter has pushed all his toys out the window. Would you be a love and fetch them for me?"

I nodded, put my sewing aside, and went outside to find the toys. I had to walk around the building, and as I passed beneath an open window, the sound of voices reached my ears.

"She's dangerous, I tell you!"

I froze, my senses heightened by the raspy whisper and the implication of the words I had just heard. A voice—low, like a man's—responded, but try as I might, I could neither identify the speaker nor distinguish the words.

"Be calm, you say," the other voice continued. "How can I be calm with her prying and her questions? She'll find out something yet, mark my words! The high and mighty Mrs. Woburn will find out your scheme yet. She's dangerous. Dangerous!"

The blood stopped in my veins. The library's occupants were discussing me! But this was no time to pause for reflection. I stood still and strained to hear more, but all I heard were inaudible murmurs as they moved away.

There was a laugh, low and ugly, and the first voice whispered, "Another accident, then?"

Without a thought for Peter's toys or my own safety, I picked up my skirts and dashed around the house to confront the speakers.

As I careened around a corner, I nearly collided with the carriage that was waiting by the front door. I barely had time to glance at the horses shying away or the liveried driver who gave me an astonished look as I sped past and went flying through the front door.

Mrs. Meadows, on her way upstairs, stopped to glance down at me as I went tearing through the foyer. When I finally reached the library, I flung open the doors without ceremony to trap whoever was there.

Sir Mark and Jane Standish were the room's only occupants.

His face was livid and his temper barely under control as he confronted me. "Do you always come charging into rooms without knocking first, Mrs. Woburn?"

Jane Standish, dark eyes wide in a face white with panic, stared at me as though I had caught her naked in bed with her lover.

"No, sir," I stammered, my mind racing. "Amabel sent me to collect one of Peter's toys. She thought it might be here."

One brow arched in disbelief. "Oh? I didn't know Peter had acquired a taste for literature."

I gave a lame shrug and began backing toward the door. "I am sorry. I didn't realize anyone was here."

As I returned to the sewing room, I felt as though someone had hit me in the pit of my stomach. Sir Mark and Jane Standish were the voices I had overheard. True, they had been whispers, but who else could it have been? And they considered me dangerous. Why? my whirling brain cried out. If my prying had uncovered some scheme, I was unaware of it.

My thoughts fled back to the time I had overheard them talking about me in the library, while I had sat hidden not twenty feet away. "I have plans for Mrs. Woburn," Sir Mark had said. And there was to be another accident.

Another accident. What had been the first? My hands began trembling. The falling stone at the abbey had not been meant for Sir Mark, as Amabel suggested, but for me, and somehow, he had a hand in it.

"Not Sir Mark," I murmured aloud.

But why had he saved me, I asked myself. He could have just moved away until the stone did its work. No, it didn't make sense.

I felt lightheaded as I entered the sewing room.

"Well, where are Peter's toys?" Amabel's voice was peevish as she tried to calm her fretful child, now squirming and whimpering in her arms.

I looked at her blankly. "Toys? Oh, I must have forgotten them."

I turned to go back downstairs, and Amabel made an exasperated sound behind me.

After searching the grass beneath the library windows once again—a now-empty library, for I heard no voices this time—I finally found all of Peter's toys, scooped them up, and started back for the sewing room. The carriage that had been waiting was gone now, having taken Jane Standish back home to her husband.

When I entered the cool, dark foyer, I was startled to see Sir Mark leaning languidly against the newel post. "You've found my nephew's toys, I see," he said smoothly.

I managed a wan smile, "Yes, I did."

He seemed disturbed about something, for his mouth was drawn in a thin, uncompromising line. "You may tell my sister not to count on your company this afternoon. I wish you to go riding with me."

"Riding?" I echoed, my heart racing in alarm. It was easy to have an accident while riding. Guinevere could stumble and I could be thrown.

"Yes. To a place called Deepwell."

"I . . . I'd rather not, if you don't mind."

He laughed. "Still afraid of horses, Mrs. Woburn?"

Not horses, I said to myself, but you. "No. I have a headache."

I really hadn't expected that excuse to work. Sir Mark gave me a level look and said, "Then fresh air will do you a world of good."

"I'd rather finish the dress I am sewing, if you don't mind."

I regretted my words the instant they were out of my mouth. Who was I to refuse my employer anything?

Luckily for me, Sir Mark didn't appear to notice my rebelliousness. "Oh, but I do mind. I'm sure my sister's dressmaker can handle your dress most expertly." He was not going to accept my refusal. "We'll leave as soon as you change into your habit." He then turned on his heel and limped off before I had time to make any more excuses.

Less than an hour later, I was mounted on Guinevere, who regarded the dancing Odalisque with a contemptuous eye. We began our ride to the place called Deepwell. Uppermost in my mind was my need to remain calm and not give myself away to Sir Mark. I could never let him suspect that I was forewarned of his intentions. He must never know I mistrusted him. My life depended on it.

Under ordinary circumstances, I could have appreciated the fine figure he cut on his mettlesome mare, who never ceased rolling the bit between her teeth, as though she resented the metal bar's dominance. But I was preoccupied with survival.

We rode in silence until we reached the moor. In desperation, I said, "You must have seen a great deal of the world, Sir Mark."

His eyes focused somewhere beyond himself. "I've climbed mountains in South America, and I've frozen in the land of the Vikings. I've even seen a man killed by a shark in the Pacific islands. I suppose I could fill a book with all the places I've been and all the things I've seen."

"But did you find what you left home for?" I could not resist asking.

He glanced at me, puzzlement reflected in his eyes. "Yes, I think I did. I discovered who Mark Gerrick is."

"If it was such a full life, why did you give it up?"

He pulled at Odalisque's mane absently, and didn't look at me. "I grew tired, Nora. Tired of wandering. I missed Devonshire. I had proved to myself that I didn't need to be a Golden Gerrick to succeed, so it was time to return."

"And what became of your business?"

"My partner runs it in Plymouth and London with only minor interference from me."

"Did you know Dr. Price had a daughter?" I asked.

His brows rose in surprise. "Sam? No, I didn't. I knew he had a wife, of course."

"His daughter's name was Lucy, like your brother's fiancée." I told him about the day I had gone into the doctor's office, and that he had been very upset over my discovery of the photograph.

"I wouldn't be offended. Sam's a melancholy, secretive sort of fellow," Sir Mark admitted. "I suspect his work makes him that way, seeing so much pain and misery."

"I suppose that would affect one's outlook."

My companion smiled. "He's only been here since Doc Bright retired, right after my father's death."

This information startled me. "Why, I thought you were old friends."

"No. But I think of Sam as an old friend." He pulled at the mare's mane. "He's done so much for us all."

A silence fell once again, and my thoughts went back to this morning. I was confused. If I was some kind of threat to Sir Mark, why had he hired me to be Amabel's companion in the first place? Why hadn't he just left me to my fate in London? I would have been destroyed soon enough. Unless, of course, I had become dangerous only since coming to Raven's Chase, with all my "prying and questions." But the only questions I had ever asked were about Damon or Amabel.

Dread made the backs of my hands prickle. Suppose Amabel was right. Suppose Sir Mark was responsible for everything. What if she were next in line for elimination, and I was in the way.

I stole a glance at the man riding by my side. He was brooding and temperamental, but a murderer? Something inside me refused to admit this was true. But, on the other hand, his concern for my welfare could be easily feigned.

Still another thought came to mind. Someone else could have been in the library before Sir Mark and his mistress. It had taken me a few minutes to run back around the house, time enough for someone to slip out of the library. But who? Nellie? Mrs. Meadows? Or even Amabel herself?

The urge to confront Sir Mark about what I had overheard welled up inside me, but I quelled it immediately. If it was true, all he had to do was deny that he had been the one I had overheard. And then he would be on his guard, and I would be the loser.

"Tread carefully, Nora, girl," I heard my father say, "tread carefully."

We pressed farther into moorland, and had now not a speck of civilization around us. Turning in my saddle, I could no longer see the Chase. No shepherds lingered with their flocks, and no coaches stirred up the dust on the narrow lanes. Except for the mournful cry of a bird coasting on the winds above, Sir Mark and I could have been the only two living things in the world.

Without warning, the moor became even wilder than I could have imagined. Gone were the long flatlands, where our horses found firm footing. Steep, narrow paths lined with loose shale slipped from beneath Guinevere's hooves, so that even she became unsure of herself. I followed Sir Mark through canyons barely wide enough for the horses, and through shrubbery that caught at my skirts.

As we broke from the rugged terrain, I caught a glimpse of what looked like a village in the distance, but even that was so remote I dismissed it as a mirage. Finally, when my arms and legs cried out in protest, Sir Mark stopped, jumped off his horse, and announced, "This is Deepwell."

I looked around, thinking to see an estate or picturesque ruin of some sort, but only cliffs and more rocks greeted me.

Sir Mark grasped my hand and began leading me up a path of packed, well-worn earth that seemed to lead nowhere. When he stopped, I found myself on a ledge looking down into a pool of unimpressive dimensions, with a surface still as glass.

"The villagers never come here at night," he said softly at my elbow. "They say a spirit lives in its depths, and is heard to speak on occasion. It speaks the name of the next person in the neighborhood who will die."

A soft ripple of fear caressed my shoulders, and I became aware of Sir Mark standing behind me, not touching, but inexorably barring my retreat. The center of the pool held me spellbound, and I found I could not tear my eyes from those black, stagnant depths that mirrored my white, terrified face.

Suddenly, the surface rippled, as if words were trying to float to the surface. "Nora Woburn," they said, and I knew I would be the next to die.

I shook my head to clear the mist from my eyes, and felt my elbow clutched from behind. With a gasp of terror, I whirled around and threw myself at Sir Mark, refusing to accept the "accident" he had planned for me.

"Nora!" Sir Mark's alarmed face swam above mine as he grasped my arms to steady me. "What's the matter?"

"Why did you bring me here?" My voice was a hollow whisper.

He looked bewildered as he replied, "You write ghost stories, so I thought you'd be interested in the supernatural and Deepwell's purported powers."

I laughed shakily and passed my hand over my eyes. "I'm sorry. It seems as though the spell of the place did overcome me for a moment."

"It happens." Sir Mark was frowning once again. He regarded me suspiciously, as if my behavior baffled him.

He remained distant and preoccupied as we mounted our horses and started back to the Chase. My hands, still trembling at my narrow escape, communicated my fear to poor Guinevere, who seemed unusually skittish.

We stopped for refreshment at a charming roadside inn, but neither of us talked about anything of significance. When we went outside and waited for the groom to bring our horses around, I discovered this eventful day had still one more surprise in store for me.

A carriage rolled into the inn's yard, and I was startled to recognize it as the same carriage that had been at the Chase this morning. In it sat Jane Standish herself, a vision in an ornate bonnet of purple plumes and ribbons, and a stern-faced young man I assumed to be her son, Dennis.

So this was the boy who had fought with Sir Mark. He certainly hadn't inherited his mother's looks, for Dennis was short and heavy, with a sullen face. He appeared to be more brawn than brains.

As the carriage passed us, I received a jolt down to my shoes. Jane's eyes were red and swollen, as though she had been crying for a long time. She turned her head to Sir Mark as though he were a lodestone.

Dennis leaned forward, snarled, "Mother!" and placed a warning hand on hers. Jane shook him off and made some reply, which was lost to me amidst flying gravel and hoofbeats.

Glancing at the man beside me, I received my second shock. Sir Mark did not so much as glance at his beautiful mistress. He suddenly grasped me by the waist, and, before I could protest, lifted me into Guinevere's saddle as though I weighed nothing. Then he handed me the reins, vaulted effortlessly onto Odalisque, and we set off for the Chase.

I could not resist glancing back over my shoulder, but hastily looked away from that woman's haunted face.

"He took you *where?*" Amabel's blue eyes were incredulous.

"Deepwell," I answered. "It's a—"

"Oh, I know what it is," she interrupted, flouncing over to the sewing room's window seat. "Damon told me it was one of Mark's favorite spots. When he was a boy—if you can believe he ever was one—Mark went to Deepwell often, to defy the pool to say his name."

I stopped, my scissors poised in mid-air. In my mind's eye, I saw a tall, thin boy on the verge of manhood standing rigid before that stark, still pool. A mixture of loneliness, despair and desperation twisted his face as he shouted his defiance, more against the Golden Gerricks than the supernatural.

And today he had almost pushed me in. Why hadn't he done so, I wondered. It would have been so easy to subdue me.

"I said," Amabel intruded on my thoughts once again, "have you heard the news?"

"I'm sorry. What news?"

She paused for effect. "Mark has thrown over the Standish."

Jane's ravaged face floated before my eyes.

"It's true." Amabel giggled. "He ended their affair this morning. LaBelle Standish went wild. All the maids heard her screaming at Mark. 'You can't do this to me!' and 'I won't live without you.'" Amabel mimicked her cruelly. "'I love you! I'll die if you send me away.'"

I gave her a wry and skeptical look. "I doubt if she went that far."

"Well, maybe not those exact words," Amabel admitted. "I heard she even tried to stab him with a letter knife." She danced around the room and stopped. "Mark has another enemy to add to his collection."

"What do you mean?"

"Don't play the simpleton, Nora. 'Hell hath no fury like a Standish scorned.' Jane will make him pay for throwing her over. You'll see."

That evening, Sir Mark announced his plans to leave for Plymouth the next day. He would stay three days. Later, Amabel came to my room as I was dressing for bed.

"You want me to do *what?*" I cried in disbelief as she sat on the edge of my bed like a conspiring schoolgirl and outlined her plan to me.

"When Mark leaves tomorrow, will you take me to Goodehouse to see Damon?" Her eyes sparkled excitedly in the lamplight as she clutched my arm. "Oh, please say you will, Nora! You'll be my true friend forever if you do."

"Take you to Goodehouse? I can't do it, Amabel. Your brother has forbidden you to go. I can't go against his wishes."

"But he wouldn't have to know. We could tell Mrs. Meadows we're going to visit an old friend of mine from Miss Firthwright's, Rosalind Walkins. She lives near Goodehouse, and it's only a two-hour ride from here. We would leave in the morning, just see Damon for an hour, then come right back. That's all I ask, Nora, an hour with my brother. We could be back before dinner, and no one would be the wiser." She sat before me, pleased with herself for concocting such a plan. But already I could see its flaws.

"Amabel, even if we did fool Mrs. Meadows, someone at Goodehouse would be sure to tell Dr. Price we were there," I pointed out.

"But then it would be too late. I will have seen Damon. I will have found out if he's really as sick as Dr. Price claims." She wrung her hands in desperation. "Don't you *see?* I'll know if I can bring him home."

I shook my head. "And if you find this to be true, what then?"

As was her custom, when required to face a flaw in her reasoning, Amabel resorted to tantrums. "You don't want to help me. You're in Mark's pocket. You don't care if he's guilty of imprisoning Damon and plotting against me, do you? You don't care about the truth, as long as you have a roof over your head."

"I can't afford to be idealistic," I snapped. "And I think it's high time you stopped thinking of yourself, Amabel Gerrick."

"I'm thinking of my brother," she replied, her lower lip thrust out.

I sighed.

"Please, Nora!"

"I'm sorry, Amabel. I can't be a party to this."

But in the back of my mind, I knew I'd be taking her to Goodehouse, because I too had to learn the truth. The memory of that deadly stone whizzing past me and the feeling of terror at the edge of Deepwell were too fresh in my mind. I had to know if Sir Mark had intentionally imprisoned his brother without cause.

Amabel read me like a printed page. "You'll do it then?" Her face shone with an eager light that was hard to deny.

Damon was her golden god, and if I had to be the sacrifice. . . . Hard luck, Nora Woburn.

Wednesday morning found Amabel and me riding across the moors to Goodehouse.

That morning, a taciturn Sir Mark had been driven to Sheepstor, from where he would take the train to Plymouth. This time, unlike his custom whenever he left Amabel alone, he did not instruct Mrs. Meadows to watch Amabel, nor forbid her to use the horses. I was overcome with guilt as I realized he did so because he trusted me to watch her. But, I rationalized, a man who would lock his own brother away was not worthy of trust.

I at least had to give Amabel a chance to prove her brother guilty of all she claimed. My father had tried to teach me to be objective at all costs, to see an issue clearly and from all sides. Truth, he claimed, was more important than convenience.

A few hours after Sir Mark's departure, Amabel informed Mrs. Meadows that we would be leaving.

"We'll be visiting Rosalind Walkins, an old friend," she announced.

The housekeeper glanced at me, then Amabel. "Sir Mark said nothing of this to me."

"I just today decided to visit Rosalind," she replied blandly. "And besides, Nora will be accompanying me."

"Very well."

We had won.

The most difficult part of the whole scheme was securing the horses without having Young Corman insist that he accompany us.

"You wait here," Amabel commanded, leaving me behind the stables while she went stalking off.

Minutes later, she returned leading Flame and a bay mare I had never seen before.

"Where's Guinevere?" I demanded suspiciously.

"You're to ride Patches today. Guinevere would never make it to Goodehouse."

Patches looked docile enough, but I felt the familiar fear rise in my stomach.

"I'll help you up," Amabel said.

"I don't know . . ."

"Don't be a baby. Patches is as gentle as a lamb."

I hauled myself into the saddle. "Where's Young Corman?"

The girl grinned. "Out chasing Odalisque halfway to Sheepstor by now. And if they don't find her, Mark will have their heads. They all know it, too."

"You turned her loose?"

Amabel swung effortlessly into the saddle. "It was the only way I could think of to get the grooms out of the way. Now, shall we go?"

Goodehouse, Amabel informed me as we rode off, was located to the north. I recalled what I had heard of London institutions, and trembled to think of what we'd find there.

Amabel would have galloped Flame all the way, but, as I so sensibly pointed out to her, neither Patches nor I could survive the pace. She made a face, then sought to frighten me into going faster by galloping almost out of sight. I refused to play her game, and soon she came trotting back to me, only to repeat the performance again and again.

I had no way of knowing exactly how long we had been riding. My most accurate calculation was the state of my own body. When my arms and legs stiffened and ached, I could be certain I had been in the saddle for a long time.

And, suddenly, we were there. Amabel plunged up a rise and stopped, waiting for me to catch up. When I joined her, she looked down at the house like a medieval knight lusting after a castle for plunder.

She pointed dramatically. "Goodehouse."

I had expected a prison. What I saw was a small, neat Queen-Anne-style house and outbuildings complete with trees and landscaped grounds. A banker or tradesman could have lived there.

Amabel started down the hill. As we drew closer to Goodehouse, I felt as though I was staring at a beauty past her prime. From faraway, she looked beautiful, but upon closer inspection, one could see the wrinkles, the sagging jawline, the pouches under the eyes.

Surrounding the structure was a high gray stone wall, which I imagined sought to deter those who wished to leave. But then, I reminded myself, if Goodehouse was the sanctuary Dr. Price had painted it to be, why would anyone want to leave?

As I had expected, it was almost as difficult for anyone to enter the place as it was to leave. The guard at the gate only let us in after Amabel gave him the imperious performance of her career and mentioned Dr. Price's name several times.

Riding through the yard, I noticed a passive group of people in gray homespun tending a garden under the watchful eye of two men. They didn't so much as glance up at us, and I wondered if these people were happy in the world they had created in their minds.

We dismounted before the building's massive door, and a white-faced Amabel pointed out the bars across every window. Other windows looked boarded up, and I shuddered to think of those poor people inside, never to see the sun again.

We knocked. A hatch opened and a face peered out, asking our business. I explained that we were here to visit Damon Gerrick, with Dr. Price's permission, and then identified ourselves. The massive door opened reluctantly on squeaking hinges, and Amabel and I found ourselves in Goodehouse.

A heavy-set woman with grizzled hair scraped back in a severe knot greeted us. "Yes? And what may I do for you?" The voice and eyes were poised on the border between friendliness and hostility.

"I am Nora Woburn, and this is Miss Amabel Gerrick. We are here to visit her brother, Damon Gerrick." I surprised myself at how authoritative I could sound.

The eyes turned hostile. "I'll have to ask Mr. Wentworth."

"And who," Amabel inquired haughtily, "is he?"

"He runs Goodehouse."

Amabel raised her proud chin a notch. "Well, we demand to see him."

The matron rose stiffly. "I'll see if he's available."

"Do you think this Mr. Wentworth will let us see Damon?" Amabel whispered in desperation.

I shrugged. It had never occurred to me that perhaps Dr. Price had told Mr. Wentworth to admit no visitors on the pretext that Amabel might find her way here someday. Perhaps that's why Sir

Mark had taken no precautions to restrain Amabel before he left for Plymouth.

"Pray that Damon is allowed to have visitors," I whispered.

Fortunately, neither Dr. Price nor Sir Mark had instructed Mr. Wentworth to keep Amabel from seeing her brother, and the caretaker did not think it odd that Damon should have visitors.

Mr. Wentworth did not fit my image of a madhouse-keeper. A little badger of a man with sharp teeth and tiny eyes, he had the sweet smile and gentle air of my long-dead Uncle Aloysius, who used to empty his pockets of coins and little toys whenever he came to visit me.

As Mr. Wentworth welcomed Amabel and me into his office, he beamed and said, "I'm so pleased you've come to visit Damon. Why, his only visitors are Sir Mark and Dr. Price."

I thought this odd, since Sir Mark and the doctor were so insistent that Amabel not visit Goodehouse. What if she did, in fact, contrive to get to the asylum, as we did today? Shouldn't Damon's jailers at least be warned not to let her see him?

If Damon was as sick as we were led to believe, why was he allowed visitors at all?

"Who are the people tending the garden?" Amabel asked, as we left his office and followed him down a hall.

"Why, our patients, of course." Then he laughed, a soft, gentle sound. "Here at Goodehouse, we try to keep our patients occupied in productive labor. Some, of course, become too violent and must be restrained. But those that are able are allowed to garden or sew."

Amabel went rigid beside me. "I've heard patients are kept in dark cells and never washed. Or beaten like animals."

Mr. Wentworth regarded her indulgently. "Miss Gerrick, this is 1863, not 1800. Things have changed. I like to think Goodehouse is a very progressive institution."

She was not convinced. "Really?"

"We are as humane as possible. Some rooms do have no windows, true. But we wouldn't want a patient breaking glass and cutting himself, would we? We try to keep patients clean, but some of them refuse to be bathed without a violent struggle. We do what we can," he concluded, as he started to mount the stairs.

Amabel flashed me a desperate look.

Mr. Wentworth caught it, and smiled benignly. "Don't worry, Miss Gerrick. Your brother and the families of our other patients pay us well to see that their loved ones have the best of care."

So, Goodehouse was progressive because it was a private institution.

"In fact," Mr. Wentworth went on, "Goodehouse used to be my family's home. It was called Wentworth House then, but certain, er . . . circumstances forced my family to consider taking boarders. So you see, Goodehouse is just like the patients' own homes."

Both Amabel and I were unconvinced.

As we went upstairs, I had to admit that the floors looked swept and the halls light and airy. Through the walls, we could hear muffled shrieks and long, low wailing sounds that made one's hair stand on end. Amabel gripped my hand until my fingers lost all sensation.

We turned down a corridor where the patients' rooms were. There was a long row of heavy barred doors with tiny barred windows set in them. I kept my eyes focused on Mr. Wentworth's back, refusing to peer into the rooms.

"It saddened me to have to convert rooms I'd loved and played in as a boy," he admitted. "But when I think how much I'm contributing to the welfare of these poor souls in my charge, it seems like a small sacrifice."

And a profitable one, I thought to myself.

Finally we stopped before a barred door, and the man inserted a key, one of many at his belt.

As he swung the door open, he said, "Good afternoon, Damon. You have visitors. Isn't that nice?"

Amabel and I entered the room, which was, surprisingly, as large as the Ming Room. But it was furnished only with a bed, upon which Damon Gerrick knelt, his face turned toward the wall. Slowly, the blond head turned to see who had entered.

"Damon!" Amabel spoke softly and eagerly, stepping forward, her hand extended toward her brother.

A rush of pity overwhelmed me for the shell of a man kneeling there. The sweetly curved lips were slack, and those beautiful blue eyes that he and his sister shared were lusterless and totally devoid of spirit. It was as though his soul had been snuffed out of him. I was horrified.

A glimmer of recognition passed across his face like a candle sputtering in the wind. Then it was replaced by one of abject terror.

"Lucy," he whimpered, his face crumpling. "Lucy. No! No! No!"

Damon drew away from Amabel, flattened himself against the wall, and covered his head with his hands, all the while whimpering like an injured dog.

"It's me, Damon," Amabel said gently. "Amabel. Don't you recognize me?"

"Lucy. No, no, no," was his only response.

"I'm sorry," Mr. Wentworth said regretfully as he ushered both of us out of the room and locked it behind us. "I'm afraid that seeing you has upset him." Then he frowned. "Usually he just stares out the window and refuses to speak at all. But you, Miss Gerrick, have done the impossible. You've gotten him to speak." Mr. Wentworth beamed at Amabel as though the triumph were hers.

"It's terrible," Amabel moaned, her cheeks glossy with tears. "He's just like that night they found him at the abbey. He hasn't changed at all. This place hasn't made him better, it's made him worse!"

We arrived back at Raven's Chase at two o'clock that afternoon. Amabel cried all the way home, and when we arrived, she locked herself in her room and would see no one.

"What's wrong with Miss Amabel?" Marianne Meadows was suspicious. "Wasn't your visit to Miss Walkins—"

"We went to Goodehouse," I said. Sir Mark would hear of my treachery soon enough from Amabel or Dr. Price.

The housekeeper stared at me, her dark eyes narrowing. "You know the master doesn't want her there."

"I know, Mrs. Meadows, I know." And I went upstairs to my room.

Despite my own folly, which was sure to get me dismissed, I could not keep my mind off Damon Gerrick. The dissimilar opinions about his condition puzzled me. On the one hand, Sir Mark and Dr. Price insisted visitors would upset Damon, while Mr. Wentworth seemed pleased to see us. A fabrication on Sir Mark's part, to keep Amabel from seeing Damon? But why? And why hadn't Mark told Mr. Wentworth not to let Amabel visit? Could it be because the caretaker would have refused?

It was a heartless thing to do, to commit your own brother to an institution to punish him for being your parents' favorite. Cruel and unjust. Some part of me refused to see Mark Gerrick in that light. Perhaps he had just wanted to spare Amabel the shock of seeing Damon in that state. And I had made short work of that.

I was disgusted with myself, astounded at my own stupidity. In my eagerness to please Amabel, to prove her wrong, I had only succeeded in upsetting her and bringing Sir Mark's wrath upon my head. I deserved to be dismissed, and I was sure that would happen as soon as he returned.

"You've done it this time, Amber Eyes," my father mocked.

Perhaps Sir Mark was blameless for Damon's condition. Perhaps. But I was not yet thoroughly convinced.

Sir Mark returned on Friday, and I, like a coward, remained in my room, waiting for the summons that would send me packing.

It came later that afternoon, delivered by none other than Mrs. Meadows herself. "The master wishes to see you in his study," was all she said, but her eyes were filled with accusation.

I took a deep breath, squared my shoulders, and swept by her, as contemptuous as Marie Antoinette going to the guillotine. At least, I reminded myself, I would not have to answer for Odalisque, who had been captured and returned to her stall.

Sir Mark was seated at his desk. If I had entertained fleeting thoughts of mercy, they disappeared with one look at his face. His quiet anger seemed to ignite the air around him. Those eyes, cold and gray as Goodehouse, held mine.

"Hello, Sir Mark," I said. "Was your trip profitable?"

"Extremely so, thank you. I understand you and Amabel have been quite . . . adventurous in my absence."

I took a deep breath. "I am to blame. I allowed her to persuade me to take her to Goodehouse."

"In spite of my orders that she never go there?"

My mind raced to think of a plausible excuse to give him. I couldn't give myself away by telling him I half believed Amabel's wild accusations.

"Yes," I admitted. "I acted against your wishes. Amabel can be very persuasive, but my behavior was inexcusable. I betrayed your trust, and I deserve to be dismissed. I'll collect my things and leave tomorrow morning." I turned to go.

"Nora. You aren't leaving."

I turned in disbelief. "But . . . ?"

"Stop acting like a chastened child and sit down." His face was somber, but his eyes danced with laughter.

As I did so, still somewhat incredulous that he wasn't even mildly annoyed, he rose and stalked over to the window. "I have been tyrannical with my sister," he admitted, more to himself than me. "Her behavior is not exemplary, by any means. I sought to protect her from the truth about Damon's condition—that he'll probably never regain his sanity—but in doing so, I've fostered wild suspicions in her mind. So perhaps it's best that you took her there to see for herself."

Had my hearing failed me? Was Mark Gerrick absolving me? Or

was he seeking to allay my suspicions? "Are you saying I'm not to be dismissed?"

"I want you to stay."

Relief flooded over me. Visions of working in a London mill blurred and dissipated like smoke. "Thank you, Sir Mark," I virtually babbled, and would have risen, but his voice restrained me. "What did you think of Goodehouse?"

"I can't say. I've no standard of comparison, never having been in a madhouse before."

He turned. "Oh, come now, Nora. That's a coward's way out. You must have formed some opinion."

I spread my hands in bewilderment. "It looks like a progressive institution, from what I've heard of others. But it still frightened me."

The harsh features softened. "And how did you find Damon?"

I told him how his brother had just sat on his bed, calling Amabel Lucy. "But he wasn't violent."

Sir Mark replied, "And you're wondering why he's there at all, aren't you? You're wondering why he couldn't be locked in a room here at the Chase, as Amabel suggests."

"Yes," I admitted quietly, avoiding his eyes.

He paced the room like a caged cat, and finally flung himself back in his chair. "Nora, how can I make you understand?"

"Tell me the truth."

His eyes widened. "And you think I haven't?"

"Have you?"

Sir Mark's hand shot out and grasped my wrist. "Yes, Nora! As God is my judge."

"I believe you," I whispered, to ease his suspicions.

He released me and fell back in his chair, as though greatly relieved. Then he began talking, all the while staring at the ceiling. "I tried to keep Damon here, but he became so violent, and flew into rages." Sir Mark regarded me solemnly. "He began howling incessantly, like a demented animal. It was not pleasant. I had no other choice but to put him in Goodehouse, where he would get medical care."

"No, I can see now that you didn't."

Sir Mark gave a weary sigh and ran his long fingers through his hair. "Wentworth's a kind soul. He treats all of those poor people well."

"He seemed . . . kind," I agreed.

A light smile touched his mouth, then he became very still, as though his mind were a hundred miles away. He said, "May I ask you something, Nora?"

"Of course," I replied heedlessly.

"It's very personal."

"Then I may not answer it, but you're welcome to ask."

"Why did you leave your husband?"

"That is a very personal question, Sir Mark."

"I know it is, and I know it's none of my business."

I looked up into his eyes for the longest time. What did I see there? I couldn't tell. But suddenly I wanted to tell him about my failed marriage. Perhaps it was gratitude for his having rescued me from Oliver. I felt there would be no harm in his knowing the whole story.

As I began my sorry tale of Oliver's courtship, my father's fury and disownment of me and the eventual dissolution of my marriage, I felt a door open somewhere deep within me. The words came easily now. But there were some things I could never tell anyone, such as Oliver's constant belittling of me in our marriage bed. The humiliation was too much to bear.

"When I discovered I was going to have a child, I was overjoyed," I continued. "Somehow, it made up for all his infidelities. Do you know Oliver's reaction when I told him?" I laughed bitterly. " 'That will bring your father around.' "

"And did it?" Sir Mark asked gently.

I shook my head, while swallowing hard to keep from crying. "No. My father is as proud and stubborn as I. Even the prospect of a grandchild wouldn't move him an inch. Finally, when Oliver and I had not a penny more—he couldn't sell any of his miserable paintings —we began arguing. They were ugly, violent quarrels. One day, he struck me. I fell down some stairs." I put my hand to my head and choked out the words: "I lost the baby."

Mark Gerrick grasped my hands and pulled me to my feet. I made a feeble attempt to draw away, but he held me fast. I was mesmerized by those gray eyes, now burning with a fire of their own.

He shook his head. "My poor Nora."

Then he drew me to him and just held me, like a lost child, my face pressed against his shoulder. "Set yourself free, Nora," he whispered.

That inner part of myself which had so freely surrendered to Oliver resisted his comfort. Another man was seeking to enslave my emotions, I thought, and I felt the old fear steal over me. The trap was yawning before me like the black depths of Deepwell, but I was stronger this time.

"I can't!" I pulled away and stumbled blindly toward the door.

Sir Mark did not try to stop my headlong flight back to the Ming Room.

7

Another week vanished, a time that lingered in my memory because of its comparative serenity after the Goodehouse debacle. It was as though the house had reached a climax, and was now slowly drifting down.

The period affected everyone differently. Sir Mark was moody and withdrawn, and I saw little of him, since he didn't even dine with us. I wondered if he was thinking about Jane Standish at all. Amabel was subdued and listless, as though our visit to Goodehouse had finally brought home to her the fact that Damon would never be the same again. Even Peter absorbed our moods and became fretful and demanding.

I, on the other hand, felt a great urge for activity. When not writing, I was riding Guinevere, exploring, with Young Corman not far behind.

I did take the time to write to Mrs. James, a task I had seriously neglected. As I described Raven's Chase, trying to make my life here come alive through words, my former home leaped vividly to mind. I could smell yesterday's cooking in the foyer, and see Mrs. James smoothing stray hairs into place. I wondered if Madame Leclerc had taken over my rooms yet, and if Miss Fowler's cough had gotten any worse. And did Harry Leeds still stand guard outside, now that I was gone? Perhaps the police had caught him at last. The thought of Harry on the treadmill formed a knot in my stomach.

Hurriedly finishing my letter, I sealed it, then propped it up on my desk, where I could see it and remember to post it. Then I took paper from the drawer and continued working on my novel. After overcoming one thorny chapter, which had to be rewritten six times, I settled down to a few hours of smooth writing. But I soon came up against another obstacle: I needed a biblical quotation for one of my characters, a minister.

Since the Bible had never been part of my father's library, I was unable to quote scripture. But surely Raven's Chase possessed a Bible somewhere. I went downstairs to begin my search.

I scanned the library shelves in vain. There was no Bible here.

"Odd," I muttered to myself as I swept out of the room. Families like the Gerricks usually had Bibles to record their births, deaths, and marriages.

The uneven sound of Sir Mark's footsteps coming down the stairs tapped through my thoughts. I looked up.

"Sir Mark?"

He stopped. "Yes, Nora?"

"Do you—that is, does anyone here have a Bible?"

A slow smile jerked at his mouth as he came down the rest of the stairs. Before he could mock me, I added, "I need to look up a quote, for my novel."

"My father always kept the family Bible in his room. He was fond of it. Regretfully, I am just on my way out, or I'd direct you there. I'm sure Mrs. Meadows would show you the room if you asked." Then he bowed, wished me good day, and disappeared out the door.

I found the housekeeper in the kitchens, and explained to her why I wanted to go into Sir Charles' room. She nodded impassively and at once took me upstairs to a corner of the house which was seldom used and contained Sir Mark's parents' rooms.

"This was Sir Charles' room," Mrs. Meadows said, standing before one of several doors that lined the corridor. Then she reached out, opened it, and stood aside for me to pass.

It was an oddly ascetic room for a man who had lived such a full life. The walls were bright white, and the rugs a nondescript shade. The bed, bureau, and few chests were of plain dark wood. And there was the Bible, reverentially sitting atop its lectern of polished wood.

As I went over to it, Mrs. Meadows ran her fingertips lightly over the top of the bureau and shook the edge of the counterpane. Satisfied with the housemaids' work, she smiled briefly and left me.

I settled myself on the window seat and cradled the worn volume in my lap. Its spine creaked and the pages crackled with age as I gently opened it. Before seeking a suitable quote, I felt the need to satisfy an elemental curiosity. Turning to the front of the book, I scanned all the many different handwritings left behind by generations of Gerricks.

The first entries were so faded and spidery, I couldn't decipher them. But as I progressed, the names matched the portraits in the gallery. Finally, I came to Katherine Cross, who married Sir Charles Gerrick in 1830 and had given birth to Mark two years later, Damon five after that, and Amabel in 1844. I was scanning through more names, which looked like Sir Charles' assorted sisters, when something strange caught my eye.

Blank spaces had been left near Mark's and Amabel's names to indicate future spouses, but Damon's name was coupled with another's, Lucy Lawton, wed 1855.

Lucy Lawton. I stared at the name as if I should know it, my brow knotted in confusion. Sir Charles had recorded his son as being married to Lucy, but everyone insisted that Damon had met Lucy in India before the Great Mutiny, and the Cawnpore Massacre had ended that. They had never married. The mutiny had taken place in 1857, and this entry had them wed two years before they had even met!

"How very strange." I was puzzled. Sir Mark would want to know about this, just to correct his family history, if nothing else.

Then I turned my attention to the quote I was seeking and, after an hour's worth of work, I found one, so I returned to the Ming Room.

Two hours later, Flanna knocked to tell me that Amabel was entertaining Dr. Price and asked if I cared to join them for luncheon. So I deserted my writing for the Garden Room, where I found Amabel all honey and enchantment.

Amabel greeted me with her warmest smile, but Dr. Price rose and glared at me as he held my chair. His coldness chilled my back as I sat down, and I instantly sized up this little scene: Dr. Price was furious with us for going to Goodehouse and Amabel was trying to placate him.

"You should not have disobeyed us!" He seated himself and included me in his wrath. "You could have easily undone all the good work Mr. Wentworth and I have done."

"But even Mr. Wentworth said my visit had helped him." Amabel frowned. "Why, Damon never said a word to anyone until he saw me."

"So I was told." The doctor mashed his peas with the back of his fork. "Called you Lucy, did he? And you think he's showing improvement because he didn't even recognize you? Because he thought you were his dead fiancée?" I was sure there was pity behind those thick spectacles.

Amabel's face crumpled under the doctor's calculated assault on her reasoning, and, to distract her, I said, "By the way, Amabel, I've discovered a discrepancy in your family Bible." I quickly explained just why I had been in Sir Charles' room. Then I said, "Do you know that your father had Damon married to Lucy in your Bible?"

"Married?" She wrinkled her nose. "They were never married."

"Not only married," I added, "but wed two years before they met."

Amabel laughed. "You're not making any sense. Father was too thorough to make a mistake like that."

"But he did. There it was in black and white: Damon Gerrick wed Lucy Lawton in 1855."

A loud crash sent us all whirling around in our seats. Mrs. Meadows, her face crimson, stood there, with several dishes of the family's best Royal Worcester in shards at her feet.

"I'm sorry," she said. "How perfectly clumsy of me." And she turned to find someone to sweep it up.

"This is all very interesting," Dr. Price murmured, as red-faced as the housekeeper, "but what does it have to do with taking Amabel to Goodehouse?"

"Nothing, I suppose. I thought it was curious, that's all."

Amabel scowled. "What did you say the woman's name was?"

"Lucy Lawton."

"That's odd. I could have sworn her name was Lucy Middlebury." Then Amabel shrugged and dismissed the problem with an airy, "Oh, well, Papa just got the name wrong, I suspect."

I looked at her in astonishment. "Do you really think your father would have made a mistake like that? To err about his prospective daughter-in-law's name? And in the family Bible?"

Now it was Amabel's turn to be exasperated with me. "Nora, you can make as many mysteries out of this as you wish. But don't involve me in them. I don't care whose name is there. I have to concern myself with Damon and Peter."

I said no more, but quickly finished the food on my plate, then rose and left.

I could not expect Amabel to be concerned about the erroneous entry, for puzzles required unraveling, and time to let one's mind wander down one pathway of conjecture, then another and another. Amabel had no patience. But the mysterious Lucy Lawton continued to haunt me for the rest of the afternoon as I sat in the library.

Why had the meticulous Sir Charles made such an error? Suddenly, I sat bolt upright, sending the book I was reading sliding to the floor. Perhaps he had made a correct entry. . . . Perhaps Damon had married a girl named Lucy Lawton, then was sent over to India with his regiment. Had she gone with him, or stayed behind? If she had gone, what was all this talk of his meeting a girl in India? And if she had stayed, where was she now?

I slumped down, discarding that theory as soon as I had formulated it. A secret marriage was highly unlikely. Surely Amabel at least would have known of it, even if Sir Mark did not.

"You're not making sense out of this, Nora, girl," my father would have said.

I sighed, picked up my fallen book, and put it back on the shelf. I wished I were Amabel, and able to accept everything at face value, but I always had to question and pry until my curiosity was satisfied.

When I left the library and crossed the foyer, I met Sir Mark.

There were dark circles under his eyes, and his limp was more pronounced than usual. But his smile was dazzling as he said, "Hello, Nora. Away from your writing, I see."

"But only for a short while." Then I told him of my discovery.

The dark brows came together in a furrow. "Damon wasn't married. Father had some secrets he kept from me, but I'm sure he would have told me if my brother had married. Besides, his fiancée's name was Lucy Middlebury, not Lawton." He shrugged. "Well, my father wasn't himself from the day Damon returned from India. Perhaps he blamed himself for sending him there in the first place. Father often became befuddled and had lapses of memory. Perhaps he confused the names and wrote down the wrong one. He was almost seventy when he died."

"Amabel said he was too careful to make such a mistake," I said, "and I agree. Wouldn't a man know the name of his daughter-in-law?"

Sir Mark gave me a thoughtful look. "Why this preoccupation, Nora?"

"Just a writer's curiosity, I suppose," I murmured. "I find myself wondering who she was, and where she is now."

A smile tugged at his mouth. "Damon's ghost wife existed in a befuddled old man's mind, nowhere else."

"Perhaps." But while one part of me wanted to accept the obvious, another part of me hesitated.

At that point, Dr. Price came trotting down the stairs, greeting Mark warmly and me coolly. I excused myself and took my doubts to the Ming Room.

Hours later, when the house was locked for the night and everyone asleep, something—a sound, a dream—woke me, and I found myself sitting up in bed. I listened, but no floorboards creaked beyond my door, and no crack of light appeared beneath it. I glanced around my room. No shadow moved to menace me, so I slipped out of bed and went to the window.

Standing in an icy patch of moonlight, I shivered as I looked out over the silver lawn and the eerie ruins beyond. They looked much more sinister than romantic tonight. I shivered again.

Suddenly I saw something move. As I watched, a cloaked figure, the hood thrown back to reveal a familiar mane of gold, darted across the lawn and hurried down the path to the abbey.

"Amabel!"

She stopped and turned for a moment, as if she had heard me, then continued down the path, finally disappearing from view.

I stood in the darkness, wondering what mischief that girl was brewing now. She was probably the same figure I had seen leaving the house at night a few weeks ago.

Where was she off to at this hour of the night, and on foot?

I couldn't ignore her actions. I had to do something. Follow her? Amabel was out of sight now, and I doubted if I could find her by myself.

I turned and put on my robe. No matter if it was past midnight; Sir Mark must be told of his sister's nocturnal wanderings. What if something were to happen to Amabel? I would never forgive myself.

I lighted the lamp and held it high as I glided down the corridors to Sir Mark's suite. There I hesitated, my hand on the doorknob of his bedchamber, and stared at the door. Biting my lip and shivering, I wondered what to do. What if he should misconstrue the reason for my being in his bedchamber at such a compromising hour?

"Now's not the time to be priggish," I scolded myself, as I turned the knob and went in. A gasp escaped my lips as my lamp illuminated the chamber. It was the most sensual room I had ever seen.

Done in blue and gold, the furniture was deeply carved and gracefully turned. The bed had a full canopy, almost to the ceiling, and was draped with heavy woven damask curtains.

A queer feeling warmed the pit of my stomach as I thought of Sir Mark and Jane Standish. Had they ever enjoyed each other in this room?

So caught up was I in the beauty of this room, that I didn't realize at first that Sir Mark wasn't in his bed. I glanced nervously around, half expecting him to leap out at me from behind the curtains.

Of course, Dr. Price had been here when I retired, and perhaps he and Sir Mark were still lingering over brandy and cigars in the study. I stood still, barely breathing as I listened for voices. Silence. I hesitated. Surely Dr. Price, with his busy practice, would not keep such late hours. Perhaps Sir Mark had fallen asleep in his study. I walked over to the connecting door and quietly opened it.

There, hunched on the sofa, was Sir Mark.

He had left his lamp burning, so I extinguished my own and walked over to where he lay.

"Sir Mark." I gently shook his shoulder. "Sir Mark!"

He groaned, and his eyes flickered open. I was shocked at his pale, feverish appearance. "Are you ill?" My mission was quickly forgotten.

He turned on his side and brought his knees almost to his chest, as a child does to relieve a stomachache. "My stomach," he said, trying to smile and fit his large frame on the tiny sofa.

And a big head as well, I said to myself as my gaze alighted on two glasses and an empty bottle of brandy.

"I'll get one of the footmen to undress you and put you to bed," I said, turning to go.

"No!" He tossed again, with a little sigh of pain, and I thought he would fall to the floor.

I stopped. "Well, you can't spend the night here. Let me help you to bed." I took his arm and gently pulled him into a sitting position, but he just scowled and doubled over.

"Sorry. Too much pain."

"I'll help you. Just try to walk to your bed."

He succeeded in grimacing. "Persistent Nora."

I had often half carried my drunken father up to bed by the thin light of dawn. Now I wryly thanked him for his training. I swung one of Sir Mark's arms over my shoulders, while I encircled his waist with my other arm and hauled him to his feet. He turned as white as paper, and his legs were unsteady, but I was determined to get him to bed. Leaning against me, he managed to stagger into his room. He collapsed on the bed with a groan of agony.

Luckily for me, he had taken off his coat, so all I had to do was pull off his shoes and draw the coverlet over him.

As I turned to go, his hand closed around my wrist. Gray eyes narrowed and filled with mockery in spite of the pain.

"And what are you doing in my rooms at this hour, Nora?"

I felt my cheeks flame, not in embarrassment, but in anger. The arrogance of the man, to assume that I had come here seeking his favors. I almost blurted out my news of Amabel, but bit it off quickly. Sir Mark was in no condition to chase after his sister to-night.

"I—I couldn't sleep, and I came to see if Dr. Price was still here, so he could give me a draught of laudanum."

He released my wrist. "Mrs. Meadows keeps laudanum for sleepless people. You needn't have sought Dr. Price."

"I'll remember that next time."

"See that you do." Suddenly he was asleep.

When I returned to the Ming Room, I found that sleep did elude me. Gradually, as I calmed down, I found myself wondering about Sir Mark's stomach pains. It couldn't have been something he had eaten, for we all ate the same food at supper. Perhaps, I thought wryly, it was too much brandy. And as for Amabel, I hoped she had enough sense to return by morning.

As I stared at the canopy, I found my thoughts becoming increasingly wanton, as Oliver would say. I thought of Jane Standish in Sir Mark's rooms, doors locked against intruders and curtains drawn against the afternoon light.

I thought of Oliver's lovemaking in our own bed, and a feeling of revulsion gripped me. I envisioned his naked body, hairless as a rat's tail, lying next to mine. It was always the same, like the scenario of a play. He'd grope in the dark beneath my nightdress to arouse himself and satisfy his passions, then fall asleep snoring, leaving me with a hunger that had gone unsatisfied night after night.

Sighing, I rolled over on my side and watched the patch of moonlight on the floor grow smaller, then disappear. Somehow, I did not think lovemaking would be so mechanical in Sir Mark's bed.

"Nora, what wicked, wicked thoughts you have," I could almost hear my father's approving voice in my ear.

I smiled and went to sleep.

When I did awake, it was almost ten o'clock in the morning. After dressing, I went down to the Garden Room for a cup of coffee in place of the breakfast I had missed. I found another late riser doing the same.

"Good morning, Amabel. Did you sleep well?"

She eyed me suspiciously, then said, "Very well."

I poured myself a cup of coffee. "I am surprised, considering there are black circles under your eyes, and I saw you walking toward the abbey after midnight."

Malevolent sparks flashed in her blue eyes. "I didn't go anywhere last night."

"Oh, come now, Amabel."

"I said, I didn't go anywhere last night."

"I saw you."

"Then you must be mistaken. And it is my word against yours."

"I'm going to have to tell your brother, you know."

She glared at me, and instead of exploding, said very calmly, "People who tell lies about other people had better watch themselves, Mrs. Woburn. Sometimes they can find themselves in dangerous situations."

The voice I overheard came back to me. "She's dangerous, I tell you." Did Amabel know who considered me dangerous?

"Are you feeling well, Mrs. Woburn? You look positively gray." Amabel rose, turned on her heel, and flounced off.

Had I really expected her to confide in me, to tell me the truth? I left the Garden Room and went to look in on Sir Mark.

I found him in the study, meticulously dressed, but still pale and drawn. A thread of vapor from a mug of black tea within easy reach curled lazily upward.

"Good morning, Sir Mark. How are you feeling?"

He rose and smiled. "Much better, Nora. I must apologize for inconveniencing you last night, but my malady, which I acquired in the tropics, plagues me occasionally."

"You needn't apologize. But I feel I must explain why I came to your rooms last night."

The pale eyes sparkled. "You needn't."

I wanted to wipe that arrogant smirk from his mouth. "I feel I must. I saw Amabel leave the Chase a little after midnight and walk toward the ruins. You were so sick last night that I couldn't mention it. Amabel, of course, denied it when I confronted her this morning."

He was grave at once. "Oh? You're sure it was Amabel and not one of my servants?"

I nodded. "The moon was as bright as the sun, and I recognized her golden hair."

"Do you know why she left the house?"

"I have no idea," I said, although the man on the moor she pretended not to know flashed before me.

"I'll have to have another talk with Amabel," he said.

Later, as I sat in the sewing room, working on my dresses, Amabel came in. Her eyes were blazing, and two spots of color dotted her cheekbones, so I supposed Sir Mark had had his talk with her. But her smile and voice were as smooth as cream as she said, "Nora, could I ask a favor of you?"

I removed the pins from my mouth and sighed. Only Amabel could issue veiled threats on the one hand, and ask for a favor on the other. "What sort of favor?"

"Well, Peter has a cold, and I haven't seen old Granny Hatch in weeks. She was my nurse when I was very small, and I've always taken a basket to her. She lives in a cottage a short distance away on the moor. Would you take the basket for me?"

I stuck a pin in the green muslin. "Couldn't you wait until tomorrow? I don't know her, and I'm sure she'd rather see you."

"No matter. I'm sure she'd enjoy your company, and I'd give you directions."

Before Amabel had time to remind me that I was paid to do her bidding, I reluctantly agreed.

"Splendid. I'll have Mrs. Baker put up a hamper and then I'll meet you in the foyer."

A half hour later, I found Guinevere waiting for me by the door, along with Amabel and a hamper.

"I'll help you mount," she said, and when I was on the mare, Amabel handed the basket up to me. The tantalizing aroma of ham tickled my nose.

"I really appreciate this, Nora. I can't thank you enough. Most of the grooms are out training horses today," she continued. "Besides, it's only a little ways away. You'll not get lost. All you have to do is take the road we always ride, until you come to the crossroads. Take a left, ride for about three miles and you'll see Granny Hatch's cottage. You can't miss it."

"Perhaps I should ask Young Corman to accompany me," I suggested.

She frowned. "I don't think Mark would like him to neglect his duties with the horses. Don't be such a worry-puss. You won't get lost."

"Crossroads, take a left," I repeated, then touched my heel to Guinevere and loped off.

Guinevere looked balefully at the overcast sky, as did I. It gave the whole landscape a full, leaden cast, and made me shiver.

I found the road and set my horse trotting, for I did not like the looks of the sky and wanted to return as soon as possible. But, since trotting jostled the hamper, I had to rein Guinevere to a walk. The air was damp and cold for a May day, and I would have turned my horse around, but I didn't want to face Amabel's wrath.

Finally, I spotted the crossroads and turned to the left. Well, I decided, I was halfway there. Or so I thought.

The road, a sheep's track at best, seemed to deteriorate even further, but I kept Guinevere on it as best I could. When that too had disappeared, I just urged the mare on, confident Granny Hatch's cottage would come within view.

When we topped a rise, my heart stopped, for all that stretched out before me was uninhabited moorland, unbroken by cottages. The horizon looked blurred and shifting, as though the gray sky had fallen to earth. I shivered, for the dampness had worn through my thin habit and felt clammy on my skin.

Reining the mare in, I said, "Guinevere, we're going back this instant, Granny Hatch or no Granny Hatch. Amabel can stamp her pretty little foot all she wants."

I turned the horse around, but all I found was fog coming toward me like a locomotive. It was a gray wall that would engulf us in a second, a dangerous Dartmoor fog that trapped the unwary. We were soon smothered in a quilt of gray, and I could not see a foot ahead of me. The total lack of sound was maddening. As I sat stock-still atop Guinevere, I fancied I could hear the fog rolling in, crushing the grasses as it came on.

I was lost.

Guinevere gave a little whinny of fear and decapitated a tussock of grass with her hoof.

"I know, girl," I tried to reassure her with a hearty slap on the neck. "I want to get home just as much as you do." The question was, how?

Perhaps someone at the Chase would miss us and send out a rescue party. But why should they? They thought we were safe at

Granny Hatch's. My spirits plummeted. I had to do something besides sit in this saddle, chilled to the marrow.

Somewhere I had heard that if you gave a horse its head, the animal would take you home. It was worth a try, so I let the reins slacken, and whispered words of encouragement to Guinevere. She cocked one fuzzy gray ear back and whickered in fear, preferring not to take the initiative. But soon she began moving, no doubt spurred on by thoughts of a warm stall and hot bran mash. She picked up a little speed, and was soon walking steadily. I felt the hamper slide from my numbed hand and crash against a rock.

Guinevere walked and walked. Sometimes she pushed ahead with confidence, and other times she picked her way carefully. Her hooves repeatedly found solid ground when strips of wet, treacherous marshland surrounded us.

I lost all sense of time and direction. I might as well have been in America. All I knew was that I was cold, exhausted, and frightened. I wanted to get back to the Chase alive.

Suddenly my horse stopped without warning. I gently nudged her with my heel, but she refused my command and would go no farther.

I groaned in desperation, the utter hopelessness of my situation soaking into my soul like the damp through my habit. My whole body ached and I longed to dismount, but I knew I was safest where I was.

Suddenly, the mare flung her head back and neighed, a loud, piercing sound. From somewhere out there, an answering neigh came filtering through the mists. I snapped to attention. Where there was a horse, there might be a rider.

"Here!" I cried. "Help me. I'm lost."

Nothing. I called out again, and again.

"Hello!" a voice answered. "Keep talking. I'll find you."

I kept shouting, and out of the grayness came two spots of disembodied light floating toward me. The muffled clop of hooves was followed by the materialization of a horse and rider.

"Ah, there you are," the rider said congenially as he drew up next to me. "No need for tears. You're safe."

My tears stopped as I recognized the man who lived in the shepherd's hut above Raven's Chase. He wore a hat and a heavy wool wrap over his smock. Lanterns swung from each stirrup to light his way.

He regarded me with something akin to disbelief. "What are you doing out on the moors alone in this infernal fog?"

"I might ask you the same question."

"What else would a shepherd do but look for lost sheep? The miserable creatures must be somewhere about." He regarded me with narrowed eyes. "You're half frozen." Before I could protest, he had placed his wool wrap around my shoulders.

"Thank you," I murmured, too selfish to refuse its warmth.

"Think nothing of it. No one should be out on a day like today, myself included. I'm surprised your groom even agreed to let you have the horse, jewel that she is. Good girl," he said to Guinevere, giving her a friendly pat on the face. "Well, enough of this teatime chatter. You're a very lucky young lady. You're just a few feet away from the mire. A few more steps and . . ." He shrugged expressively, and I shivered. "Well, now, where do you live? If you follow me, I'll try to get you out of this."

I stared at him for a second before saying, "But you know where I live."

"Do I?"

"You've seen me riding with Amabel often enough."

Bright blue eyes seemed to laugh at me from out of that faceful of hair. "Amabel? I know no Amabel."

"I see," I said softly. "So you're both going to play that game. Well, you and she can deny knowing each other until doomsday for all I care, but I would appreciate being taken to Raven's Chase."

And he did just that. I was amazed to learn that Guinevere had indeed almost found her way home, but had wisely stopped at the edge of the bog. The bearded young man, who obviously knew these moors inside out, led me to the door of Raven's Chase. He jumped off his pony and lifted me from the saddle. When I removed his wrap and handed it back to him, he grinned and gave me a mocking bow. Then he mounted his pony and prepared to leave.

"Wait! I don't know your name, and I haven't thanked you for saving me."

He smiled. "Then we're even. I don't know yours." And he disappeared in search of his lost sheep.

I didn't even bother to knock, but opened the great doors myself. Marianne Meadows, crossing the foyer, regarded me with cold disapproval. "Why, Mrs. Woburn. Where have you been? The master's been looking for you all afternoon. He was just getting ready to send someone out for you."

"I got lost on the moors," I replied. "Will you have someone take poor Guinevere back to the stables, please?"

Just as I was about to mount the stairs, Sir Mark rounded the corner. "Nora, where have you been? We've been looking all over for you." He scowled at me. "Good God! You look as if you've spent the afternoon out in this miserable weather."

I explained that I had done just that. I told him how I had gotten lost, and how I had been rescued by a shepherd.

He was furious with me. "Whatever possessed you to go riding on a day like today? Old Corman knows the weather. I'll have his head for even letting you have a horse today."

"He's not to blame. Amabel wanted me to take a basket to Granny Hatch, and since I am paid to be her companion and to do her bidding—"

"She should have known better," he snapped, still angry.

I shook my head. "I can't understand it. I never even saw the cottage. And I did take the left road at the crossroads." I began shivering again.

Sir Mark was regarding me strangely. "You took the left road, did you say?"

I nodded. "That's the one Amabel told me to take."

"Amabel *told* you to take the left road?" His voice was so harsh I winced.

"Yes."

"Nora, the road to the right leads to Granny Hatch. The one you took leads . . . nowhere."

I stared at him. "But Amabel said—"

"Amabel said what?" Amabel demanded from the top of the stairs.

Sir Mark looked up at her. "Amabel, which road did you tell Nora to take to get to Granny Hatch's cottage?"

She looked at me and said, "Why, the road to the right, of course."

8

"The right!" I cried, my voice edged with hysteria. "You told me to take the road to the *left*. I heard you."

"My dear Nora, are you accusing me of lying, of deliberately sending you down the wrong road?" Her voice was ice, with eyes to match.

Then I understood what she had done. It was my word against hers, the mistress of the house. Who would believe me? My whole body began to tremble, while Sir Mark and Amabel floated far away from me.

"Mrs. Meadows!" Sir Mark's angry voice was close now, and when I managed to open my eyes, I saw his pale, furious face inches from my own. I felt myself being lifted, and by the erratic movement I knew he must be carrying me.

"What in the hell have you done now?" his voice boomed from a great distance.

Before I could reply, another voice answered, "Nothing! Can I help it if she misunderstood my directions? Are you going to believe her instead of me?"

"Amabel, she could have died out there."

"It's always my fault, isn't it?" And the voices faded far, far away.

When I next opened my eyes, the latticed canopy of my bed greeted me. Someone had gotten me out of my sodden habit and into my nightdress, then piled blankets atop me. Judging from the blackness beyond my windows, I had slept until nightfall. But I felt better, and shakes no longer wracked my body.

As I lay there, safe and warm, I thought about Amabel's deception. She had purposely sent me onto the moors, knowing I'd lose my way and possibly fall into a bog. But why? What had I done to her to cause this sudden turning against me? Chills shook me again as one explanation came to mind. Perhaps Amabel was afflicted by the same malady as her brother Damon. Perhaps the Golden Gerricks had one serious flaw. Amabel's outbursts and wild fantasies about Sir Mark certainly could indicate an unstable mind.

My thoughts flew back to the rock that had almost crushed me at the abbey. Amabel had accused Dennis Standish of that, when, in fact, she could have easily used a lever to move it herself.

But what of the conversation I had overheard about my "prying"? Amabel had been up in the sewing room with Peter, so it couldn't have been her. Two faithful friends then—one of them Sir Mark—seeking to keep me from finding out the truth about Miss Amabel?

Just as I shuddered again, the door opened and Flanna entered, bearing a tray. She was followed by Sir Mark.

"Feeling better?" he inquired, as Flanna set the tray on a table near my bed, then left.

I nodded, and thought it best to allay his suspicions. "Forgive me for my hysterics, Sir Mark. I must have been wrapped up in my own thoughts and failed to hear Amabel's directions."

He stood there, hands clasped behind him, looking down at me out of narrowed eyes. "Did you now? I was under the impression she gave you the wrong directions on purpose."

"For what purpose?"

"I don't know. You tell me."

"I can't imagine why she would want to harm me."

His mouth tightened. "There are many things one can't imagine happening at Raven's Chase, but they do. As long as you are well. . . ." He bowed. "Enjoy your supper, Nora." Then he left, pleased that I had not accused his sister of trying to murder me.

Avoiding Amabel would be as difficult as avoiding a cold night in December, so I resolved to behave as if nothing had happened, as if she hadn't purposely tried to harm me. Amabel accepted the unspoken truce and responded in kind, but the openness between us had disappeared. We smiled, we exchanged pleasantries and were together every afternoon, but each of us had erected our own wall against the other.

As she had promised, Amabel had her seamstress work on my dresses, and when the garments were completed, even I had to agree that the clever woman had salvaged my amateurish efforts and transformed them into modish London creations.

In spite of this kindness, I now dreaded my afternoons with Amabel. I refused to go riding with her unless Young Corman followed. Amabel did not press me, for she knew she had demonstrated her control over me and had won.

But I wholeheartedly indulged in her other diversions. Amabel was an unparalleled planner of diversions, especially picnics. This might mean a simple, impromptu affair consisting of lunch in the folly, or an expedition past the black stone cottage up to the Eyrie. Amabel would march Nellie, with baby Peter in her arms, myself, and sometimes Flanna or a footman carrying a heavy wicker basket up to her favorite spot. Once we were atop the steep rocky ledge overlooking a thick wooded grove and chugging stream, a white cloth was spread out on the ground, and a feast set upon it. While Nellie kept a sharp eye on the baby, we would enjoy cold chicken and fruit with our fingers.

Life was never better.

Of course, there were endless games of archery and croquet. Laughter took the edge off competition when Nellie tried to draw the bowstring and either failed or sent the arrow careening off course.

Evenings were quiet or festive, depending on Amabel's mood. Fond of drama, she'd choose a play and recruit members of the household to take part. Or sometimes she would treat us to a musical evening by accompanying herself on the piano.

As I stood there turning pages for her, a feeling of sorrow welled up inside me. Without her albatross, Amabel could have become the toast of London and secured an eligible connection, perhaps some titled son with political aspirations. Her beauty, charm, and social graces would have made her a superb political hostess. There was no chance of that ever happening now.

Amabel enjoyed light and sound and activity, but I preferred more quiet moments spent with Sir Mark playing chess. My father was a great believer in the game—"Sharpen your wits, Nora, girl. Teach you to think like a man."—and I was a skillful player, in all due modesty. Sir Mark had a well-honed mind that even a day of inspecting farms and mills couldn't dull, and he played with the precision of a general planning a battle. We spent hours in his study, the chessboard between us, and only the sounds of our breathing and the clock ticking broke the silence of concentration.

Contentment settled on Raven's Chase like a gentle rain. But unlike rain, it did not wash away whatever plagued those who lived here. It merely refreshed them for new battles.

For me, any contentment I had known was shattered when I was summoned to the library a week after my harrowing experience on the moors.

"Good morning, Nora," an all-too-familiar voice greeted me as I entered.

"Oliver!"

He smiled, a lazy expanse of white teeth, as he flipped through a book he was holding. "Why, my dear wife, I've spent a month tracking you down. I've traveled across the country to rescue you from this godforsaken place. You could be a little more appreciative."

I laughed. "If anything, I need rescuing *from* you, not by you, Oliver." My words wiped the smile from his face, and before he could erupt, I said, "Who told you where I was?"

"Mr. John Burke." He came toward me, but I moved fast and put a chair between us. "After your . . . friend so rudely dispatched me from your rooms that day, I had no desire to see you ever again. But I love you so much, Nora, that I just had to make you see reason, to come back to me, to—"

"Spare me the theatrics, Oliver."

He looked like he wanted to throttle me, but he controlled himself. "I went back to your rooms a week later, but your dim-witted proprietress couldn't, or wouldn't, tell me where you had gone. Well, I went to your solicitors, and Mr. Burke told me the whole story. Burke's a good man, as morally outraged by your behavior as I was."

"Oh, I'm sure."

Oliver held out his hands to me in supplication, and his gold wedding ring winked insolently at me. "Don't you see, Nora? Your reputation is in tatters. All of London—your publisher, your father's friends—is buzzing with the story of how Nora Woburn went off to Devonshire with this Lord Raven, a rake, a libertine, a man of no reputation at all." Oliver managed to look self-righteous. "Everyone thinks you're his mistress, living here openly with him."

I smiled ambiguously. "And what am I to do to redeem myself, Oliver? Go back to London with you, I suppose?"

"Would that really be so bad, Nora?" He made a move toward me, but I kept the chair between us. "I'd take care of you . . . you could write."

"I'd take care of you, you mean," I retorted.

"Your father is in London," he said quietly. "I saw him and talked to him. He wants you to come back to me."

"Liar! My father wouldn't give you the time of day."

"But he did. And he'll tell you himself once we're back in London."

"Oliver," I began, trying to keep my temper in check, "my father himself could beg me on bended knee to go back to you and I wouldn't. And it would take more than my publishers to accomplish that. Whether the Queen herself thinks so or not, I am here as a companion to Lord Raven's sister, and here I'm going to stay."

"Companion to his sister," he snorted. "My dear Nora, you are a fool, or an innocent. Why should Lord Raven do a kindness for the daughter of the man who crippled him?"

I felt my face turn white.

"Oh. I see he hasn't told you that tidbit."

I still could say nothing.

"Yes, I've checked into Mark Gerrick's background quite thoroughly. I even struck up a friendship with a seaman who was on that voyage to Italy where the 'accident' occurred. Seems your father and Gerrick got into a brawl over some Italian wench in a Roman *taverna*. My esteemed father-in-law broke a table over Gerrick's leg." A grin lit Oliver's face from ear to ear. "Gerrick swore revenge, dear wife, before they patched him up and sailed away."

"You're lying, Oliver." But my voice didn't sound convincing.

"Oh, no, Gerrick is. What a perfect scheme he has concocted." Oliver was cocky again, now that he had implanted a seed of doubt in my mind. "Kill Ivor Stokes and he dies once, but hurt his precious daughter, and he dies over, and over, and over."

I fought to regain my self-control, to wipe the shock from my face. I took a deep breath and said, "Whether you are telling the truth or not, I prefer to take my chances with Mark Gerrick."

Before I could blink, Oliver lunged at me, grasped my wrists in a viselike grip I thought him too frail to possess, and jerked me toward him. "All right, Nora, I've had quite enough of your nonsense. You may not care if the great Ivor Stokes' daughter is the object of scandal, but I care what people say about *me!*" His eyes bulged as he shook me like a rag doll. "I'm a laughingstock because of you!"

"I see it all very clearly now," I whispered. "You haven't come to rescue me from Mark Gerrick's vengeance, or because you love me. You want me for appearances' sake, so people won't mock you. You want all the drawing rooms of London to buzz about how Oliver

Woburn won his wife back." And became a man again, I thought to myself.

Again that murderous glint in his eyes. "Taunt me all you want, dear Nora, but listen and listen carefully. If you don't do as I say, you'll be very, very sorry."

"There's nothing you can do to me that will make me change my mind."

"I know that. But perhaps there is something I can do to your father that will."

I felt myself go numb inside. "What do you mean?"

"He wouldn't see me, that's true. But he is in London." Oliver smiled slowly. "You lived near the rookery. You know there are people there who would do anything for a price, even murder."

"If you ever harmed my father, I'd—"

"Do what?" He shook me again.

"I'd kill you myself."

Oliver laughed. "Brave words, my dear. But then"—he looked around the library—"there's always this house. And your lame lover and his sister. Amabel, is it? Charming girl, I'm told. Often likes to ride alone on a frisky horse. Nasty accidents can happen to girls who ride frisky horses."

A red mist passed before me, and I clenched my fists to keep from clawing Oliver's eyes. Before I had the opportunity, the library door swung open and Sir Mark limped in. He stopped short as though we had startled him, and I saw the question in his eyes as he glanced at Oliver, then me.

"Please forgive the intrusion, Nora," he said. "I didn't think anyone was here."

"Sir Mark, this is Oliver Woburn."

"Nora's husband," Oliver added unnecessarily.

Sir Mark inclined his head slightly, and said only, "Woburn," which placed Oliver at the disadvantage of having to explain his presence at Raven's Chase.

We stood like wax figures in a tableau, and when Oliver saw he would get no help from me, his pale face turned angry red.

"I've come to take my wife back to London where she belongs," he said.

I waited for him to accuse Sir Mark of keeping me here to avenge himself on my father, but he said nothing. Had Oliver made it all up, then? I had never thought him that clever.

Sir Mark, meanwhile, looked at me backed up against a table, clutching it for support. "Nora is not a prisoner here. She is free to go wherever she chooses."

Oliver relaxed. He had not expected this.

"However," Sir Mark continued, "if she chooses to remain here, you're not taking her anywhere, Woburn."

"Now, you listen here, Gerrick." Oliver sounded like a snarling dog. "Nora's my wife. I have the right to take her wherever I please."

"You have no right," I whispered. "I have nothing left that you can take from me."

"Aptly put," Sir Mark agreed.

"You're asking for trouble, Gerrick," Oliver continued. "Do you want a court battle and scandal? There are laws to protect people from libertines. I'll fight for what's mine."

Sir Mark's eyes turned cold, but he smiled and said, "Take whatever action you wish, Woburn, but I promise you it'll do you no good." Suddenly he looked at his watch. "As it's almost lunch time, would you care to join us?"

I stared at Sir Mark in disbelief. Oliver of course accepted the invitation. I could restrain myself no longer. Mumbling excuses, I bolted from the library like a startled doe and ran upstairs. On the landing, I almost collided with Dr. Price, who had been attending a sick footman.

"Mrs. Woburn, are you ill?"

"You might say I've just seen a ghost," was my wry reply. "My husband has come down from London. And there he is now."

From our position on the balcony, Dr. Price and I watched Sir Mark and Oliver cross the foyer below. Dr. Price seemed to stare intently at Oliver, and I asked him if he recognized my husband.

"No, no. I thought he looked familiar, but I must be mistaken. Well, if you'll excuse me, Mrs. Woburn, I think I'll look in on Peter while I'm here." He turned and went off down the hall.

Dr. Price did not join us for luncheon in the Garden Room. Mrs. Meadows informed us that he had other patients to attend to, so he had sent his regrets and left for Sheepstor.

Amabel came down, bursting with curiosity about the man who had married me despite my singular lack of feminine accomplishments. She waltzed in, a vision in cream and pink, and I knew she had changed into a new dress just for Oliver's benefit.

He grinned and bowed with a courtly flourish.

"You don't mind if I sit next to your husband, do you, Nora?" she inquired, with a coquettish flutter of lashes at Oliver.

"Not in the least," I replied.

While Sir Mark carved the slab of cold roast beef, Amabel chatted away with Oliver and I stared sullenly off into space. Every once in awhile I'd raise my eyes and catch Sir Mark watching me.

"And what is your profession, Mr. Woburn?" Amabel asked.

Oliver smiled. "Call me Oliver, please. I am an artist, like Nora's father." He followed this statement with a warning glance in my direction.

Amabel was all admiration. "How exciting! What do you paint? Are you a member of the Pre-Raphaelite Brotherhood?"

"Not a member, but merely an admirer of their style and goals. As a matter of fact . . ." And Oliver went on to recount an anecdote my father had once told him about the formation of the Brotherhood.

As Oliver began to bore all except Amabel with tales of his unremarkable childhood, I found myself comparing him with Sir Mark. Physically I wondered how I had ever found Oliver's fragile, slender body exciting. Perhaps my girlish romantic fantasies wove him into another Shelley, who needed me for inspiration. But now he looked ineffectual and foppish next to the dark, glowering Sir Mark. I wondered which was the more dangerous.

Their differences went deeper than the mere physical. While Oliver clamored for recognition of a talent he lacked, Sir Mark claimed nothing except that which he had earned. Oliver wanted to own me, to bend me to his will, but Sir Mark treated me as my own person. Was it only a facade, I wondered, while he plotted his revenge?

"Nora and I have our differences," Oliver was saying, "but what happily married couple doesn't? But I do want her back, Miss Amabel. Won't you take my part, dear lady?"

Sir Mark's brows came together, and I felt myself redden.

"Oh, Nora, how can you refuse him?" Amabel cooed. "I think he's so terribly romantic. Imagine, coming all the way down from London just to woo and win you."

"Amabel . . ." Her brother's voice held a warning.

"Please reconsider, darling," Oliver pleaded like a besotted lover, as he reached across the table for my hand.

I pulled it away, sickened by his display. But even more frightening was an absurd fear growing within me that, somehow, Oliver would have his way in the end. I saw my father beaten to death in a London alley, or Amabel lying on a bed of gorse, her golden head shattered.

Or, what if Oliver was right about Sir Mark? Was I fleeing one horrible nightmare, only to fall into another, more sinister?

"You must excuse me." My trembling hand sent my fork clattering against my plate. Before anyone could stop me, I fled past a startled Marianne Meadows and up to the Ming Room.

I lay on the bed, my temples throbbing. I had let my emotions have free rein, and the pillow felt damp beneath my tear-stained cheek.

I decided to remain at Raven's Chase, even though it might mean putting my life in danger. Somehow, that alternative was preferable to what Oliver had planned for me.

"Risks let you know you're alive, Nora, girl," my father had once said to me.

This risk could cost me my life.

A knock on my door interrupted my thoughts. I sat up and murmured a trembly, "Come in."

It was Flanna, dreamy-eyed as usual. She didn't even notice I had been crying, just bobbed me a curtsy and said, "The master wishes to see you in his study, ma'am."

"Thank you, Flanna." I swung off the bed as I dabbed at my eyes with a handkerchief.

Sir Mark was staring out the window as I entered. "He's gone, Nora." He indicated a chair for me. "I've forbidden him to come to the Chase again." Then he smiled. "I'm sorry. Can I have Mrs. Baker make you a tray? You had no supper, and you barely picked at your lunch."

I was hardened to Oliver's abuse, but Sir Mark's tender concern for me was difficult to cope with, especially since it might not be genuine. Ask him if it's true, a tiny voice prodded me. Ask him if he wants to hurt your father through you. I opened my mouth, but nothing came out.

"I'm no Elizabethan buccaneer," he said with a deprecating smile. "I won't lock you in a tower room and force you to stay here against your will, if you'd rather go back to London with your husband."

"No." The fear began again.

"I didn't think so."

I blew my nose with a dreadful honking sound, then said, "But I may have no choice. Oliver said if I didn't go back to him, he'd—he'd harm my father, or you or Amabel."

Mark started, and I watched his eyes narrow. "Threatened you, did he?"

I nodded miserably, not feeling very self-sufficient at all.

"Nora," he began gently, coming over and taking my hands in his. "You have nothing to fear. Ivor Stokes can take care of himself. And when he receives my letter about his son-in-law's threats, he'll be on guard." He smiled again. "And as for Amabel and me, we're Gerricks."

I had an absurd longing for him to take me in his arms and just hold me, this man who could want me dead. I, Nora Woburn, who despised my weaker sisters their romantic fancies. Why, you're no better than Amabel, I told myself.

But Mark Gerrick became very remote suddenly, as though a thought had entered his mind. He dropped my hands and walked back to the window, his limp labored and pronounced.

True to Mark Gerrick's word, I didn't see Oliver once during the next four days that crawled by. But, knowing my treacherous husband as I did, I could not believe that he had just shrugged me off and gone back to London. No, Oliver Woburn was out there somewhere, like a panther in a jungle, waiting patiently for his prey to pass.

I felt as Damon must feel, locked in his room at Goodehouse. His room, however, kept the world at bay. There was danger under my roof.

All evidence logically pointed to my enigmatic employer, but some stubborn core of my being refused to believe him guilty. "You're being illogical, Nora, girl," Ivor Stokes warned me. "Just like your mother, God rest her soul, letting your heart rule your head."

On the fifth day, I could stand it no longer. I abandoned my writing to look for Amabel.

"Nellie," I said as I entered the nursery, "is Miss Amabel here?"

Peter crowed and grinned at the sight of me. I stroked his fuzzy head while Nellie prepared to change him.

"The mistress is with her dressmaker, Mrs. Nora, and I wouldn't disturb her under pain of death."

I gave a little snort. "I see. Well, Peter, it seems as though you shall go walking with me." I sighed. "Oh, if you were only older. . . ."

Nellie chuckled as she turned him over expertly. "Aye, what a blessing that would be."

I left nurse and baby and went to the stables, hoping to get a little fresh air and exercise. Sir Mark had warned me not to go riding alone now, and to always take Young Corman or one of the other grooms, in case Oliver should appear. But Young Corman was nowhere to be found, and the other grooms seemed so busy that I hated to take them from their work just to jog behind Guinevere.

I decided I would go for a walk. Oliver was really not as dangerous as I imagined, and I would keep close to the house.

My good intentions vanished quickly as I started walking toward the moors. The sun fell lightly on my shoulders and relaxed me, as did the scented air softly touching my cheeks. Who could be impervious to spring's sweet seduction? Before I realized it, I was below the shepherd's hut.

Suddenly the door opened, and the secretive young man who had saved my life came out. He did not see me at first, so I had the opportunity to study him. Although attired in a homespun laborer's smock, he lacked the look and mannerisms of one. And, I told myself, no coarse laborer's hands had ever touched Amabel's white skin. No, there was something decidedly strange about my young rescuer.

He turned and saw me, so I waved and climbed up the hill to his hut.

"I want to thank you for saving my life," I said.

"No thanks needed," was his laconic reply.

"Did you ever find your sheep that day?"

He grinned. "I'd be a poor shepherd if I didn't, now wouldn't I?"

"I owe you my life, Mr. . . ."

"Lamb," he said, "John Lamb."

"A shepherd named Lamb. How appropriate."

The blue eyes twinkled. "If you insist I have a name, that one will do."

Where had I seen those eyes before?

"Can't you tell me your name?"

He grinned again. "No, ma'am."

"I'm curious about you," I admitted frankly. "You pretend to be a shepherd, but you're not. You also claim not to know Amabel Gerrick, yet I've seen you converse intimately."

The man seemed more amused than threatened. "You know what they say about curiosity, miss."

"You know it was Amabel who sent me out on the moors that day, don't you? She tried to send me to my death."

His grin was replaced by wide-eyed indignation. "Amabel would never—" he began, then stopped when he saw my trap.

"But you don't know Amabel," I reminded him as I smiled slyly and turned to go.

I felt a restraining hand on my arm. "You think that was rather clever, don't you?"

"Yes, I do," I said as I turned to face him. "It told me what I needed to know."

The young face was grave. "I trust you will keep what you know to yourself, Mrs. Woburn. It's the only prudent thing to do."

I shrugged. "I shall keep your secret for as long as it serves my purposes."

That seemed to reassure him. "Fine. It's all I can hope for. My life is in your hands."

"You saved my life. I owe you that." Then I smiled, wished Mr. Lamb good-day, and left him.

"I do have my reasons," I heard him call after me.

As I kept on walking, both the hut and its occupant disappeared behind a high hill. More gorse and heather grew here, and I had to pick up my skirts lest they catch on the grasping branches.

Suddenly I noticed a horseman riding toward me. Fear rose in my throat when I recognized Oliver's golden head. I decided I would not give him the satisfaction of running me down like a hound running a hare to earth.

He smiled as he reined in his dusty rented hack. "Why, Nora. What a pleasure to find you out here . . . alone. I've been spending every daylight hour watching that house, hoping you'd grow careless and come out without a watchdog." His eyes glowed. "And now you've come to me."

"If you think I came out here looking for you, you're mistaken."

"Why do you pretend to resist me? You know as well as I that you'll come back to me in the end."

"Will I?"

"Yes, you will. Or you'll be sorry."

I exploded. "How can you profess to love me when you've bullied and threatened me and those I care for? You can't base a relationship on threats. If you really loved me, you'd want me to be happy. And I am quite happy without you, Oliver."

"You think that now, Nora, but once we're back together, you'll realize what happiness you've missed. You're being stubborn, and I have to make you see reason. If threats will bring you back to me, then I'll threaten."

"I'm not going back to you, Oliver."

I turned and began walking away, while my heart hammered against my ribs. Suddenly I found myself pulled into Oliver's arms. His lips, wet and expectant, came down hard on mine, and he tried to force his knee between my legs. In a great rush of strength born of desperation, I struggled like a madwoman and succeeded in flinging him from me. But this only angered him further, and he lunged for me again.

"Would you take me in the bushes like a scullery maid?" I spat at him, as his fingers dug into my shoulders and forced me to the ground.

"It's time someone taught you obedience," he snarled.

Then he was on me, pinning my whole body to the ground, while twigs dug into my back. I screamed as his urgent fingers tugged at the bodice of my dress, which seemed to come apart in his hands. His face, contorted by lust, swam above me.

"Oh, God, not this!" I pleaded silently. "Anything but this."

Just as the fight went out of me, I felt the ground beneath me tremble and shake. Suddenly Oliver's weight was plucked off me. I sat up in time to see Sir Mark hit my assailant in the face. Oliver staggered back, then regained his balance and flew like an enraged bull at my rescuer. I heard someone grunt, and scrambled to my feet. Both men went crashing down into the heather. More grunts were punctuated by curses from Oliver and the dull thud of pummelling fists. It looked as though Oliver was winning.

But it was Sir Mark, hair disheveled and face bruised, who staggered to his feet. Oliver lay still, face down.

Sir Mark's gray eyes flickered darkly as he stooped over me. "Nora, are you all right? He didn't . . ." Mark swayed.

I jumped up, my torn dress forgotten. "No, he didn't . . . hurt me. But are you all right? You came just in time."

"I was coming from the Tarrant's farm when I saw Woburn there, looking like a hawk that's spotted a pigeon. I followed him."

"It's a good thing for me that you did. Thank you, Sir Mark."

I took his arm to steady him. He was breathing heavily through the nose, but he appeared to be recovering rapidly. Suddenly I became very conscious of my torn bodice, and so did he, for a wry smile tugged at the corners of his mouth. He bent down to retrieve something in the heather.

"He ruined your new dress," Sir Mark said, as he draped his cloak over my shoulders.

Until that moment, I had been more or less in control of myself, but those words snapped something inside of me, and I felt the tears slide silently down my cheeks.

Sir Mark whistled through swollen lips to Odalisque, who trotted over and stood docilely while her master lifted me onto her back. Then he swung into the saddle and encircled me with his arms. I looked back just once to see the distressed hack nuzzle Oliver desperately.

I sighed and leaned against Sir Mark mindlessly. Odalisque walked slowly and smoothly, as though she understood that I had already been jostled about enough for one day.

"I thought I told you not to leave the house," he said.

"I wish now that I hadn't. But the day was so beautiful, I just couldn't resist."

"Must you always be so willful?"

"Must you always scold?" I retorted.

With one hand, Sir Mark started picking twigs and nettles out of my hair. Before I realized what was happening, he had entwined his fingers in it and pulled my head back, so I had to look up at him. Cool gray eyes, suddenly warmed, gazed deeply into my own.

"Oh, no," I thought to myself. "Please, no."

He lowered his head and kissed me, tentatively at first, as though afraid to hurt me as Oliver had. I felt as if I were melting into a surging flame, and it was he, not I, who drew away first.

I hid my face in his shoulder and we rode in silence for a while.

When he spoke, his voice was husky. "My golden-eyed witch," he said tenderly. "I've wanted to do that for a long, long time."

9

For the hundredth time, I told myself I must leave Raven's Chase, and for the hundredth time, reminded myself that I could not. On the one hand, there was Mark Gerrick, and on the other, Oliver Woburn. I didn't have much of a choice.

I treated Mark's kiss as a gesture of comfort in my time of torment, nothing more. He meant nothing by it, of that I was certain. There were no nocturnal attempts to seduce me, no passionate declarations of love. And even if there were, he would find me cold and unresponsive. I had resolved not to fall under the man's spell, for he would use me as coldly and ruthlessly as he had Mrs. Standish. I had let my heart rule my head with Oliver Woburn, and regretted it deeply enough never to let it happen again.

And I was convinced of the rightness of my decision the day Jane Standish came to call.

Two days after Oliver had tried to force his attentions on me, Sir Mark, Amabel, Dr. Price, and I were having lunch in the Garden Room. Amabel, who seemed more carefree and less obsessed with Damon these days, was chattering brightly about a headstrong colt Young Corman was training. Dr. Price, who knew as little about horses as I, listened politely.

It was a quiet, pleasant lunch. Damon and Oliver were forgotten, as was Amabel's hostility toward her older brother. Smiles came easily to this plagued household for once, but they were not to be repeated for a long, long time.

Out of the corner of my eye, I saw a footman appear at the door and motion to Marianne Meadows, who glided silently over to him. Suddenly, the housekeeper turned and hurried toward Sir Mark.

"Sir Mark—" she began.

"You must pardon me for this intrusion," a dusky voice interrupted Mrs. Meadows.

Five heads turned to stare at Jane Standish, who had somehow contrived to get past the footman standing guard at the door. She was now bearing down on us like a regal ship pulling into port. Sir Mark and Dr. Price automatically rose to their feet, while one glance from LaBelle Standish sent Mrs. Meadows retreating to her post at the sideboard.

In spite of myself, I stared at the woman. At first glance, one would never guess she had been discarded by a lover. Her dress and bonnet were exquisite and expensive. Even her face was perfectly composed. But one look at Jane Standish's eyes, and you saw her anguish. I had to look away.

"Mrs. Standish," Sir Mark said formally. "I think you have met everyone here: Dr. Price, Mrs. Woburn, Amabel."

"Yes, of course." She nodded collectively at us, but her eyes were locked on her former lover.

"To what do we owe the pleasure of this call?" He had his back toward me, so I could not see his face, but there was no mistaking his tone, one of cold indifference.

Jane winced, as though he had struck her. "I would like to speak to you."

"Feel free to do so."

Her eyes flickered nervously over each of us. "Alone?"

"Madam," Sir Mark began, "there is nothing you have to say to me that cannot be said in front of my family and friends."

Jane's collected facade crumbled, and a look of desperate hunger replaced it. "Please, Raven." She placed a hand on his arm.

All he said was, "I'm sorry," very softly.

"Don't do this to me, Raven! You must talk to me. I'll make you understand."

Disgust and pity welled up in my throat. Dr. Price, still standing, was plainly embarrassed, for he kept fidgeting from one foot to the next as his gaze slid from his plate, to me, and back to his plate. Amabel was obviously enjoying this, for she gloated at her enemy.

"Control yourself!" Sir Mark hissed. "Have you no pride?"

"Not where you're concerned," she murmured.

I could take no more of this. "You must excuse me," I said as I pushed my chair away from the table. Before anyone could utter a word of protest, I was out of the Garden Room and running for the Oriental refuge of my own room.

Later that afternoon, I went down to the library. Not until I had closed the door did Sir Mark make his presence known. Too late to escape, I took a deep breath and confronted him.

I said, "That was cruel of you."

The mocking gray eyes looked down at me. "Sometimes," he said, selecting his words carefully, "it's necessary."

"But Jane Standish loves you!" I protested. "She was your—your . . ."

"Mistress." He smiled. "You sound like Sam."

"Don't you owe her something?"

He looked away as he slid his fingers down a row of books, then stopped. "I never told Jane I loved her, and I certainly never even hinted at marriage. Her husband had been ill for a long time, and my family was placing a great strain on me. Jane and I diverted each other." Sir Mark's voice took on the patronizing drawl I hated. "I assumed she entered into our relationship with her eyes open and unclouded by a romantic schoolgirl's fantasies."

"Evidently not," I remarked dryly.

"Evidently not," he agreed. "It's unfortunate she's being decidedly difficult about the whole business."

My temper soared to the ceiling. "You men are all alike!" I slammed my book down on the table with a startling crack that forced him to look at me. "You use women for your own pleasure, then discard them when they're of no use to you. 'She's being decidedly difficult about the whole business,'" I mimicked him.

Sir Mark smiled, but it was a smile devoid of warmth. "Are you presuming to choose my mistress, Nora?"

His words doused my anger as water did fire. I was, after all, his employee, and had no right to speak to him that way. "I presume nothing, Sir Mark," I replied quietly.

"Good. For I shall choose my own mistress—or wife, for that matter—as you chose your husband."

"Forgive me for speaking out of turn."

He cocked one sardonic brow at me. "First Amabel, now Jane. You have a kind heart, Nora. I wonder . . ."

"Wonder what?"

"Nothing." Then he smiled, bowed, and left me.

Jane Standish was still in my thoughts the following morning when I decided to go riding. But this time I had Young Corman follow me, in case Oliver should spring out from the heather.

As Guinevere jounced down a narrow, bog-bound lane, a day from my youth suddenly came rushing back to me. I saw my father poised before his easel centered in the studio, while I sat nearby, watching him as I hugged my knees. If my memory served me correctly, I had been suffering from unrequited love, and Ivor Stokes was quite out of patience with my languishing looks and sighs.

"What ails you, girl!" he roared, without taking his eyes off the model or letting a brush stroke falter.

Both the model and I jumped, but I knew he had addressed me.

"I'm hurting inside," I wailed. "I love someone who doesn't love me."

He stopped, turned around, and stared. "Nora, my dear, you mustn't be a slave to your emotions, as most of your sex are. You must learn to control them. For if you don't, there will always be some man ready to play upon them for his own ends. He'll leave you shattered and aching inside, while he goes blithely on his way, quite unscathed. I should know," he added under his breath, but I heard him.

Instead of taking his advice, I had promptly fallen in love with Oliver Woburn. And now, years later and miles away, my emotions were seeking to master me once again.

"Not on your life," I resolutely informed Guinevere.

She snorted, whether in disbelief or approval I couldn't tell. I smiled at that, touched my heel to her ribs and sent her into a jolting trot that required all of my meager skill to keep me in the saddle. We continued along this way until my mount started slowing down of her own volition.

"I don't blame you," I said, patting her lathered neck. "It is very warm today."

When I turned Guinevere around, I noticed the woman on the rock.

At first I thought she was a farmer's wife, for she wore coarse homespun and a black shawl was draped over her head and shoulders. She sat atop one of the many rocks that cropped up out of the moor, and she was watching me. The woman seemed so alone that I

—after a quick glance at Young Corman, who had stopped his horse within waving distance—rode up to her.

As I drew close enough to see her face, I recoiled in surprise. It was Jane Standish, and I was trapped. To just turn my horse and ride away would be unspeakably rude, but I was not looking forward to conversation.

"Hello," I said, halting Guinevere.

She stared at me, those great eyes piercing me to the backbone. Then her sensuous lips curled. "You bitch."

I felt as though she had struck me. "What have I done to you to merit such vile abuse?"

"What have you done, did you say?" She flung back her head so the shawl fell away, and she laughed, a shrill, bitter sound that caused Guinevere to whistle in surprise. "I would have expected affected innocence from Amabel, but not you."

"Mrs. Standish, I wish I knew what you were talking about."

She snorted in disbelief. "You do know."

"Well, I don't."

The woman regarded me thoughtfully for a long time, and I felt like a prisoner waiting for sentencing. Finally, she said in a bemused tone, "No, I don't think you do."

"Please enlighten me, then."

Instead of complying, she drew her shawl back over her head and looked out across the moors, as though she were a seaman's wife scanning the sea for his return. I could have been invisible.

"Mrs. Standish, you called me a bitch, and I'd like to know why."

She turned to me and snarled, "You took Raven away from me."

"What?"

She met my shocked gaze. "You heard me."

"That's absurd. You're imagining things."

"For one who appears so worldly, you're incredibly naive. Don't pretend you don't know Raven's infatuated with you. Ever since he bought that damned portrait, all I've heard is *Amber Eyes* this and Ivor Stokes that. I could feel his love for me growing cold. He was slipping through my fingers like sand and I was powerless to stop it. And when I met you, I saw he finally had what he wanted. Damn you!"

She cradled her head in her hands. I could think of no words to comfort her.

"I love Raven," she said, her voice old and drained. "When I first saw him riding across the moors, I knew I had to have him, for we're two of a kind, you see. I lived for him and the time we were together.

Nothing mattered—not my husband, not my son, not my self-respect. I'd give my life for Raven! And now he says he doesn't want me. Oh, God! What will I do?"

She began rocking herself to and fro, like a hurt child.

Sickness clawed at my insides. Now I understood why Mark Gerrick had ended their liaison. Jane Standish didn't love him, she was obsessed with the idea of loving him, and that destroyed her beauty.

I shuddered, and turned Guinevere to go.

"Wait!" The harsh command caused me to twist around in the saddle.

A gust of wind flung her words at me. "You will regret loving Raven."

She was a witch of Endor now, hollow-eyed and scheming, but I did not fear her. "Are you threatening me, Mrs. Standish?"

Without another word, I pointed Guinevere's head toward Raven's Chase, then kicked the mare into a startled canter. Behind me, a wail of anguish rode the wind.

But I did not go directly to the house. I was too unnerved and agitated by what Jane Standish had told me to risk coming face to face with Mark Gerrick just yet. When I halted Guinevere in the stable yard and slid off her back, I had already made up my mind to avail myself of the peace and calm of Amabel's Eyrie.

Several thoughts were racing through my mind at once, so I resolved to think of only one of them at a time. Uppermost was the woman's accusation that Sir Mark was infatuated with me. This so amused me that a smile crept out unawares. I, Nora Woburn, the unassuming brown mouse.

I reminded myself, as I passed the black stone cottage and began the arduous climb to the Eyrie, that Mark Gerrick had always seemed rather reserved with me most of the time, not at all like an ardent lover seeking to make a houseguest his mistress. Even if he was infatuated with me, I was certain I could hold him at arm's length, if I ever had to. What worried me were Jane's threats.

My breath was coming in sharp, shallow pants as I climbed higher and higher, my skirts held up so they wouldn't impede my progress. When my brow was damp from exertion, I hesitated a moment to catch my breath.

Anyone else would have dismissed Jane's threats as a futile means of lashing out in her grief, but I was genuinely afraid of what she might be plotting. For she was the type of woman who needed a man to provide her with a purpose for living. I myself had seen her in her prime, basking in Mark Gerrick's achievements, radiating beauty, charm, and confidence. And just now, I had seen her bereft, all her beauty gone as she wandered the moors like a lost soul. She reminded me of a doll I had once had. It was beautiful until I pricked a hole in it and drained all the sawdust out. Only a limp shell remained. I sighed, and drew the back of my hand across my eyes.

Her husband would be dead by the end of summer, and her son would probably cast her out. Even her lover had left her. Jane Standish had nothing to lose, and that's what made her dangerous.

I began walking again, and soon left the sun-seared hillside to plunge into the inky shadow of the trees that hovered close together, protecting the Eyrie from the prying eyes of curlews and crows. The muted chuckle of the stream far below me came to my ears as I stepped out onto the rocky platform.

The sound of voices caused me to freeze. I listened, not daring to breathe as I strained my ears to determine the direction the voices were coming from, and whether they were friendly or hostile. Gurgling water mingled with words, until a sharp bark of laughter burst above nature's whisperings. I followed it to the opposite side of the brook, far below the ledge on which I stood.

It was Flanna, naked to the waist, her arms extended upward to the man who stood over her. But it was the man who held my attention. He was Dennis, Jane Standish's son.

My eyes widened in astonishment. Dennis was Flanna's lover. Suddenly, everything came together with lightninglike clarity.

Dennis hated Mark Gerrick for his liaison with Jane Standish. The boy had sworn revenge, but to do that effectively, he would have to have access to Raven's Chase. And what better way to do that than by wooing a susceptible serving girl? Someone to spy on the family. Or even to unlock doors, when all were asleep. An enemy masquerading as a friend in our midst. Despite the warm day, I shivered as though snow were swirling about my ankles.

Flanna smiled beguilingly at Dennis, and said something I could not hear. It was just as well, for he started to unbuckle his belt. That was my cue to leave, and I did so, backing away without so much as the snap of a twig underfoot. When there was no chance of them hearing me, I turned and started back toward Raven's Chase.

My thoughts were in a turmoil as I hurried down the hill. Today I had seen the storm clouds gathering to make their assault on Raven's Chase, but unlike a storm's thunder and lightning, the form this violence would take was unknown. Perhaps it would take aim at Sir

Mark, perhaps myself. Or both. Or Amabel. Or even—God forbid—baby Peter.

For some inexplicable reason, thinking of Peter made me recall the baby-farm letter I had found when I had first come to the Chase. I halted in midstride. Had Flanna been responsible for it, I wondered? A woman who bares her breasts to her lover can expect results in nine months' time, I thought wryly to myself. I had found the baby-farm letter over one month ago, and if Flanna was "knapped," as Gentleman Harry would say, she had a long way to go before her condition became apparent. Perhaps she had rid herself of the unwanted child already. There were ways, even down here in Devon.

Later, I told Sir Mark about my meeting with Jane, but only about her threats against him, not those to myself, for that would lead to a discussion of why she had threatened me. I wished to avoid that at all costs.

He listened attentively, his fingers entwined behind his head as he sat back in his chair. Finally, he said, "Jane is apt to be melodramatic at times. I wouldn't take her threats seriously."

"I would," I said with a shiver. "She's so hurt she's apt to do anything."

"'Hell hath no fury . . .' and all that," he replied with a smile. Then he regarded me thoughtfully. "I shall be on my guard. Thank you for warning me."

"There's something else. Your maid, Flanna—the red-headed one—she and Dennis Standish are lovers." I felt my face redden.

"And how did you come to find this out?"

"I saw them in a compromising situation up at the Eyrie," I replied, as I blushed even more.

"And what business is it of mine what my housemaid does with her time?"

"Don't you see?" I cried in desperation. "Dennis hates you. He's sworn to kill you. Couldn't he be using Flanna to spy on this household? What a perfect situation!"

Sir Mark suddenly became grave as he weighed my words. "I see. I've often wondered if Dennis hasn't been responsible for certain occurrences as of late, and this could be the proof I'm looking for."

I thought of the rock that almost crushed us to death at the abbey. "I don't wish to condemn him without proof," I said, "but I think Dennis Standish is a young man to be wary of."

"I most certainly agree," Sir Mark said grimly, and his face became as cold as steel.

It rained for two days.

During this period, I found myself haunted by Damon. My brain had collected every bit of information I had ever heard about him since I came to the Chase, and over these two wet and dreary days, my mind fed each bit back to me. I was obsessed by him, so much so that I couldn't concentrate on my writing. Even my sleep was dream-riddled. . . . Damon adored. . . . Damon in exile. . . . Damon out of his mind.

While I thought of Damon more, Amabel seemed to be thinking less of him. She seldom spoke of him now, and dinnertime outbursts had ceased. Conversation between her and Mark was civil and intelligent.

On one of these torrential afternoons, I remarked to her how pleased I was that she had finally cast off her fancies about Mark being responsible for her other brother's madness.

Her round blue eyes regarded me thoughtfully over Peter's head. "Oh, Nora. How wrong you are. I still hate Mark as much as ever. I've just become more adept at hiding it, that's all."

Amabel thought herself so clever she had to tell me just how clever she was, which in itself wasn't very clever at all. I was relieved. She had not yet become truly sly.

"I'm sorry to hear that," I said.

"Have you decided to go back to your husband, Nora?" She gently pried open Peter's fist to remove a button before he had time to swallow it.

"I'll never go back to him, Amabel. I've told you that. There's been too much damage done already."

She stared moodily out the window. "I think it's frightfully romantic to have someone so in love with you that he'll follow you halfway across the country."

I sighed. It was pointless to tarnish Oliver's shining armor in front of Amabel. She refused to hear ill of him, and I was tired of defending myself.

"Did you like being an artist's daughter?" she asked.

"Yes. Yes, I did."

"What was it like?"

"Very free and what I suppose you'd call unconventional. People dropping in at odd hours. Picnics every Sunday. That sort of thing. And we'd visit other artists to see what they were painting. Writers were always bringing over their manuscripts for criticism and we'd stay up half the night discussing literature or the state of the world."

She sighed and flopped down on the nearest seat. "It sounds so wonderful."

"The grass is always greener somewhere else," I reminded her.

"You don't know how lucky you are, Nora. You're free. I'm tied down with a child, although I love him deeply, and am virtually my brother's prisoner." She shuddered.

"You mustn't say that, Amabel."

"But it's true." She hugged herself. "And one day Mark will try to harm me. I know it."

I went over to her and put my hand on her shoulder. "Why do you say that?"

Her brow furrowed. "Because he said something that killed Papa. Then he locked Damon away. I'm next, Nora, I'm next!"

I shook my head. "Mark doesn't want to hurt you, Amabel. You musn't have this wild fantasy."

The girl's lips turned white as she silently watched me. "Oh, Nora. Why won't you believe me? Has he fooled you, too?"

I didn't answer her. I went instead to the window to watch the gray wall of water advance and retreat. Somehow, I felt besieged, and the storm was only delaying the inevitable. Beyond these encircling walls and the implacable rain, our enemies were amassing to destroy us. Oliver lurked somewhere out there, of that I had no doubt. So did Jane and Dennis. Would mother and son now join forces to bring about Mark Gerrick's downfall? I wondered.

But what of the danger from within? The fortress had been infiltrated by Flanna. There was Amabel's hatred to contend with. And what about me? There was a very real possibility that I was in danger.

Watching the raindrops merge and run down the windowpane, I pondered Oliver's accusation that Mark Gerrick sought to injure my father for laming him. Yet all I had to do was confront him and demand to know the truth. Somehow, I couldn't bring myself to say those words. Was I afraid they might be true?

"I hope the rain stops," Amabel said with a sigh.

I agreed.

The following morning was dazzling, with the well-scrubbed freshness so common after a long cleansing rain. After being imprisoned for two days, I could not resist the impulse to take a long, leisurely stroll.

I wished the Gerricks socialized with their neighbors, for I missed the stimulation of meeting new people. Certainly Mark knew a great many people besides Dr. Price: the gentry, business acquaintances, townspeople. But he chose an insular life and seemed to shun company. Was it because of Amabel? He had mentioned the many doors closed against her because of her illegitimate child, but surely this was no reason why Sir Mark should deny himself stimulating company.

I stopped, poised to pick a flower. Perhaps he did care for his sister's feelings after all. Not wanting to make her feel excluded, he neither invited others to his house, nor called upon anyone else. I shook my head. Why couldn't Amabel open her eyes?

When I returned an hour later, my slippers and hem soaked from the wet grass, I felt invigorated and able to face those formidable blank sheets of paper. So I kicked off my slippers, ignored the damp hem clinging to my ankles, sat down, and wrote.

My fingers were cramped when I finally set my pen down. My neck also ached, and the clock on the mantel told me I had missed breakfast long ago.

I slipped my manuscript into a drawer and rose to go downstairs to the Garden Room for lunch. I was halfway across the room when I noticed the neatly folded square of white paper lying a foot inside the room.

It was a note. Someone had slid a note under the door while I was writing. The backs of my hands tingled as I bent down to pick it up. I unfolded it and began reading.

Nora,
There is something we must discuss. If you care about the Gerricks at all, you will meet me at the ruins tonight at midnight. Come alone. Tell no one, or you shall regret it.

Oliver

Rage coursed through me like a locomotive as I read the familiar handwriting. Wrenching open the door, I peered down the empty corridor, but whoever had left the message hadn't lingered to be caught. I stepped back into the Ming Room, reread the note as if I couldn't believe my eyes, and then struggled to compose myself.

Who put the note under my door, I wondered? Oliver himself? That was impossible. He'd never risk it. Perhaps he had bribed one of the servants, a scullery maid who came from her cottage to work at the Chase, a guileless girl who fancied herself love's messenger. Even Amabel would have done it, so sympathetic to Oliver was she.

I would confront her with it. I had my hand on the knob when I hesitated. "Tell no one," Oliver had said, "or you shall regret it." What if I did show the note to Amabel or Sir Mark? Oliver was a desperate and vindictive man. If I caused any harm to befall the Gerricks. . . .

Groaning aloud in exasperation, I crushed the note into a tight, angry ball and flung it into the wastepaper basket. I wanted to rid myself of that which Oliver had touched.

What did he have to discuss with me, I wondered peevishly. More reasons why I should go back to him, no doubt. Well, there was no harm in keeping this absurd assignation and hearing what he had to say.

I stopped short. Nora, you fool! Had I forgotten so quickly how Oliver had tried to force himself on me? The ruins would be dark and deserted. If I should scream, no one would hear me. Not Sir Mark, not Amabel. No one would be there to come to my rescue this time. Perhaps Oliver planned to kidnap me. He was not beneath such high melodrama.

Or did he plan to commit the ultimate outrage that would force me to go back to him? Loathing welled up inside of me. I shivered, thankful these four walls separated us. I was safe in this house. Oliver could not harm me here.

My whole being straightened with resolve and purpose. Let Oliver plan his clandestine meetings and esoteric messages. I refused to play his games. He could threaten all he wished, but nothing was going to lure me out to a deserted ruin alone and at midnight.

Such antics were fine for silly heroines of romantic novels, but I credited myself with some intelligence. No, Oliver could die out there before I left the security of Raven's Chase.

10

And Oliver did die that night.

I was awakened at five o'clock the following morning, as I lay secure between the sheets and quite unconscious of the furor racing through the kitchen and servants' quarters. A hand on my shoulder shook me. "Nora, wake up!"

My eyes flew open to see Mark Gerrick sitting on the edge of my bed. There were dark smudges beneath his eyes, and his mouth was set in a grim line. His clothes looked as though he had thrown on his shirt and stepped into his boots and pants. And when he spoke, he whispered.

"Wake up, Nora. Your husband is dead."

The last word instantly purged sleep from my mind. I sat bolt upright. "What did you say?"

"Oliver Woburn is dead."

"Oh, my God!"

"One of the tenants' girls who works in the kitchens found him this morning as she crossed the fields. She came screaming to Mrs. Baker, who in turn told Mrs. Meadows. . . . You look quite pale, Nora. This has been a great shock, I know." He squeezed my hand. "Shall I have some hot tea sent up, or some brandy?"

"Both," I said. As he jerked the bellpull at my bedside, I heard a voice unlike my own say, "How . . . how did it happen?"

Sir Mark looked down at me. "He had a fall, I think. The back of his head was crushed. I'm sorry, Nora. I was the one who brought him in. It could have been caused by a fall. Sam Price will know soon enough."

My face felt cold. "Oliver dead. I can't believe it. Dead!"

A light knock sounded. Sir Mark rose and answered it. The person left and he came back to me.

I looked up at him. "Where is he?"

"In an empty guest room."

I laughed inwardly at that. Oliver had never been a guest at the Chase.

"I've sent Young Corman for Sam. He'll have to examine the body, of course. Cause of death must be determined, and whatever else is necessary."

"May I see him?"

Sir Mark hesitated. "He's not a pretty sight, Nora."

"But surely his face—?"

"Perhaps later, when you've rested."

Perhaps later, when the blood has been discreetly cleansed away, and Oliver's clothes changed.

A knock, bolder this time, intruded on my thoughts. Sir Mark answered it and returned carrying a tray laden with a glass of amber brandy, a steaming crockery pot of tea, hot muffins and fruit bread, all kindly placed there by Mrs. Baker, I had no doubt. It was plain food to soothe and comfort. I felt like a cosseted child again.

Somehow, Sir Mark understood that I wanted to be alone, for he smiled, touched my hand, and left without a word. When the door had closed noiselessly behind him, I rose, downed the brandy in a few searing, choking gulps, then poured myself a cup of tea.

My husband was dead.

I took the cup and walked over to the window. The tea tasted strong and bracing as I sipped it. The sun had not yet risen, but the unblemished sky was touched with pink around the horizon, as a virgin blushing in anticipation of her lover's coming. I smiled sadly. Whether we live or die, the sun rises and sets.

"Well, Nora, girl," I could hear my father say from a long way off, "how do you feel now?"

"I feel sorry," I said aloud. "No one—not even Oliver—deserves to die. But I am also glad that I am free."

Memories of the Oliver Woburn I had first known flooded my thoughts. Would I ever forget that spring day when I was walking through Hyde Park with Georgina Burne-Jones? A handsome young man I had never seen before introduced himself and managed to appear everywhere I did. Or the foggy, drizzling afternoons we spent strolling through galleries and discussing paintings and painters? It all came rushing back. Oliver was sweet, sincere, and unspoiled then, and he had made me feel that I was beautiful.

I put my hands to my eyes, and for the first and last time in my life, wept for him.

"Mark, you know I've got to report this to Constable Tibbins," Dr. Price announced as he joined us in the library. He looked tired and grave as he unrolled his shirtsleeves.

Sir Mark and I were the only ones keeping a vigil here. Lucky Amabel was still asleep, although it was nine o'clock already. There would be time soon enough for her to know.

"Why must the constable be notified? Oliver's death was an accident." I looked first at the doctor, then at Sir Mark. "Wasn't it?"

Dr. Price looked at me and Sir Mark. "It doesn't appear so," he said.

My hand flew to my mouth. "You mean Oliver was *murdered?*"

"I found an iron rod not far from the body," Sir Mark said, as gently as he could. "There can be no doubt that it's the murder weapon. Nora, sit down."

He helped me to a chair before my knees could buckle. "How horrible!"

"It happened about midnight," the doctor said. "Robbery was probably the motive. A farmer with a dozen children to feed, some thief down on his luck. Who knows? But what ever possessed the man to wander about the ruins at midnight?"

"He was waiting for me," I blurted out, suddenly remembering the note.

Both men stared at me. Sir Mark said, "Woburn's been prowling around the Chase for days trying to persuade Nora to go back to London with him."

"I see," was all the doctor said.

"But there was something else," I added. "Yesterday, someone slipped a note under my door. It was from Oliver." I went on to explain how he wanted me to meet him at the abbey, and that I was to tell no one. "I decided he probably wanted to kidnap me or harm me, so I never went to meet him last night."

Dr. Price smiled slightly. "Very wise of you. You probably would have come to harm yourself."

Or seen who had murdered Oliver, I thought numbly to myself.

When I glanced up, Sir Mark was watching me with an expression of astonishment on his face. Then he looked away, leaving me puzzled.

"Well," said Dr. Price, rising, "I must put things in order for Tibbins. I have no doubt he'll arrive soon." He nodded in our direction and left.

Mark turned to me, his face threatening. "Why didn't you tell me about this note?"

"Should I have? It seems so inconsequential."

"It may or it may not be. Are you sure it was from Woburn?"

"It was in Oliver's hand, and in his belligerent tone."

"Did you see who delivered it?"

I shook my head. "Perhaps Oliver bribed one of the maids to do it, someone who could get into the house easily and who knew my room."

"That's possible."

My head began to ache dreadfully, and I pressed my fingers to my temples to relieve it. "Oliver was cruel to me. He tried to use me. But now that he's dead . . ."

Sir Mark smiled gently. "You did love him enough to marry him."

"Yes, I did." A vision rippled before my eyes, then disappeared forever.

"Tibbins will be here soon," Sir Mark said. "If anyone can discover who killed Oliver Woburn, he will."

Tibbins. The name conjured a Cruikshank caricature, a portly man whose addiction to drink buffed his cheeks into ruddiness and widened his girth. The man himself, contrary to what his name implied, was neither bluff nor stout. Clyde Tibbins was a tall whip of a man whose candid eyes devoured details while his sharp mind sorted them out. He appeared to be the kind of man who relished ale and pork pie, and cases that were black and white. I wondered if Gentleman Harry had his kind to reckon with in London. If so, I felt sorry for him.

Our first meeting with the good constable took place in the library with only myself, Sir Mark, and Dr. Price present. I had just come from viewing Oliver's body, and was still shaking. But Sir Mark's calm, level voice soothed me as he told of being awakened by Mrs. Meadows at five A.M. It was she who had informed him that one of the kitchen maids had come upon a dead man in the ruins. The maid had run screaming to the Chase. Sir Mark told of dressing quickly and going out to the abbey to investigate, and finding Oliver's battered body and the rod that had been used to club him to death. Sir

Mark then sent for Dr. Price, he said, and carried Oliver back to the house.

Constable Tibbins listened without comment and occasionally scribbled in a green-bound book he carried.

"I would like to speak to the girl who found the body, your lordship," he said.

Effie Cooper, a nervous, wispy thing with red swollen hands, was sent for and ushered in. She kept twisting her fingers in her lap and looked as though she wanted to cry, but dared not.

"Now, there's no need to be afraid," the constable said, making an attempt to calm her, but only succeeding in making her even more skittish. "We just want the truth."

"I lives on a farm down by Rye's ditch," she began. "I works for the Gerricks in the kitchen, like my sister does, only she comes later. I gets here early, usually before dawn, so's I can start the fires. This morning, I comes through the abbey, as I usually does, when I saw this man just lying there." The young face lost its ruddy bloom. "At first I thinks he was drunk. Then I looked and sees that his whole head was smashed in and bloody. There was blood on the grass near him, too. I got so scared I just screamed and screamed and ran as fast as I could to tell Mrs. Baker."

"Did you see anyone there, Effie?" Tibbins asked, so gruffly that the girl started and shook her head wildly.

"I didn't stay around waiting to get murdered myself!" she replied.

"That will be all." The constable dismissed her.

As Effie bolted out of the library like a startled cat, Clyde Tibbins turned to me. "You are the victim's wife, are you not? Nora Woburn?"

I nodded.

A brow rose suspiciously. "May I ask what you were doing here at the Chase, while your husband was out there? Did you quarrel?"

"About three years ago." I spent the next half hour telling the man just why I was here. And I also told him about the note.

"I see," he said, when I had finished. Disapproval tightened his mouth. In Constable Tibbins' narrowly circumscribed world, wives stayed with their husbands. "Mrs. Woburn, who could have killed your husband?"

"Many people. Oliver had a talent—perhaps his only talent—for making enemies, but all of them are in London, as far as I know."

"I see. There's no one else."

Oh, I threatened to kill him on several occasions, I felt like saying, but one could not be offhand with a man like the constable.

"No one," I said.

Tibbins turned to Sir Mark. "I must inspect the area where the body was found, and also make some inquiries in town. I also want to question everyone in this household about various matters that puzzle me. I must ask your lordship, and Mrs. Woburn, to remain here and make yourselves available for further questioning."

I felt as though I were watching the next day pass before me through a gauze veil. People once so familiar to me had become strangers, observing me from a great distance, and when they spoke, their words sounded slow to me.

When Amabel was told what had happened, she turned white and stared hard at me for a moment.

"I'm sorry for him. I liked him," she said, then drifted back to the nursery like a ghost.

Dr. Price insisted I should rest, and gave me laudanum to make me sleep. Through the haze, I remembered Sir Mark at my side whenever I opened my eyes.

Constable Tibbins returned the next day.

He summoned us all into the library late that morning. As I seated myself across from Sir Mark, I noticed a long object wrapped in sacking on the table by Tibbins' side. I knew what it was, and instinctively recoiled.

When we were all seated, including Amabel, Tibbins' cold eyes swept over us, and he said, "Thank you for being so prompt. As you know, I've been investigating the site of the murder out near St. Barnabas' Abbey. All we found there was this," he said, unwrapping the parcel and producing a long iron tool, the murder weapon.

Amabel shuddered and turned away, but I could not.

"This is what killed Oliver Woburn," Tibbins intoned. "Hit from behind, he was. Doubtless he never knew what hit him. Mrs. Woburn, where were you at midnight on the night before last?"

I jumped. "Why, in bed, sleeping."

His face was a mask. "You did not go to the ruins to meet your husband?"

"No. As I told you, I ignored his note and did not meet him there as he wanted me to."

"Then how do you explain *this?*" He whipped a crumpled piece of paper out of his pocket and thrust it at me.

As I unfolded it and began to read, the constable said, "That note, Mrs. Woburn, says that *you* wanted your husband to meet *you* at the ruins at midnight on the night before last."

The damning words in my own handwriting leaped out at me. "But this can't be! I never wrote this. There is some mistake!"

"That is your handwriting," he insisted, producing another wad of paper. "It matches the writing we found in your wastepaper basket."

All I could do was shake my head. "It may look like my handwriting, but I swear I never wrote this."

All eyes were on me. Amabel gaped at me in shock, and Dr. Price looked baffled. Sir Mark, however, tapped his fingertips lightly together and regarded the constable through narrowed eyes.

"We found that note in your husband's rented room in Sheepstor," Tibbins said. "How do you account for it, if you didn't write it?"

"I don't know. All I do know is that I didn't write it."

"Let's see the note you claim to have received."

"It's in the basket by my desk," I replied softly. "I threw it away."

While Tibbins sent Dr. Price to fetch the basket, the rest of us sat in shocked and hostile silence. Who would want to play such a monstrous trick, I wondered dismally. Finally, the doctor returned with the basket, and he and the constable began to go through it, rapidly unwrapping each wad. Soon all of them were smoothed out.

"There's nothing here," Tibbins announced.

I sprang to my feet. "But there has to be!"

"There's a simple explanation for that," Sir Mark intervened. "One of the maids usually empties the baskets when she does her cleaning."

"But in that case, the basket would be empty," Tibbins said. "I would like to speak to the maid who cleans Mrs. Woburn's room."

Within moments, Flanna entered the library. She looked prim in her white starched apron and cap, and for once was not dreamy-eyed. But all I could envision was the voluptuous creature reaching up for Dennis Standish in the wooded grove.

Constable Tibbins asked her if she had emptied the basket.

"No, sir," she answered promptly. "The last time I emptied the wastepaper basket was two days before yesterday. I'd be emptying them today, sir."

"I see. Thank you, miss. You may go." As the door closed behind the maid, Tibbins put his hands on the table and leaned forward. "Well, Mrs. Woburn, where is your note? It's not in the basket."

"I don't know. All I know is that I did throw it away."

Suddenly, I realized just where all this relentless questioning was leading. "You think I killed Oliver," I whispered, staring at Tibbins. "You think I lured my husband out to the ruins and hit him with that —that thing!" I cried, pointing to the iron rod. "Well, you're wrong!"

The constable said very softly to me, "And where were you at midnight, the night before last?"

"Just where the lady says she was," Sir Mark replied smoothly from the depths of his chair.

We all looked at him, while Tibbins said, with exaggerated politeness, "And just how would you know that, your lordship?"

He smiled. "Because I looked in on Mrs. Woburn a little before midnight the night her husband was killed. She was sleeping quite soundly in her bed. I rather doubt that she could have dressed, raced to the abbey, killed her husband, and got back into bed within five minutes."

The constable was as tenacious as the mastiff I was sure he owned. "If I may ask, sir, how did you happen to look in on the lady at that particular time?"

Sir Mark tapped his fingers together and smiled. "I was at the stables that night, because one of my best brood mares was about to foal. When she had accomplished that feat, I returned to the house."

"And you just happened to look in on Mrs. Woburn? Very convenient, if you ask me, your lordship."

Sir Mark smiled.

Tibbins continued. "And how can you be so sure of the time?"

"Because the colt was born at eleven thirty. I looked at my watch to be sure. And when I returned to the house, the clock in the foyer was just chiming midnight."

"Begging your pardon, your lordship, but why didn't you tell me sooner? It all sounds highly suspicious to me."

Everyone seemed to hold their breath as a spark of anger touched Mark Gerrick's eyes, then disappeared. He smiled disarmingly. "Because I wanted no slurs on Mrs. Woburn's good name."

What is this leading up to, I wondered, as I slid back into my chair.

Tibbins looked unsure of himself now. "And how is that, sir?"

Sir Mark's face was the picture of incredulity. "I thought it quite obvious."

"It is not," the constable replied sourly.

"I had dishonorable intentions." He leveled those mocking gray eyes straight at me. "Why else would I go to a woman's bedchamber at midnight?"

A shocked gasp popped out of Amabel, and Dr. Price's freckles stood out on his forehead. I knew I was as white as the sheet of paper Tibbins held.

The constable was thrown off balance. "Did anyone see you enter her room?"

He was rewarded by a contemptuous reply. "Would I bring guests to witness such a proposition?"

I almost laughed aloud.

Tibbins tried to restrain himself, but turned crimson anyway. "Begging your pardon, your lordship, but why should I believe you? You could be making this all up to save the lady."

One black brow shot up. "You doubt my word, Constable Tibbins? The word of a Gerrick?"

It was a dirty trick. The constable was backed into a corner and he knew it. I could see him thinking of his wife's family, the ones who worked on Gerrick farms or in Gerrick mills. Sir Mark had him by the throat.

"Of course not, your lordship."

Sir Mark sat languidly in his chair, looking every inch Lord Raven, master of Raven's Chase and owner of half of Sheepstor. Master of moor and manor. And who was Clyde Tibbins to doubt his word? I would have thought Mark Gerrick's years at sea had pounded rank and privilege out of him, but I was wrong. He was not above being ruthless.

To give Tibbins credit, he responded with great dignity and chose his words with care. "It's just my job to discover the truth, your lordship, no offense meant. There will, of course, be an inquest into the death of Oliver Woburn. No doubt you will all be asked to give evidence, so I must ask you all to be available to the court. Good day."

And he left.

So I was not accused of Oliver's murder, thanks to Sir Mark, I reflected as I strolled slowly through the garden toward the folly. Had he really come to my room that night, or had he made up the story just to save me?

I trembled in spite of the warm afternoon sun. If either was true, Mark Gerrick had lied to me.

If he had come to my room, seeking to seduce me, as he claimed, then Jane Standish was right. He was infatuated with me and had brought me here for reasons other than to be Amabel's companion. My treacherous emotions fought for control. I felt Sir Mark's mouth on mine the day he had saved me from Oliver, and felt something stirring deep inside me.

"No!" I cried aloud, my hand flying to my mouth in shock.

Think, Nora, think! I was not Jane Standish, that a man would plan such an elaborate deception to seduce me. No, there had to be some other reason why Mark Gerrick was going to such lengths to save me.

I stopped, one foot poised on the folly's first step. Oliver had told me why Sir Mark wanted me at Raven's Chase. I was his means of hurting my own father for laming him. Could Oliver have been right? Suspicion gnawed at me.

"All you have to do is ask him," I said aloud as I entered the folly and seated myself.

The cool silence welled up around me, bringing me peace. Once or twice a bird twittered. My mind sorted the many scents of flowers that wafted my way. Roses. Violets. Lavender. I closed my eyes.

I sensed, rather than saw, Sir Mark walking across the lawns toward me. Strange how one got used to his limp, as though it didn't exist. I fancied his pale eyes were mocking.

Finally, his shadow fell across me, and I shivered.

"May I come in?"

"Please. It is yours."

He smiled and seated himself across from me. "My mother always came here when she was troubled."

I opened my eyes. "Lady Katherine had troubles? I find that hard to believe."

"Of course. What color ball gown to wear . . . which jewels went with it—that sort of thing."

I closed my eyes again. I did not want to hear about Lady Katherine.

"Nora, I hope what I said to Tibbins won't force you to leave."

I roused myself to look at him. "Why should it?"

The sardonic smile tugged at his mouth. "Stay in the same house as a man who has openly declared designs on your virtue? Any woman of sensibility would have purchased her train ticket by now."

"As my father constantly reminded me, I possess very little sensibility. Besides, I cannot leave. There is still the inquest."

He made no reply, but turned his head to stare across the lawns at something far beyond my point of vision. The silence lengthened like shadows.

Go on, a tiny voice inside me urged. Ask him. Now. "Why did you lie to Tibbins?" I said instead.

He looked at me sharply. "I did not lie."

My face began to grow warm, but I couldn't stop. The words came in a rush. "Thank you for trying to protect me. But it really wasn't necessary. I can fight my own battles."

"I meant what I said, Nora."

We stared at each other across the folly. Finally, he said kindly, "Do you find it so difficult to believe I went to your room that night?"

"Yes. I am not Jane Standish. Men don't throw themselves at my feet."

"Someday we'll have to discuss that. But right now is neither the time nor the place," he said.

"You speak in riddles."

"Not really."

I hugged myself against a chill that gripped me. "But it's all so pointless. No one will ever believe I just went to bed. Did you see the way Tibbins looked at me? He was measuring me for the gallows."

Sir Mark's voice was hushed. "This hasn't been easy for you, Nora."

"It's been a nightmare." I rose and paced around the folly. "But who wanted to kill Oliver? He knew no one in Sheepstor, except me. And who copied our handwriting and sent us both notes? Someone wanted us both at the abbey at the same time." My eyes widened. "Perhaps someone wanted to kill me."

"It is possible," he agreed. "But then, why lure your husband out there? Why not just kill you? Or did they want both of you dead?"

My head began to spin, so I quickly sat down. He made no move to touch me.

"No, I think someone merely intended for you to find Oliver's body," he continued. "It would have been impossible for you to explain your way out of that."

"And even the word of a Gerrick couldn't save me then."

Sir Mark smiled.

"But *who?*" I cried out in anguish.

"I wish I knew."

Jane Standish, witch of Endor, floated into my mind's eye. Her words swarmed around me like angry wasps: "You will regret loving Raven and he you." Would she murder Oliver just to hurt me?

"The inquest will be difficult, of course," Sir Mark was saying, "but I doubt that Tibbins will be able to find evidence against you."

"He may. He's not stupid."

Sir Mark gave me an exasperated look. "I don't underestimate Tibbins for a moment."

"You treated him like a fool yesterday."

"Breeding always wins out, in the end," he replied, and I longed to slap him.

"Rank is an unfair weapon."

Sir Mark rose and towered over me. "When I fight, I fight with everything I've got."

And he bowed and walked back toward the house.

Later that night, as I lay beneath the canopy of the pagoda bed, thankful that I couldn't hear any nighttime noises beyond my locked bedroom door, more thoughts pressed against my mind.

First, the attempts on my life, and now, an attempt to make me look like a murderess. I'd give anything to trade places with Damon Gerrick now.

But what have I done? I shrieked silently. Why must I be blamed?

If I could answer that question, I'd know my enemy.

Was this Jane Standish's handiwork? Perhaps Dennis was involved. How easy for Flanna to bring him a paper with my handwriting on it, and how easy for her to slip another note under my door. Who would question the maid who cleaned my room? Restless, I turned over on my side. I dismissed any thought of questioning the girl as useless. She would only give me her dreamy stare and deny my accusations.

And what of Amabel, who had nearly sent me to my death on the moors? But I could not picture Amabel killing Oliver, even to hurt her brother. Still, she was a member of this household, and she did have access to my room. . . .

That made as much sense as suspecting Dr. Price or Marianne Meadows or Mrs. Baker, not to mention Nellie.

I tried to discount Sir Mark as a suspect, and then recalled Deepwell. If he had sought to drown me, why had he saved me from Oliver, and why had he lied about coming to my room? Nothing made any sense.

Suddenly I sat up, a cold knife of fear sliding between my ribs. Sir Mark had despised Oliver. If Mark Gerrick wanted me, as his former mistress claimed, was he capable of murder to get what he wanted?

Oh, Nora, why didn't you think of this before?

With Oliver dead, there was no one to stand in Mark's way now.

11

"I wonder if Mark really went to your room that night," Amabel said, brushing the baby's silken hair while he wriggled in her lap, "or if he's just trying to protect you."

She made this remark while we sat together in the sewing room on the afternoon before the inquest. I was forcing myself to do embroidery, for I found it kept my hands from shaking, and kept my mind free.

"I don't know, I didn't see him come in," was my tart response. "I was sleeping, despite what Constable Tibbins thinks."

"Well, I don't think you killed Oliver," she said.

"Thank you."

"The whole house is humming, and I'll wager half of Sheepstor is too, by the time Effie Cooper gets through telling everyone about finding the body. Peter, stop that!" The baby grabbed the brush out of his mother's hand, then laughed.

"It couldn't have been very pleasant for her," I said.

"Mrs. Baker doesn't think you did it," Amabel went on. "Neither does Nellie. I don't know what Mrs. Meadows thinks on the subject, but then, one never knows what she is thinking, anyway. Now, Flanna . . ." Amabel's eyes lit up. "I heard her talking to one of the other girls today, and she said—"

"Amabel, I don't want to hear it," I snapped. "What Flanna

O'Brien thinks is of no concern to me. And I'm surprised at you for listening to idle gossip."

She began bouncing Peter on her knee. "I think Mark was lying."

"Why didn't you tell Constable Tibbins then?" I jabbed the needle so forcefully through the material that I pricked my finger. "This would be your perfect opportunity to hurt your brother, as you claim he has hurt you."

She shrugged. "What good would it have done? Who would believe me? My brother is a very powerful man. I can see that. He's got a tight rein on me. I know that." A slow smile touched her mouth. "And now he's got control of you, too."

I looked up. "What do you mean?"

"If it weren't for Mark's story, you would not have a witness to your whereabouts that night. And with that note they found in your husband's room. . . ." She shrugged eloquently. "You owe Mark your life."

I stopped and looked at her. "I know that."

She set Peter down on the carpeted floor, where he was delighted to roam at will. Then Amabel walked over to the window.

"One day, not even Mark's power is going to save him. All of the people he has hurt, all the ones he has tried to control, are going to have their revenge." Her voice became dreamy and faraway. "One day, we are—" Suddenly she snapped out of it and looked at me furtively, as though she had said too much already.

I stared, appalled at the change that had come over the girl. I preferred the old spirited Amabel, with her outbursts and flashes of temper, for once the thunderstorm had passed, all was calm, if not forgotten. But this Amabel was pensive, and there was a furtive look in her eyes. And what had she started to say before catching herself?

"One day, we are going to do what, Amabel?" I prodded.

"Nothing," she said quickly. To distract me, she added, "Did you ever think that perhaps Mark killed Oliver?"

"No. I haven't. Why would he want to?"

The slow smile came again. "He wants you. And your husband was in the way. Now no one is in his way. Mark has a knack for eliminating people who get in his way. He got rid of Damon very neatly, and legally, too."

"You really should take up writing yourself, Amabel. You have a talent for concocting the most imaginative plots." I threw down my embroidery in disgust and reached for Peter, who was just about to pull a table down on his head.

"Not only does he give you an excuse, he gives himself one as well," Amabel continued.

"What are you talking about?" I demanded as the baby howled in my arms, his curiosity thwarted.

"I see you didn't think of that possibility."

Didn't think of it, or refused to think of it, I thought to myself.

"No one knows where Mark was that night, do they?"

I reminded her that he was up with a mare about to foal.

Amabel frowned thoughtfully. "Of course, and all the grooms will swear to it. He left the stables at eleven thirty and claims he went to the house. But no one saw him return. Not the footmen, not Mrs. Meadows. No one. He had ample time to run out to the abbey, kill your husband, and return."

"You're groping at straws."

She shrugged. "Perhaps."

"If you're so convinced, why don't you present evidence to Constable Tibbins?" I asked.

"As I've said, what good would it do?"

Somehow, I survived the inquest.

To this day, I remember few details of it, for I felt as though I was not participating, merely watching from a great distance someone who looked like me. The carriage ride into Sheepstor was interminable. Sir Mark scowled at the passing scenery, consulted his pocket watch every five minutes, and said little. Amabel chatted away brightly, as if to fill the silence rather than say anything of consequence. My replies were mechanical and forced, and finally stopped altogether, like a child's top that has run down slowly.

As we drew up in the courtyard of the Headless Horseman Inn, where the inquest was to be held, Amabel smiled briefly and patted my hand before stepping down from the carriage. Then it was my turn.

Well, Nora, it's now or never, I said to myself as I took a deep breath and prepared to step down. All of Devon seemed to be packed into the courtyard, staring. I felt like a doe who sees the huntsman's rifle just before the bullet rips through her.

"Nora?" Sir Mark's gentle whisper destroyed the illusion as his reassuring fingers gripped my own.

I joined him and Amabel, and Mrs. Meadows, Flanna, and Effie Cooper, who had followed us in a second carriage. Mrs. Meadows was white-faced and preoccupied; she had just learned that her mother was gravely ill in Surrey. Flanna looked at the crowds with frank curiosity, and Effie cringed and twisted her red swollen hands constantly.

A forest of faces—curious, hostile and even a few solicitous—bobbed before me as they parted for us as neatly as if someone had drawn a comb through them.

"That's the one, the one with the brown curly hair," someone said.

"Don't look like no murderess to me."

"Aw, she did it, all right."

We ignored these faceless rumblings. But when someone shouted, "Jezebel!" Sir Mark went white.

He stopped and scanned the crowds for whoever had said the name. No one spoke again.

"Now I know how Gentleman Harry feels," I muttered as we mounted the steps.

"Who is he?" Sir Mark asked.

"A thief I knew in London."

Strong fingers bit into my elbow. "Nora, get ahold of yourself," he hissed under his breath. "You'll never make it through this if you don't."

I nodded.

The dining room had been converted to a courtroom, and I immediately noticed the magistrate seated at a long, low table, whispering to another man with a pinched, censuring face. He was the court's solicitor. They stopped talking as we were seated, and looked straight at me. I knew I could make a favorable impression if I lowered my eyes and contrived to blush in maidenly modesty, but I could not. I just stared at them coolly, and, in the end, they looked away.

The room filled quickly, the crowd scrambling and scurrying for seats, then fell silent as the inquest began. The solicitor with the pinched face was named Mr. Davenport, and when he began speaking, I could see he had been well briefed by Constable Tibbins.

Davenport began by questioning the constable. Oliver's body, the blood-stained rod, the notes . . . I had heard all of this so many times before that I just closed my mind to it. When my own name was called, I rose and was seated across from the jury, to the accompaniment of a buzz of conversation.

Davenport was relentless and ruthless, and I found myself bridling at the picture he was painting of me. I was a woman of no morals, who had left her husband to consort with bohemians, and who could have had a motive to kill him. But I forced myself to remain calm and not lash out at him as I would have liked to.

I was conscious of Sir Mark seated almost across from me. He sat negligently in his chair and stared at the floor. To the casual observer, he looked totally uninterested in the proceedings. Only I saw his eyes grow cold and his brows come together as Davenport assaulted me verbally, trying to wear me down, to break through the barrier I had erected to protect myself.

Davenport then called Effie Cooper, but had little luck with her. The girl just twisted her red fingers together and jumped whenever the solicitor raised his voice. Then he called Dr. Price, who elaborated on the more grisly medical details of Oliver's death, much to the delight of the spectators. After Flanna and Marianne Meadows were questioned, Amabel was called.

As she sat there, a blue and yellow vision, I waited for her to denounce her brother, or to suggest that Mark himself had killed Oliver, but she didn't. She was cool and polite, and answered Davenport's questions in a calm, level voice.

"And would you say, Miss Gerrick, that Mrs. Woburn hated her husband?" the solicitor asked.

"Oh, no," was Amabel's wide-eyed reply. "She was always civil to him. She just didn't want to return to him, that's all."

And so it went on. By the time Sir Mark was called, my insides were shaking and my mouth was dry. Just the fact that I had left my husband condemned me in the eyes of these good people. Add that to the note that I had allegedly sent Oliver. . . . I was in trouble.

Then Sir Mark rose and took the stand.

He sat there tapping his fingers with the same insolence that he had so often displayed. The gray eyes were amused and mocking, and his mouth twisted imperceptibly into a sardonic smile. In a deep, level voice, he repeated his claim that he had looked in on me at midnight and that I had been sleeping. A murmur of disbelief rippled through the crowd, but it was quelled by Mark Gerrick's defiant stare. He challenged them to call him a liar.

Would these good people allow him to shut down the mills and mines, put their husbands out of work, let their children starve? Davenport's face fell. He was beaten and he knew it.

Within fifteen minutes, it was over. Even as the jury stood there, with its verdict that person or persons unknown had killed Oliver Woburn, I could see the resentment in their eyes and on their faces. They were not convinced that I was innocent, but they could not prove my guilt. I was free.

Raven's Chase was at peace once again.

Old Corman drove Mrs. Meadows into Sheepstor, where she

boarded a train for Surrey and her ailing mother. Amabel was ever Amabel, engrossed in her son. Dr. Price came to the Chase even more often now, and I wondered how he could afford to neglect his practice so.

The day after Mrs. Meadows left, I walked out to the abbey, which I had avoided since Oliver's death. I felt jubilant, for I realized I was now a free woman. Free of Oliver's domination. Free of suspicion that I had killed him. I was my own woman again.

So what, I asked myself as I entered the ruins, was I still doing here at Raven's Chase?

"Nora!"

I turned toward the sound of the shout to see Sir Mark in shirt-sleeves, waving at me from across the ruins. I waved back and started toward him. When we met, his smile made my stomach give a queer little lurch.

"I haven't been here since—since Oliver died," I said, glancing nervously about.

His smile faded. "Don't think about it, Nora. He caused you much pain."

"I know. But I'd still like to know who killed him. Wouldn't you?"

The square jaw hardened. "Not really. Probably some poor soul in need of a few guineas. Woburn just happened to be in the right place at the wrong time."

"That was the story of poor Oliver's life," I said, as I seated myself on a stone pile.

He sat down beside me and stretched his leg out before him. "Is something wrong? You don't seem yourself."

I sighed. "All those people in the courtroom thought you were lying. I could see it in their faces. Suspicion. Resentment."

"As I said before, I wasn't lying."

My cheeks were on fire. "Then why have you made no further attempts?"

He grinned. "Because you would reject me. And, my dear Nora, I refuse to be rejected. When the time comes, I won't be."

"You are quite sure of that."

"Quite sure."

This entire conversation was incredible. Here I sat, verbally sparring with a man who openly declared his intentions to make me his mistress, and I reveled in it. Sir Mark made no move to touch me. And what would I do if he had? Claw and scratch, or go willingly into his arms?

It was all a trick to hide his desire to harm me. The backs of my hands began prickling, sensing danger. Run, Nora, before it's too late.

I rose, but was stopped by his words. "Running again, Nora?"

"I don't know what you mean, Sir Mark."

"Yes, you do. And it's Mark, Nora, Mark. Or Raven, if you prefer."

I thought of Jane Standish. "No, not Raven."

He smiled as he read my mind. Then he rose. Suddenly his eyes widened and he pitched forward.

"Mark!" I cried.

I knelt beside him and rolled him over, cradling his head in my hands. His eyes flickered open, but he looked at me without recognition.

"What happened?" I whispered.

"Dizzy," he muttered.

"I'm sending for Dr. Price. You're ill. First that stomach complaint, and now this."

He got to his feet, and stood tottering there like a newborn foal. "Damon used to get these dizzy spells, too." Then he gave a bitter bark of laughter. "Perhaps I've inherited an unstable mind, like my brother. Perhaps they'll lock me in Goodehouse, too."

I was horrified. "We must get back to the house."

"First, I have to find my lantern."

"Where did you leave it? I'll get it for you."

"Down near the cellars."

I shuddered uncontrollably. "Why do you wander around down there? It's horrible, and a wall could fall on you."

He grinned feebly. "Do I detect a note of tender concern in your voice? I'm trying to find who drove my brother mad."

I stared at him as though his wits were addled. "Who drove your brother mad? I don't understand."

"You could say I'm looking for Lucy."

"Lucy? But she died in India. Her existence here was just in Damon's poor sick mind. He envisioned her out here in the abbey. Didn't he?"

Mark shook his head. "Oh, she was quite real."

I was shocked speechless.

"No, I'm not mad, Nora. One night when I came here to look for Damon, I saw someone, a woman, out here with him. She disappeared before I could come closer and confront her."

My legs gave way and I found myself clinging to him. "You mean this Lucy is alive? She wasn't just in Damon's mind?"

He shrugged. "I don't know. But whoever she was, she disappeared without a trace. I searched these ruins from top to bottom and couldn't find anyone."

He swayed again, and I straightened up to support him. "Damned dizziness," he muttered. "It must have been someone. I don't believe in ghosts."

"Neither do I," I said. "What do you think happened?"

He looked at me for a long moment, as if debating something. Finally, he said, "I think a real person was out there, no ghost. I think something happened to Damon in India that he's not telling us. Perhaps Lucy didn't die in the mutiny at all, but is here and alive. Perhaps my dear brother dishonored her in some way and she was here to repay him."

"That sounds rather farfetched," I said dubiously.

"Yes, I suppose it does. But I don't have any other answers at the moment."

I frowned. "But why hasn't she made herself known to you? And how did she disappear?"

Mark scanned the ruins. "This place is full of secrets. The old abbot managed to disappear with the three crowns, much to King Henry's chagrin."

I looked up at him. "The secret passage."

"It's the only explanation."

"But how did a girl from India ever find out about the abbot's secret passage, when all of you have been looking for it for years?"

Mark laughed as he shook his head. "You tear all my theories into little pieces, Nora."

"The theory has to fit the facts, not the other way around. The mysterious Lucy theory seems highly doubtful to me for many reasons. Perhaps it is someone else who does know about the passage."

He agreed, then added, "But that would restrict it to someone here, who knows the Chase."

"But who? The Standishes? Dr. Price? Amabel?"

A wry grin touched his mouth. "Absurd, isn't it? We Gerricks have our share of enemies, but I can't for the life of me determine who would want to harm Damon in such a way. Do you see my dilemma? Everywhere I turn, I face a blank wall." He straightened. "Shall we find my lantern and go?"

We found it near the cellars, where the rock had almost fallen on us. I left Mark leaning against the wall and skipped down the steps to fetch the lantern, all the while trying to avoid looking into the black hole. When I returned, Mark, ashen around the mouth, smiled and thanked me.

I said, "I'm going to Sheepstor to get Dr. Price myself. A dizzy spell shouldn't go unchecked."

"They'll go away. They always do."

I shot a reproachful look. "You've had these before?" When he nodded, I said, "I'm going for the doctor at once."

After pressing one of the younger stable boys into service, I started for Sheepstor and Dr. Price. The lad and I said little to one another, and finally arrived shortly before noon.

As the cart rumbled through the town, a strange uneasiness gripped me. A farmer leading a pair of yoked oxen stared as we trotted by, while a gray-haired woman pulled her grandchild into the house, as though my look would turn them into stone. Two men lounging in front of the apothecary watched me insolently. One of them whispered something to the other, who laughed. I was thankful I could not hear what they said.

We finally pulled up in front of Dr. Price's house. A movement at the upstairs window caught my eye, and as I glanced up, I caught a glimpse of a face before it quickly disappeared behind the curtain. Somehow, I had the feeling I had seen that face before, but it had been such a fleeting impression that I couldn't be certain.

I shrugged as I stepped down from the cart. It was probably someone else staring at the murderess.

I rang the bell and waited. No one answered, so I rang it again impatiently. Just as I was about to open the door and let myself in, the doctor himself answered it.

"Oh, Mrs. Woburn. Forgive me for not answering the door immediately, but I had mislaid my spectacles. I'm blind as a bat without them, you know. Can't see my nose in front of my face."

I could believe him, as I stared into the thick glass.

"I'm sorry to disturb you, Dr. Price, but Sir Mark has been having dizzy spells and I was wondering if you'd be so good as to ride out and examine him?"

The thin lips narrowed. "I was just out there yesterday. Why didn't he inform me then? I do have other patients."

I was taken aback. This was the first time I had ever heard him complain about visiting the Gerricks. He was so friendly with Mark and had never begrudged him his time before. What had caused this fit of pique, I wondered?

"I know you were there yesterday," I said, trying to mollify him, "but you know Sir Mark is the last one to complain of an illness. He's had these spells before, but he's just shrugged them off."

"Very well. If you'll wait right here, I'll get my bag." Then he bustled off into his inner office.

I glanced around as I waited, remembering the time I had come for Amabel's medicine and had violated the sacred office. "Shall we go?" he said as he emerged from the room and closed and locked the door behind him.

"But you aren't going to leave your patient all alone, are you?"

He regarded me with a blank expression. "Patient?"

"The one I saw at your upstairs window."

"Oh. Mrs. Drewe. Yes. Well, I have a woman coming to tend her in a few minutes, so it's all right to leave."

"Then you had better leave the door open for her."

"Yes. Thank you for reminding me. Mark's illness must have unnerved me for a moment. Well, now, for the second time, shall we be off?"

"Exhaustion," was the doctor's pronouncement to me as he emerged from Mark's bedchamber. "Nothing more, nothing less." And for this you dragged me all the way out here, he silently seemed to say.

"Will he be all right?"

"With rest, and a change of scene."

The bedchamber door opened and Mark joined us, buttoning his waistcoat as he came. "Sam says I shan't die today, at any rate," he said, a mischievous smile twisting his mouth.

Dr. Price was not amused. "Your health is no laughing matter, Mark. As I was telling Mrs. Woburn, you're suffering from exhaustion. Your father's death, then Damon's breakdown, not to mention Amabel's hysterics. . . ." He threw up his hands. "You push yourself too hard, and it has affected you more than you realize. You may think you can handle all this and the estate at the same time, but your body rebels."

"What would you suggest I do?" Mark laughed. "Get away for a while? With Damon locked away and my sister at my throat?"

"Yes. I mean exactly that. You needn't go to Italy for a few months, although that would be ideal. Even London would do."

Mark was silent, with a thoughtful look on his face. Finally, he said, "What about a few days in Plymouth? I think I could spare that."

"Better than nothing," the doctor said.

Mark turned to me. "Nora, would you like to go to Plymouth for a few days? With Amabel as a proper chaperone, of course," he added when he saw the doctor's shocked face.

"I would be delighted."

Then his face grew cold. "Do you think my sister could bear my company?"

"All you can do is ask," Dr. Price commented dryly.

When asked at dinner that evening, Amabel's reply was a bored, "Well, it's not London, but I suppose it will do." Only I could see the glimmer of excitement in her eyes as the caged bird contemplated freedom.

Mark gave us one day to prepare for our holiday.

"One day!" Amabel wailed. "It will take me one day just to decide what dresses to take."

I persuaded her to take only one piece of luggage, for by the time she had bought out the Plymouth shops, she would need three others. So, by the following morning, both of us and our bags stood in the foyer, waiting for Mark.

But it was Nellie with Peter in her arms who descended the stairs. "I just thought I'd bring his lordship to see you off," she said, as the baby reached eagerly for his mother.

"Oh, my precious!" Amabel showered him with kisses, despite the havoc he was wreaking on her elaborate bonnet. She hugged her son and made faces at him until Mark joined us.

"Good-bye, my precious," she crooned, kissing him one last time. "Be a good boy for Nellie, and Mama will bring you a present when she returns."

As we headed out the door, Peter's chubby face dissolved, then he wailed as though he'd never see his mother again. All of us laughed and boarded the carriage that would take us on our holiday.

The train ride down to Plymouth drew me back to my childhood and the trips my parents and I had sometimes taken down to the sea on stifling summer Sundays. Of course, there were many differences. Now, the three of us were isolated in a first-class compartment, but then I had sat sandwiched between my parents in a noisy common coach, the acrid scent of old clothes mingling with bread, wine, and sweat. I remembered holding my breath for as long as I could to escape it.

The Amabel I knew appeared to have changed overnight, for she chatted amiably with her brother, and even made us laugh with her witty observations. Perhaps all she had needed after all was a chance to behave like a carefree girl again.

As I drank in the soft, mellow beauty of the fields and towns flying past, I could see Mark Gerrick watching me. I had often caught my father and mother looking at each other in that same intense way when neither knew I was watching. It was a look of deep emotion that I had been too young to understand, but I had envied my mother those looks my father gave her. Oliver had never bestowed them on me. I had waited so long for a man to look at me in the way Mark Gerrick was looking at me now.

He acts like he desires me, I told myself, startled in spite of his previous declarations. Somehow, I had not believed him.

I would be lying to myself if I said I wasn't attracted to him. But, like the moth's attraction to the fatal flame, mine would be just as disastrous if I succumbed. The wild, uninhibited part of me inherited from Ivor Stokes urged me to throw caution to the winds, while its levelheaded counterpart intoned circumspection.

How could I even consider a liaison with a man who might now be plotting to kill me? My common sense must have deserted me. I was irrational. I belonged in Goodehouse, with Damon.

No, not Goodehouse, but perhaps London would do. With Oliver dead, I was free to continue my literary career. Perhaps Mrs. James would let me have my rooms back. I would pretend I had never met Mark Gerrick or Amabel or Peter. I would be in London. Safe.

Our four days in Plymouth passed too quickly.

Amabel was like a child turned loose in a toy shop. She floated from one shop to the next, each one more enticing than the last, and there was little Mark refused her. Dresses, ornate bonnets, slippers and gloves of paper-thin kid, parasols—they made our hotel rooms look like Fleetwoods. I wondered how the mountain of boxes would find its way back to the Chase.

But her favorite purchase was a homely cloth pig she bought to amuse her son.

Mark's guided tours of the seaport were my most memorable times. We visited the heart of the city, a dark cluster of buildings, and walked on the very green where Sir Francis Drake had played his famous game of bowls while the Spanish Armada snapped at English shores. Mark also took us outside the city, to point out the smugglers' coves that had been so well-used until recently.

And then we toured the docks and the Raven Line. Two ships, *Raven's Pride* and *Black Raven,* were in port, and, as Mark explained, three others were in London. Then he pointed to one being constructed. It was hard to believe the hull, just bleached ribs of a ship, would fill out like the *Pride* or *Raven*.

Amabel was plainly bored until her brother introduced us to young Captain Fiske, a serious man who plainly found ships less disconcerting than winsome, blue-eyed maids. Soon Amabel had enchanted him into explaining the merits of sail and steam.

Our last day came and disappeared. After dinner, Amabel retired early, eager now to return to the Chase and her son. I volunteered to pack our bags, and I was halfway through when a soft knock interrupted me. It was Mark.

"Where's Amabel?" he whispered.

I pointed to the door that joined her bedroom with the suite's drawing room. "Sleeping," I whispered. "She could barely keep her eyes open at supper." I continued to fold clothes, trying to ignore the excitement in Mark's face.

"Nora, will you stop playing ladies' maid and look at me?"

My heart hammered at my ribs. "Yes?"

He came toward me. "I want you, Nora."

I drew away. "I have no desire to take Jane Standish's place. I will be no man's mistress."

"Mistress?" He stopped, a shocked expression on his face. Then he laughed softly and put out his hand to me. "Silly darling. I love you. I want you for my wife. This is not the most romantic place in the world for a proposal. If I had my way, I'd propose to you on some tropical island with the warm sea breezes and moonlight overhead. But I couldn't wait any longer. Will you marry me? You are free now."

"I can't. I won't."

He laughed, as though I were joking. "But why not? You know I love you. I've loved you from the day I saw *The Edge of Experience* hanging in a friend's house in London. Do you remember the day you ran past me in John Burke's office? I wasn't there on business. I was there to find you. When I overheard you talking, I saw a way of getting you to come to Devon."

My mouth went dry. "So you were planning . . . even then."

"Yes. I couldn't believe my good fortune when you said you would come as Amabel's companion." He turned and walked over to the window and stared down into the street. "I drove myself insane worrying that the real Nora Woburn might be cruel or shrewish or grasping." The gray eyes sought mine. "But you're not, Nora. You're a kind, sensitive person, as well as beautiful, and I know I don't deserve you."

"You flatter me. But I'm afraid I can't return your feelings. I . . . I don't love you. I'm sorry."

His exultant laugh mocked me. "No? You're lying, Nora. When I kissed you after Oliver tried to—"

"Please go."

"No." Before I could move, he was by my side and had my wrists imprisoned. Those eyes dared me to look away. "I know you love me, Nora. I've seen the way you look at me. And I want to know why you pull away from me."

The time has come, I said to myself. Now I had to confront him with Oliver's accusation. What could I say to him? I rehearsed the words in my mind: Mark, is it true my father lamed you, and now you want to have your revenge? Or: Have you been trying to kill me?

I took a deep breath and my lips moved, but no words came out. I just could not bring myself to utter those terrible words of accusation.

"Well, my darling?" he said, staring at me with such intensity I had to look away. "I've just asked you to marry me, and your hesitancy overwhelms me."

I twisted my fingers together and walked over to the window to avoid answering him for a moment. My brain was speeding like a runaway train. I couldn't tell him that I suspected him of trying to kill me.

"It's just that I don't love you," I said, staring into the street.

He was silent for a moment, then said, "I don't believe you. No, there's something else. You've been very distant lately. Something has thrown up a wall between us and I would like to know what it is."

Once again, he had read my mind. It was going to be very difficult to convince Mark Gerrick. I smiled brightly and turned to face him. His hands were thrust deep into his pockets and his head was lowered like a belligerent bull's.

I forced myself to laugh lightly, like Amabel at her most coquettish. "Why won't you believe me? Do you think all women fall at your feet, like Jane Standish?"

"I love you," he said. "I've never been so happy as during the weeks I've spent with you." He dropped his arms to his sides, all the arrogance gone. In a voice so humble it almost broke my heart, he said, "Will you have me, Nora?"

"Such pretty speeches, Mark." I sounded like the heartless flirts I had always hated. "You are a darling, but I can't accept you. You offered me a way out of my difficulties with Oliver, and I'm grateful. But love? I'm afraid my only love is my literary career, which I am going to resume in London now that Oliver's dead."

"Why are you doing this, Nora?" he demanded. He was not going to accept my refusal. "Why are you pretending to be Amabel, or Jane?"

I looked affronted. "And why do you refuse to believe I could possibly reject you?"

Now his face darkened with anger. "Because you love me!"

"But I don't. What can I say that will convince you?"

In three strides he was at my side, and, for a moment, I thought he would strike me. Cold, furious gray eyes burned into mine. Suddenly he was kissing me with a savagery that made me want to melt. But I knew I would never convince him I didn't love him if I surrendered, so I went rigid and forced myself to think other, less treacherous thoughts. Finally, he tired of kissing an unresponsive stick of wood.

"I'm sorry, Mark," I said with a brief smile.

"For the love of God, Nora, what is wrong!" he bellowed. Then, remembering Amabel asleep in the next room, he lowered his voice. "Why are you doing this? You've changed overnight, and I want to know why."

"I've told you a dozen times. I don't love you."

"You went into my arms willingly enough when Oliver tried to rape you."

I shrugged. "You rescued me, and I was appreciative."

His face had lost all color, and I knew he was finally starting to believe me. Mark's hands clenched into fists at his sides. "I can't believe it. You're a different person."

I smiled. "I can be whatever person the occasion warrants. It suited me to be one Nora Woburn with you, and another with my husband."

"We have to talk, Nora." He grasped my elbow and shook me violently. "Why are you lying, damn you!"

"It really isn't necessary to shout at me. I realize your pride is injured by my refusal, but please believe me, Mark. I don't love you."

I had never seen a man so devastated. His eyes, once so mocking, were lifeless and dull, and there was a helpless, pleading expression on his face that made me sick inside. I had reduced the arrogant Mark Gerrick to a dejected child. I almost wished he would fly into a rage and strike me. Anger would have been easier to deal with than this quiet desperation.

Suddenly he turned on his heel and started for the door. I watched him drag his useless leg along, and felt my resolve weaken. I started for him, but held myself back. At the door, he suddenly stopped and turned. "I hope your literary career warms your bed at night and comforts you in your old age."

And he was gone.

As the door clicked shut, the tears began to slide down my cheeks. I should have felt triumphant, or at least relieved, but I only felt empty and hollow inside. I finished packing, then went to sleep. When morning came, I felt like I hadn't slept at all.

I found a note from Mark under my door waiting for me when I did rise.

Madam,
Since you do not wish to remain in my home any longer, I trust
you have other plans, once we return to Raven's Chase.

Raven

Quite irrationally, I burst into tears.

"You fool, Nora!" I chided myself. "Why should you cry for getting what you wanted?"

Sir Mark was waiting for us in the lobby. His face was impenetrable, although his cold eyes met mine for just an instant. Then they slipped away, as though he could not bear the sight of me. Deep lines of anger and bitterness were etched into his face, and he looked like he had had an evening of too much drink.

When I informed him I was leaving for London, he merely said, "As you wish."

Our strange entourage—black-faced Mark, myself, and Amabel, the chattering parrot—finally boarded the train and left for Sheepstor.

Mark and I said nothing to one another. Amabel looked from one of us to the other, and tried to draw us into conversation with her aimless chatter.

"I can't wait to give Peter his pig," she said brightly. "Nora, do you think he'll like it?"

I smiled. "I'm sure he'll adore it."

Once again, silence overtook us. Finally, Amabel said, "I say, is there something wrong? One would think we were going to a funeral."

"Nothing is wrong, Amabel," I said. "Nothing at all."

But there was something horribly wrong, as we discovered in Sheepstor, where the carriage awaited us.

"Why, there's Nellie," Amabel exclaimed as we stepped onto the platform. "And Dr. Price and Constable Tibbins." She flashed a worried look up at her brother as the trio approached us.

Suddenly Nellie burst into tears and flung herself at Amabel.

"Oh, miss," she wailed. "Peter's been kidnapped!"

12

Confusion exploded on the platform.

"My baby!" Amabel began shaking poor Nellie by the shoulders. "Someone has stolen my baby!"

"Amabel, stop it!" Mark pulled his sister off the hapless nurse and handed the girl to me with a curt, "Take care of her, Nora."

As I comforted the sobbing Amabel, Mark turned to Dr. Price and Constable Tibbins. "Sam, what is going on here?"

Dr. Price was a picture of gravity and dejection. "It's true, Mark. Someone has taken the child. Yesterday afternoon, Young Corman came to my office to tell me Peter was missing and couldn't be found."

"Some blackguard drugged me," Nellie cut in, "when I had my breakfast in the nursery." She began to wring her hands like an actress in a melodrama. "One of the girls brought my tray up to the nursery. I stepped out to get some fresh linen, and when I returned I ate my breakfast. Before I knew what was happening, I had dozed off. When I woke up, it was ten o'clock and Petey was gone."

"Did you search the house and grounds?" Mark demanded.

"We searched everywhere," Nellie moaned. "But someone had to take him out of his crib. He couldn't have gotten out of his crib by himself." Nellie blew her nose. "After we searched the whole house, we got Young Corman to search the grounds. Nothing."

Mark frowned as he said, "Why wasn't I notified sooner, Sam? You knew our hotel in Plymouth."

"I didn't think it was necessary, your lordship," Constable Tibbins said. "By the time I was notified it was evening yesterday. Since you were to return this morning, we thought it best not to worry you."

Amabel broke away from me. "Worry us? Constable, my son has been kidnapped! He may be dead for all we know, and you say not to *worry?*" Her voice rose hysterically, then she collapsed into my arms.

Mark took charge of the situation. "There's no point in standing around here. Constable, would you prefer that we go to your home, or back to Raven's Chase?"

"The Chase," he replied, "where the crime occurred."

Amabel had somehow gotten herself under control during our carriage ride back to the house. Her face looked ravaged, and her eyes were bright with unshed tears, but when she stepped into the foyer, she was calm and self-assured. Nellie appeared incredulous that such a thing could happen to her, while Mark and Dr. Price wore solemn masks of concern. Constable Tibbins of the penetrating stare—he reminded me so much of Harry Leeds—kept assessing each one of us, as though trying to discern who was capable of telling the truth. I could tell by the stubborn set of his jaw that *this* crime was not going unsolved.

Mark ushered us all into the library, where the constable addressed us. "The first thing we have to do is find the boy. I've got men combing the moor and towns from here to Goodehouse. All of the train stations have been notified to keep an eye out for someone with a child answering to the lad's description," he said.

I thought of the dozens of women who took their children on trains every day, and my heart sank. But I said nothing.

"Who could have done such a thing!" Nellie sniffled into her handkerchief.

The constable looked us all over before saying, "Someone who knew this house and the people who live in it. Someone who knew you'd be away, and who knew the nurse's habits."

"Are you suggesting one of my friends or servants kidnapped the child?" Mark said.

The constable bristled. "I'm not suggesting anything, sir. But people have a way of talkin' to their friends. One of your servants mentions when the nurse has her breakfast, or which doors are unlocked. Or that the master is goin' away. Do you see what I'm gettin' at?"

"Yes," Mark replied.

"I feel so responsible," Dr. Price spoke up. "I'm the one who suggested you take this trip. If I hadn't . . ."

"Sam, it's not your fault," Mark said.

"But how did the kidnapper get in to drug Nellie?" I asked. Five pairs of eyes focused on me.

Tibbins said he didn't know. "I suspect someone just walked in and hid." He looked around the room. "There's lots of hidin' places in a house like this. He—or she—waited for the nurse's tray to be brought up, then hid until the drug did its work."

"That has to be the answer," I said. "I can't believe Mrs. Baker or one of the kitchen maids would be a party to this." Then I scowled, as a thought occurred to me. "No one heard Peter cry when he was taken?"

Nellie insisted that no one heard anything.

"Which leads me to suspect the child knew who was takin' him," Tibbins added. "I've talked to some of your servants last night, but there's a few more I've got to talk to yet. Now, have any of you seen any strangers lurkin' around?"

Mark and Nellie shook their heads, but I thought of the bearded young man who lived in the shepherd's hut on the edge of the moor, the one who had saved me from death on the moors. "I have seen someone," I said, and told of the shepherd.

Amabel suddenly snapped out of her morose state, all claws and acid tongue. "That man is no stranger. He is a friend of mine, and I know he would never kidnap Peter. Leave him out of this, can't you?"

A ripple of interest spread among us at the girl's outburst. Who was the man and why was she protecting him, a man she had denied knowing?

Mark looked at me. "Yes. The shepherd who uses the stone hut on the moor. I've passed him many a time on my way back to the Chase, but I've never thought anything of it."

"He may be a friend of yours, Miss Gerrick," Tibbins said, "but if we are to find your child, I must talk to everyone and leave no stone unturned."

Amabel leaped to her feet as though the kidnapper had entered the room and she was ready to do battle for her child. "It was you, wasn't it?" She pointed her finger at Mark in a performance worthy of Drury Lane. "You had someone kidnap Peter to hurt me. First, you killed Papa, then you drove Damon insane, and now you've taken my baby away from me!"

Mark couldn't have been more astonished if Amabel had suddenly slid a dagger between his ribs. He was so dumbfounded he couldn't think of a sharp retort.

Dr. Price was the first to come to Mark's defense. "That's preposterous."

But I didn't think Constable Tibbins found the idea so preposterous, for I had seen a glimmer of interest flash in his eyes. He was a very determined man, our constable.

"Oh?" he said. "That's a dangerous accusation you're makin', miss. Anyone can make accusations, but it's proof you need to back them up."

"Mark ran away to sea when I was just a child. When he returned, things started happening. My father died, of a bad heart, they said. But I say Mark told him something that brought on his death. And then Mark locked my younger brother in an asylum." Her voice deepened with emotion. "He's hated us all. And the only one left is me. Mark always did torment me by not letting me visit my brother in Goodehouse, and by keeping me a virtual prisoner here. And now he has found the ultimate weapon against me—taking my baby away." She collapsed, bursting into tears.

The doctor and Nellie assisted Amabel to her feet and led her away. I, however, remained behind.

"My sister is often given to making hysterical outbursts," Mark said, his face unnaturally pale. "Her accusations are untrue."

"I see," Constable Tibbins said, but it was plain that he didn't.

I said, "Amabel has not been kept prisoner here. She may go anywhere she pleases. And as for her brother being locked in an asylum against his will . . ." I smiled. "I'm sure Dr. Price will confirm Damon Gerrick's insanity."

"Thank you for the defense," Mark said across the room, but the sarcastic sting to his words took away their meaning.

Tibbins listened politely, but I could see he did not believe me. I, after all, had barely escaped being accused of murder. In his eyes, I was not to be trusted.

"I appreciate your speaking up, Mrs. Woburn," Tibbins said. "But I must leave no stone unturned." It was his way of saying that he had to consider everything anyone said, no matter how preposterous or hysterical, whether Mark or I wished him to or not. He continued with, "I would like to speak to you privately, Sir Mark, and then to the rest of your servants."

That was my cue to leave.

"I've given her something to make her sleep," Dr. Price whispered to me as he was leaving Amabel's room. "She has suffered too much already." He shook his head. "All she does is clutch that absurd toy pig as if it were a child."

I explained that Amabel had bought it especially for the baby. Then I asked, "Does she really believe Mark had Peter kidnapped?"

"She does. When you've hated someone for as long as Amabel has hated Mark, it's easy to understand why. He's the focus of all her suspicions, from their father's death to this."

"You don't think Constable Tibbins believes her, do you?"

We had reached the balcony overlooking the foyer. Dr. Price stopped and said, "I can't say. He may. Tibbins has one unsolved crime hanging over his head, and I suspect he will do his utmost to solve this one."

We walked to the library in silence, each with our own thoughts.

Mark and the constable stopped talking as soon as we entered.

"Sam," Mark said, "would you ride with us? We've got a group of men together and we're going to search some of the cottages."

"Certainly," he replied.

Mark turned to me. "Would you stay with Amabel?"

"Of course."

"Thank you."

The three men started to file out the door.

"Mark?" He stopped and looked back at me, a quizzical expression on his face. "Good luck."

He nodded, and went off to join the others.

When they had galloped off, leaving me virtually alone, or so it seemed, in the big house, dejection settled on my shoulders like a shawl. Even the house seemed gloomy. I felt houses took on the moods of their inhabitants. Our house had seemed mournful to me after my mother's death, and this one seemed so to me now, with the baby gone.

Was he all right, I wondered, as I slowly climbed the stairs back to the Ming Room. Did they give him enough to eat, and did they keep him warm? He was such a dear little mite. The thought of him being mistreated brought tears to my eyes. He was not old enough to take more than a few tottering steps, but he was old enough to drink from a cup. How convenient for a kidnapper, I thought bitterly; small enough to carry inconspicuously, yet old enough to do without a nurse.

Why had he been taken? Money, most likely, and the Gerricks had plenty of that. No doubt Mark would be receiving some sort of note very soon, telling him how much and where to leave it, if they ever wanted to see Peter again. I hesitated, my hand on the doorknob. What if they had already killed the baby? "Please, God," I prayed, "not that."

Once inside, I kicked off my slippers and let my toes luxuriate in the plushness of the carpet, while my eyes wandered over the coromandel screen and the blue-and-white floor vases. I would miss this room very much. I walked over to the window and looked down into the garden below. Could Mark have hired someone to take his nephew, just to hurt Amabel? No, I could not believe him capable of such a monstrous act.

"But you have believed him capable of murder, Nora, girl," the voice of my father echoed in my mind.

"I don't know what that man is capable of," I snapped back.

Putting all thoughts of Mark Gerrick out of my mind, I sat down at my desk, pulled out a fresh sheet of paper, and began writing. I waited for the creative urge to take hold of me, to enslave me, but nothing came. I felt empty, dried out. It will come, I told myself, and relentlessly put words down on paper. When I stopped, I saw that all I had done was string words together, without life, without meaning. In consternation, I crumpled the papers into tight balls and flung them across the room.

Peter was still on my mind. I rose and headed for the nursery.

Nellie was sitting there, as I expected, staring at the empty crib. Her swollen eyes glanced up at me briefly when I entered, then turned back to the crib. She stared at the tiny blue blanket folded neatly at its foot.

"How are you, Nellie?" I placed a gentle hand on her shoulder.

"I fear for that little boy," she said, sniffling. "I lost my own two little boys, you know, right after my husband ran off on me. I heard there was a position open for a nurse up at the Chase. I didn't have to go into service. My brother and his wife up in Northumberland wanted me to live with them, but I didn't want to be a burden. So I applied for the job as nurse here. Miss Amabel didn't want Petey's wet nurse for his regular nurse—the girl was dim-witted." Nellie smiled, caught up in her reminiscing. "Petey took to me from the minute he saw me. He just broke out into a grin and laughed and laughed."

"I know you love him, Nellie."

She looked up at me and clasped my hand. "You don't think anything's happened to him, do you, miss? You think they'll treat him well, don't you?"

I squeezed her hand. "Of course they'll treat him well. No one has anything to gain by harming him."

"I hope you're right, miss," she said with a deep sigh. Then she became practical Nellie once again. "It's past noon, and I think we both need a bit of food in our stomachs. I'll ring for some lunch."

She pulled the bellpull, and, fifteen minutes later, yanked on it again.

"Where is that girl?" Nellie demanded after another quarter hour had gone by. "Wasn't around yesterday either, the slattern," she grumbled. "Probably giving some lad a tumble in the hay."

I asked her who she was talking about.

"Who else?" She gave a little snort. "Flanna O'Brien, of course."

An alarm suddenly went off in my head. "Flanna? You mean Flanna wasn't around all day yesterday?"

Nellie nodded, and informed me that the "slut" never came in yesterday morning, and hadn't been seen since.

My mouth went dry as pieces of the puzzle began to fit together. It was a shame no one had noticed Flanna's absence before. I had to find Mark, and there was no time to lose.

"Nellie," I began, "I'm riding after Sir Mark. If he should come back here before I find him, tell him I have something very important to tell him, and to wait for me."

"But, miss—"

"Please, Nellie, do as I ask. I have no time to explain."

And I went flying out the door.

A few minutes later, I was mounted on Guinevere and galloping off with one of the few remaining grooms at my heels. Old Corman, too old to ride with the searchers, had indicated the general direction Mark had taken, and I took off after him, praying I could overtake him.

After I had wandered aimlessly down steep slopes, up rocky tors, and across boggy moorland, Lady Luck finally took pity on me and conjured up Mark and Dr. Price. My arms felt as though they would fall off at any moment, and my legs were beginning to cramp from urging the mare to cooperate.

"Mark!" I waved frantically. The two men stopped, then started toward me. We met at the base of a slope.

"What's wrong?" Mark grabbed Guinevere's bridle, for I no longer had the strength to stop her.

"I think Flanna is the one who has taken Peter."

"What!" Dr. Price almost fell off his horse.

Mark's lips compressed into a thin, hard line. "You had better know what you're talking about, Nora."

I took a deep breath to stop from shaking. "Nellie told me that no one has seen Flanna since the day before yesterday."

"That doesn't mean she took the child," Mark pointed out.

"Of course not!" I snapped. "But she and Dennis Standish are lovers. And you know how he feels about you. Flanna knows the house and Nellie's habits. How easy it would have been for her to do it. And if any of the other servants questioned her, she could have said she was just playing with the baby."

Mark still looked skeptical, but Dr. Price said, "It certainly is a possibility, Mark."

He shook his head. "Dennis hates me, and has threatened me on several occasions. But to kidnap a child, just to get to me? I find it hard to believe that even he would do such a thing."

"But what would be the harm in checking?" I demanded.

"Sam, why don't you take Nora back to the Chase before she falls off that horse. I'm going to try to find our good man Tibbins." And before Dr. Price or I could say a word, Mark had whirled Odalisque around and galloped off.

"Flanna," the doctor said as he shook his head. "I never would have believed it of her. She was always dreamy-eyed, with her head in the clouds, but I never thought she was a bad girl."

"I hope for her sake she didn't take Peter," I said as we started our ride back together. "But she could have."

I then went on to explain how I had come upon Flanna and Dennis in a compromising situation. The doctor turned scarlet, so I hastily pointed out how Dennis could have persuaded Flanna to spy on the household.

"I was just at Kent House the other day," he said. "Mrs. Standish seems to have gotten over her . . . her association with Mark. She's devoting herself to her husband, something she should have done a long time ago."

His words surprised me. I could still see Jane Standish on the moors that day, vilifying me, spewing hatred. It was difficult for me to imagine her complaisant and resigned to her fate.

"Dennis is still bitter," the doctor continued. "He'll never let his mother forget that she betrayed his father. I wonder what will happen to Jane when her husband dies and her son inherits?"

"What do you mean?"

Dr. Price looked at me. "I'm just wondering if Dennis will allow his mother to live there, or if he will throw her out."

"He wouldn't!"

He sighed. "I think he would. Dennis was always lacking in brains."

"Well, I'm sure Jane Standish will have no difficulty finding a new husband," I replied, with more tartness than I had intended. "Since you know Dennis better than most, would you say he's capable of involving Flanna in such a scheme?"

The doctor was silent as we rode along. "It's possible. As I've said, Dennis is not too intelligent. And Flanna . . . " He shrugged.

"I know. Her head is filled with such romantic nonsense that she'd believe anything Dennis told her. He must have really dazzled her. Flanna O'Brien, a mere serving girl, loved by a gentleman." I smiled bitterly. "Great romance, is it not?"

The doctor nodded. "I hope this 'great romance' doesn't land her in prison. Or swinging from a rope."

Two days later, Constable Tibbins announced that he had found Flanna O'Brien.

Those two days of waiting were the worst I had ever experienced. Nerves were stretched to the limit of human endurance, setting everyone on edge. When Amabel wasn't sniffling into a handkerchief or clasping the toy cloth pig to her breast, she was staring into space. Occasionally, she would rouse herself to lash out at Mark. Her vitriolic words were always returned in kind by her brother, who reduced her to tears time after time.

Mark was usually in a foul mood, his face dark with anger and his black brows in a perpetual scowl. We usually avoided each other, and the few times we did pass in the hall, he barely glanced at me.

You asked for it, Nora girl, I reminded myself. But somehow, victory tasted like sawdust on my tongue.

I had little time to dwell on Mark Gerrick, for on the afternoon that Constable Tibbins arrived, he summoned us all to the library and announced that he had found the missing Flanna.

"She's at Kent House," he said.

Amabel leaned forward expectantly. "And my son?"

"Flanna O'Brien—or Dennis Standish, for that matter—didn't steal your child. The maid flew to get married. She's now Mrs. Dennis Standish."

"So much for that theory," Mark remarked, giving me a crushing look.

"Yes," I agreed, suddenly quite ashamed of the ease with which I had been ready to blame Flanna for Peter's kidnapping. But it had seemed so logical.

"Well, what do we do now?" The hysterical note was starting to creep back into Amabel's voice again. "My baby has been gone for *three days!* No one has seen him or heard him. Where is he?"

"I don't know, miss," Constable Tibbins said sincerely. "But we're doing all we can. Everyone's on the lookout for the lad. All we can do now is hope and pray."

"Well, it's not enough!" she wailed.

"Have you talked to the shepherd yet?" I piped up.

Tibbins shook his head. "He's not been in his hut for these two days."

I leaned forward in excitement. "Then perhaps he is the one who has Peter."

"Why must you persist in accusing everyone except Mark of Peter's kidnapping?" Amabel demanded. "I've told you once and I'll tell you again, the shepherd didn't take Peter!"

"And how can you be so sure?" was my challenge.

We all jumped in our seats as the library doors flew open as if of their own accord. The bearded young shepherd strode in like a god, golden and fierce.

Amabel jumped to her feet. "Colin!"

He said, "I've come to find out what has happened to my son."

As I stared at Colin, I began to see bits and pieces of Peter in him: the same bright blue eyes, the identical set of head and chin. In his black suit and waistcoat, he looked more like a banker than a farmer. His shoes looked expensive and freshly polished, and his beard was neatly trimmed. If I had just met the man, I would never have suspected that he had been living in a cramped, draughty stone hut, chasing sheep on foggy afternoons. This Colin was the father of Amabel's love child, and yet she had denied knowing him. I wondered why.

"Well," said Mark mildly, "Peter's father in the flesh. Why have you waited so long to present yourself?"

"I had my reasons, Sir Mark."

"I wouldn't let him," Amabel said.

"Well . . . Colin, is it?"

"Colin Trelawney."

"Before we proceed, this is Nora Woburn, Amabel's companion."

"Mr. Trelawney and I have already met," I said, and he smiled.

"And this is Constable Tibbins."

Tibbins kept staring at Colin with narrowed eyes, as though trying to see past the thatch of beard to the face beyond. "I keep gettin' the feelin' we've met somewhere before."

Colin rolled his eyes with impatience and said, "Perhaps you have, but what does this have to do with my son?"

"All right, all right." The constable proceeded to tell Colin everything about Peter's abduction, including our false starts and lack of success.

"I still say Mark had a hand in it." Amabel glared at her brother from the shelter of her lover's arm.

Colin shook her. "Amabel . . ."

Mark stretched out his leg in front of him and smiled. "I see you use a firm hand with my sister. Admirable. There is hope for her yet." And he tapped his fingers together, aloof and unapproachable.

Colin said, "I want to help find my son."

"You're welcome to join us," Mark said. "You're also welcome to a room here at Raven's Chase. Amabel could use some comforting."

"There is nothing more for me to do here." Tibbins rose to his feet, bowed, and left.

After that, Amabel and Colin drifted off, arm in arm with their heads touching. I had never seen Amabel so content, and for a moment I envied her.

Mark and I were left alone. He cocked a quizzical brow at me. "I'm surprised you haven't left yet. Left the last of the Gerricks stewing in a tragedy of their own making."

"I wanted to wait until Peter was found." My voice caught on the lump in my throat as I said, "If he is ever found, poor lamb." When Mark made no response, I asked him what he thought had happened.

"I don't know. My thoughts haven't been about Peter, horrible as that sounds. All I can think of is how beautiful you are, and how much I want you." I remained silent. "Oliver—toad that he was—was right in one respect. It's pointless to be gentle with a woman like you. You're like a high-strung filly daring any man to tame her."

"I do so enjoy being compared to a horse," was my dry comment.

"You see? I was right. You are the Nora who first came to Raven's Chase. That poor imitation of Amabel in Plymouth no longer exists." He sprang to his feet, as lissome as a cat. "Why did you playact with me that night, Nora? What was the purpose of your charade?"

I matched his defiant stare. "I did it because I had to convince you

I could not marry you. I felt if I presented myself as someone frivolous and unfeeling, you would stop pressing me."

"I never believed that of you for an instant."

"Oh, but you did."

"Perhaps. But now that I know the truth, why, Nora?"

My brain was racing again. I should have known I could not fool Mark for long with my absurd parody of an empty-headed bit of fluff. I had always been a poor liar. But I could still not bring myself to tell him the truth.

"I did it because you would never have believed my real reason for refusing you."

The gray eyes narrowed. "And what is that?"

"I need my freedom."

A glimmer of hope lit up his whole face. "But you do love me then. Because if you love me, nothing else matters."

"But yes, it does!" I cried out in consternation. "Men like you think that just because you love a woman and marry her, she is supposed to accommodate her life to yours. She is supposed to entertain your guests and bear your children with no thought to a life of her own. Well, my father taught me to be my own person, and I've worked hard at achieving a literary reputation for myself, small though it may be. I'm not giving it up for anyone."

I had finally admitted my real reasons for refusing Mark Gerrick. It was not because I thought him capable of harming me, or my father, and it wasn't because I didn't love him. I was afraid of being dominated by him, of being swallowed whole. Perhaps what I feared most is that I might even learn to accept it.

"Marriage shackles women," I said. "I've made up my mind to be a spinster for the rest of my life."

"What a tragic waste." Before I could dodge him, Mark's hands shot out and caught my arms. A look of revelation crossed his face. "You're afraid to love me, aren't you? You're afraid of love's responsibility and its pain. You're afraid of experiencing true desire and vulnerability. You put them down on paper, where you can control them." He took me into his arms as if he were comforting a child. "Nora, oh, Nora! There is nothing to fear, believe me. I'm not Oliver."

When I made no response, he looked down at me. "Do you love me at all?"

I was silent at first. I had to choose my words carefully. "I think I do love you. But not enough to give up my freedom. So let us part friends, shall we, Mark?"

"Nora—"

"No!" I cried, pulling away. "Please, Mark. Don't press me. I've made up my mind, and there is nothing you can say that will change it. I will not marry you."

He extended his hand toward me in supplication. "Isn't there anything I could do?"

"No, Mark. Nothing."

His face turned livid. "Fine. I won't harass you any longer, since marriage to me would be so distasteful to you." He strode out of the room.

As I look back, I think it was seeing the crumpled wads of discarded paper lying on the floor in the Ming Room that made me think of the baby-farm letter again. If I hadn't, Peter would have spent his short life in a crate.

Once I closed the door securely, the sense of turmoil Mark had inspired deep within me subsided. My breathing became steady once again, and I felt in control of myself. As I walked over to my desk, I noticed the paper balls I had flung across the room earlier, and stooped to pick them up. I began smoothing them out to see if they could be salvaged by rewriting.

Now, as I smoothed out the paper, my mind flew back to the morning Flanna had discarded my manuscript, and I had stood here smoothing papers in just this way.

And that's when I had found the baby-farm letter.

I felt as though I had been struck by lightning. The baby-farm letter. Of course! What better way to get rid of a stolen child, no questions asked. And the culprits had a three-day head start.

I flew down to the library and flung open the doors without ceremony. Mark and Colin turned to look at the whirlwind crashing into their midst.

"Nora," Mark greeted me pleasantly.

"I think I know where Peter might be."

Colin started forward. "Where?"

"You thought at one time that Flanna had taken him," Mark reminded me.

I dismissed that with a wave of my hand. "Do you remember the baby-farm letter I found when I first came here? Well, I think someone was planning to take Peter even then, someone who would pay some London baby farmer to keep him."

Mark scowled. "Take the child all the way to London? It's so damned inconvenient. Why not just kill him—sorry, Trelawney—and be done with it?"

"London is perfect! No wonder Tibbins hasn't been able to find Peter. It's because he's not in Devon at all, but somewhere else."

Colin cut in with, "You've lost me. What is all this about a baby farmer and London?"

As quickly as possible, I told Colin about the baby-farm letter I had found, and what the despicable purpose of the "farmer" was.

His face turned deathly pale. "Oh, my God! Do you think that's possible?"

I shrugged helplessly. "I can't say. I was wrong about Flanna, after all. But surely the child's life is worth investigating every possibility, isn't it?"

"Every possibility," Colin agreed.

Mark was still skeptical. "What will you do, Nora? You don't even have the original letter. There must be thousands of these people all over London. Do you propose to knock on every door searching for Peter?"

"I have lived near the rookery long enough to know its ways." I thought of Harry Leeds. "I also have . . . acquaintances I think could help."

Mark just shook his head.

"We have to try," Colin said. "What is your plan, Mrs. Woburn?"

"That I leave for London this afternoon. I had intended to do so anyway." I could not meet Mark's gaze.

Colin frowned. "You mustn't draw attention to your leaving. No one except us three should know the real reason why you're leaving."

"Not even Amabel?" I asked.

"Not Amabel, not the constable, not Dr. Price," Colin insisted.

"I'm going with you, Nora," Mark said.

Colin shook his head. "That would draw too much attention. And if Peter's kidnapper is someone you know. . . . No, Sir Mark, I think it would look less suspicious if you remained here. You are the lord of the manor"—did I detect a touch of acid in his voice?—"here at the Chase. Tibbins will want you around to assist him with the investigation."

"Nora can't go off chasing kidnappers alone," he protested.

Colin volunteered to go with me. "After all," he said, "that little boy is my son."

We left for London by train a few hours later.

13

"May I ask you a personal question?"

At my inquiry, Colin stopped staring at the placid towns and turned to face me. He wore the conventional black suit again, and while he resembled any other gentleman in our carriage, a mere change of clothing could not eradicate the wildness of the moors that still clung to him, like barnacles on a Raven ship. His level gaze held mine.

"Yes, Mrs. Woburn?"

"Nora. If we are to share an adventure, it must be Nora."

"Nora then. Ask me anything you wish."

I confronted him with what had been plaguing me for days. "You are Peter's father, and you obviously love Amabel. Why have you spent your days masquerading as a shepherd, pretending you didn't know each other, never telling anyone who you were?"

He turned his attention to the fields again, and when he spoke, his voice was heavy and weary. "It's a very long, very sad story."

"I have time to listen."

Colin jerked his head around, and his eyes burned into mine. Then he looked away, and began, as if talking to himself.

"First of all, I was not masquerading as a shepherd. Beneath these fine clothes and manners lurks just that—a farmer. I was not born a gentleman, Nora, by any means. I acquired the trappings of one much later."

"I don't understand."

"I am making little sense. I realize that. I must start from the beginning." I waited while he collected his thoughts.

"My father owns a fairly prosperous farm near Ashcroft. That's where Constable Tibbins had seen me before, as a clean-shaven boy on my father's farm. Until I met Amabel, I was content with the life that my father had planned for me. I don't expect you to understand this, being the Londoner that you are, but there's something enduring about working the soil. Your life becomes ruled by the land and the seasons. I was looking forward to someday taking my bride there, raising sons to work the fields, harvest the crops."

"And then you met Amabel."

He nodded. "And then I met Amabel. I was trying to pull a calf out of the bog, and was up to my ears in mud and slime, when this Diana on a half-wild horse rode up. She was like no other woman I had ever seen, and so . . . so *above* me." He laughed. "Do you know what she did? She looked down her blue-blooded nose at me and said, 'You'll never get the poor thing out that way.' Then she got right into the bog and helped me pull the calf out. She ruined her dress and shoes, so I insisted she come back to the farm with me to change. At first she hesitated, but then she just laughed and agreed."

Colin leaned back in his seat and stared dreamily at the roof. "I'll never forget the look on my mother's face when we came riding in. Poor Mother. She blushed and stammered and kept looking at me like I had betrayed my class, which I had, because Mother could see that I was smitten with Amabel even before I knew it myself. And then when I saw her in my sister Mary's homespun dress, and she looked as fresh as spring water . . ." He shrugged.

"Amabel often visited the Ashford sisters," he went on, "and sometimes she stopped at the farm, or near the field where I was working. Knowing her as I do now, I see that it was an amusing diversion for her to disrupt a poor, blushing farm boy at his work. But one thing led to another, and we became lovers in a small deserted barn on my family's property."

The young man's voice trailed off into silence, and I could see him thinking of those sweet stolen moments with Amabel.

"She fell in love with you in spite of herself," I said, breaking the spell that held him.

He nodded. "Finally, I became obsessed with her. I had to make her my wife. She was driving me mad. But when I asked her to marry me, she became frightened by my earnestness. She was, after all, a

Gerrick, and I was only an uncouth farmer who smelled of cattle and had dirt under his fingernails."

"She was young," I said, trying to ease his bitterness. "She wasn't ready for the life you had to offer."

"I know that. I knew she would never accept a farmer's life. So if she wouldn't change for me, I'd change for her."

"How?"

"I emigrated to Australia. I heard there was gold just waiting to be mined," Colin clenched his teeth and declared, "I was going to make myself worthy of Amabel or die!"

Amabel, I said to myself, it is you who are not worthy.

"That was almost two years ago. I'll spare you the sordid details of my first year there. But we did find gold, Nora, my partner and I. By all standards, I'm a wealthy man." He ran his fingers down the fine worsted of his coat. "Wealthy enough to wear fine clothes. Wealthy enough to erase the crudeness from my speech and manners. Wealthy enough to be worthy of a *Gerrick.*"

I shook my head at the senselessness of it all.

"I was so confident she would have me when I returned," he continued softly, "especially when I discovered she had borne my child and was living as a social outcast. But not Amabel. She still would not have me. She would bear her shame, she said." He looked up at me. "For all of Amabel's protests of Mark keeping her a prisoner at Raven's Chase, I feel that she enjoys her velvet-lined prison and the comforts her brother provides."

"Why didn't you give up?" I asked him quietly. "A man can be spurned only so often."

"But I love her." As if that explained everything. "So I made myself as inconspicuous as possible, hoping one day she would change her mind."

"Why didn't you go back and stay on your father's farm, rather than hide in that miserable hut?"

Colin snorted softly. "Because they would have nothing to do with me. I had disavowed my heritage and they were hurt. Especially my father."

"I know how you felt," I said, thinking of Ivor Stokes.

"So I bought a flock of sheep and played shepherd. It enabled me to be close to Amabel. Mark had returned by this time. You know the rest."

I said, "And all this time Amabel had nothing to do with you?"

Colin shook his head. "We did meet once or twice at night. I gathered scraps of information from servants—Old Corman, mostly. I had to be content with just being near her to protect her."

"Amabel is luckier than she'll ever realize."

He sighed. "Perhaps when this is over, and we have Peter back, God willing, we can build a future for ourselves. Perhaps then Amabel will accept me." Colin regarded me solemnly for a moment. "Do you think her accusations against Mark are true?"

"I don't know."

"Neither do I," he agreed, "in spite of what my beloved says. You stare at me in disbelief, Nora. I can assure you I know my Amabel's faults and weaknesses quite well."

I smiled. "You're a wise man."

He became sober once again. "Thank you for helping me find my son."

"The odds against finding him are one thousand to one," I warned him brutally. "London shelters thousands of baby farmers who go to extremes to see that their identities are kept secret. Even if we should find Peter, we may never learn who stole him."

My companion clenched his hands into fists. "I just want my son."

Paddington Station.

As I stepped down onto the platform, a strange feeling of excitement gripped me. Nothing had changed. It could have been hours ago that I was waving good-bye to the tearful Mrs. James and embarking on a journey which would profoundly change my life.

It was early afternoon, but Colin suggested that we book rooms in a hotel. Once we had secured a cab and found a hotel to our liking, he politely asked me if I cared to rest and begin our search the following morning. But I could see how anxious he was to begin, so I brushed off my weariness and urged him to start.

"Watch your pockets," I warned him as our cab headed toward the great rookery of St. Giles.

He just grinned boyishly, and I thought, "Oh, Amabel. You fool!"

Some minutes later, the cab rocked to a halt in front of Mrs. James' house. As Colin helped me down, I noticed the spiked fence still surrounded it, but no Gentleman Harry Leeds stood guard. A queer sense of uneasiness began gnawing at me, for the house had a closed, guarded look that it had never had before.

Had Madame Leclerc appropriated my rooms, I wondered, as I mounted the steps and rapped smartly on the door, eager to see Mrs. James once again.

An unfamiliar face peered cautiously at me through a crack between the door and jamb. "Who are you, and what is your business?"

I was taken aback. "My name is Nora Woburn. I want to see Mrs. James. I am a friend of hers."

"Who?"

"Mrs. James."

The crack widened as the door was thrown open, but no scent of yesterday's cooking greeted me.

"Oh, you must mean the woman who used to live here," a fat woman in a faded, stained dress said.

"Used to?" I looked back at Colin. "Where are Madame Leclerc and Miss Fowler?"

The woman wiped the back of her hand across her mouth. "Oh, them. Those two left when me and my Horace took over. Claimed the rent was too high. The two of them are probably in the workhouse somewhere."

"And when did you and Horace . . . take over?"

"After that Mrs. James person died. I can see you didn't know. Some vicious criminal broke into this house; smothered her, he did, and cleaned the place out. The two upstairs were damned lucky he didn't get them, too."

I felt cold flow up my spine as I turned and stumbled down the steps. "What's wrong with her?" the fat woman demanded from somewhere behind me. "She sick or something?"

Colin's worried face was just inches away from mine as he steadied me. "Are you all right, Nora? You are positively gray."

"Mrs. James is dead and I didn't even know."

I felt adrift. All that had once been so familiar to me suddenly became hostile and strange. It was as though someone had turned my world inside out.

"I'm sorry," Colin said kindly. "You've had a terrible shock. Would you rather go back to our hotel, or stop somewhere for tea?"

I clutched at him for support and shook my head to clear it. "No. I'll be all right. Finding Peter must be our first concern. We mustn't waste time drinking tea. But first we've got to find Harry Leeds."

We found Posies first.

"Lavender! Fresh posies!"

I blinked hard, just to be sure, but there was no mistaking that rolling walk and the basket balanced on her hip. Sadness overcame me as I noticed the black patch over one eye. Change had touched all I had known, like a plague.

"Posies!" I called.

"I can't believe me eyes!" She lifted up the patch and gave me a broad wink. "It's Mrs. Nora with a proper young gentleman."

I laughed as I hugged her. "Oh, Posies. I never thought you'd go in for the scaldrum dodge," I said, referring to her feigned lost eye.

She pulled the patch back in place and gave an offended sniff. "The patch makes 'em feel sorry for me, and gets me a few more coppers, it does. Now, who is this young man here?"

When I introduced Colin, Posies eyed him warily. She dropped him a parody of a curtsy when he tipped his hat, then said to me, "Why'd you come back, Mrs. Nora?"

"We've come to find a kidnapped child." I quickly explained what had happened, and why we were there.

"I've got to find Harry," I added. "If anyone can help us to find the child, he can."

Posies shook her head as she shifted her basket to the other hip. "Don't count on Harry helpin' you, Mrs. Nora. He ain't been himself since you left. He's been dabbing it up with this blower—a real judy, she is—and to top it off, he's losing his touch. I heard he almost got nabbed by the jacks, he did." She gave a sour grunt. "Never thought I'd live to see the day they get their fingers on him. It would be the boat for sure, if not worse."

My hopes plummeted. "Do you know where I can find him, Posies? I've got to try to get him to help us."

She stared skyward, as though Harry's address were written there. "Last I heard, he had a drum on Nicolls Street."

"I know where that is."

"Number twenty-eight, upstairs."

"Thank you, Posies." I gratefully tried to slip a guinea into her pocket, but she pushed my hand away.

"What's that for? We're friends, Mrs. Nora. Information is free to friends."

Blushing, I thanked her again, wished her well, and started back toward our waiting cab with Colin in tow.

Once inside, he said, "What was that woman babbling about?"

I quickly translated Posies' thieves' cant. "Apparently Harry's career is on the decline," I told him, settling myself in. "According to Posies, he's living with a woman of low reputation, and is losing his talents at thievery. He was almost arrested by the police. Needless to say, if Harry were ever caught, they'd leave him on the treadmill for the rest of his life, or transport him."

Colin eyed me wryly. "You have strange friends, Nora. Thieves, pickpockets."

"Those strange friends are going to help us find your son," I reminded him.

He had the grace to blush. "I'm sorry. That was snobbish of me."

"I daresay many people who live in the rookery don't want to steal or become prostitutes. But when your alternative is starvation. . . ." I shrugged. "Can you blame them?

"When I lived at Mrs. James', the people, especially Harry, looked out for me. I would have soon died otherwise. But they also taught me that all people, whether poor or criminals, have something you can admire in them. It was an education in itself."

"I'll wager it was," Colin muttered, chastened.

When the cab finally pulled over to a halt and Colin helped me down, I felt fear and a terrible foreboding. Even the driver seemed to sense this, for he refused to wait for us, but whipped his horses and clattered off to safety.

Tenement houses surrounded us like trees in a forest, packed so tightly together one could scarcely peer between them. A black film of soot and grime was everywhere, permeating the once-rosy bricks, and even seeming to smudge what was surely a blue sky overhead.

A putrid stench almost caused me to heave, until I thought of the people who couldn't escape the overflowing sewer.

Two men with hungry faces and rags for clothing eyed us dismally from across the street. I clutched at Colin's arm as they started to advance on us, but the object of their attention turned out to be a white-haired wretch swilling gin in an alley. They snatched his bottle away, and when he protested, began kicking him.

Colin started forward in anger.

"Don't." My voice was no more than a hiss. "They would all be on us in a second."

I pulled him toward number 28, and he reluctantly followed me, as did the pitiful screams of the drunk. The door swung open easily onto a foyer so dark I was temporarily blinded. I heard sounds of whining and scuffling and as my eyes became accustomed to the murkiness, I saw what was making all the commotion. Two filthy, naked children squatted in a corner by the stairs and fought a starving puppy for a piece of meat.

They stared at us with dark eyes like trapped animals before they darted off, the puppy snapping desperately at their heels. Above us, shouting voices rose and fell in a hum.

"This is worse than I imagined," Colin murmured. In spite of his tanned face, he looked white. I knew he was thinking of his son, alone and frightened in such a place.

"Let's try upstairs," I whispered.

We took a wrong turn at the top of the stairs, and had to retrace our steps down a corridor. I was thankful the doors were closed, and all we could hear was the din from the rooms behind them.

Colin whipped out his handkerchief. "The stench in here. How can you stand it?"

Smoke from cooking fires, mingled with stale air and sewer odors, rendered the air unbreathable. I could almost feel it clinging to my clothes and skin and hair. I couldn't wait to strip off my clothes and give my body a good scrubbing.

And there it was, the door to Harry's "drum." I swallowed hard and knocked boldly, my mind's eye envisioning a large, common room clogged with people.

The door swung open to reveal a sullen-faced gypsy with large silver loops in her ears. Dark eyes swept over me insolently before she said, "Yes?"

"I want to see Harry." My tone was sharp, and brooked no nonsense.

She placed a hand on her hip and looked us up and down again, more slowly this time. "What you want?"

"That's only for Harry's ears."

Her silver loops jingled. "My ain't we the flash one. Well, he ain't here."

"Then we'll wait." I took a determined step forward.

The gypsy arched her back like an infuriated cat, and hissed, "You ain't!"

Colin now stepped forward. "Look, miss . . ."

"Colin, let me handle this." I faced her once again, and in my most authoritative voice said, "Now look here. Harry and I have been very good friends for a long time. And if he ever finds out you turned me away . . ." I smiled and jerked my finger across my throat.

Terror filled the girl's dark eyes, and she stepped back into the room. She was obviously no stranger to the back of Harry's hand.

"I'm Nora Woburn and this is Colin Trelawney," I said, more gently this time, trying to ease her hostility.

Colin whipped off his hat and bowed, as though he had just met the Queen.

"I am Sarella. Sit down, if you wish. Harry will return soon." Without so much as a backward glance, she seated herself in a carved, high-back chair near the fire in the center of the room. She sat there staring straight ahead, leaving us to seat ourselves at the table.

Taking a handkerchief from my reticule, I proceeded to wipe the seats before we sat on them. Colin said nothing, but his looks spoke volumes. I don't think he had ever experienced this, even in the rough Australian mining camps.

As the silence widened in the room, I had ample opportunity to study how Harry Leeds lived. The room was large and luxurious in the sense that Sarella and he were its only occupants. It was furnished by Harry's trade. There were unmatched chairs, probably stolen from four different houses in Mayfair, and a stately, but badly tarnished, four-armed candelabra on the table. There was also a door leading somewhere, probably to a separate bedroom, which was a rarity in St. Giles.

Housekeeping was not one of the gypsy's virtues, for the window overlooking a central courtyard was coated with grime from the cooking fire. A missing pane had been stuffed with an old rag to keep out the elements.

And all of this could have been mine, I reminded myself. I could have been the queen of St. Giles. Men and their promises. I was shaking my head as Harry walked in.

"Sarella!" His booming voice split the room, causing the girl to start out of her chair in a jangle of silver. Then he spied me, and stopped in his tracks as if shot.

"Hello, Harry." I smiled as I rose. "How are you?"

He stared at me in astonishment. A dark red flush stained his puckered face. I doubted if he had ever blushed in his life, but he did so now.

"How are you?" I asked again, while Colin remained silent in the background.

"Out!" he snapped at Sarella, who edged her way around the room and out like a whipped dog. Then he turned to me, but his eyes were wary and distrustful. "How are you, Mrs. Nora?" he said. The warmth in his voice was gone.

"Harry, meet Colin Trelawney. We need your help."

Colin stepped forward and offered his hand. "My pleasure, sir." Harry stared at him, seemingly bewildered at someone offering him his hand and addressing him with respect. But he did offer his hand, though warily, to Colin. Then he turned to me. "Why do you need my help?"

Once again, I found myself telling the story. Harry listened attentively, sometimes scowling, sometimes rubbing his scarred jaw.

When I finished, he said, "Do you know which farmer has him?"

Colin and I exchanged glances. "No."

"Do you know how many farmers work St. Giles alone?" Harry asked in exasperation.

"Thousands," I replied.

Harry rose to his feet while shaking his head. "I can't help you, Mrs. Nora. This plan of yours is harebrained. You'll never find the boy."

Colin's face fell, but I would not give up. I jumped to my feet and clutched at Harry's arm. "Please, Harry. I know the odds are against us. But all I ask is that you take us to the farmers you know. Then, if we can't find Peter, we'll give up. But please help us."

He looked down at me and hesitated.

"For me, Harry. Please."

The dark eyes burned into mine. "For you, anything, Mrs. Nora."

The next three days were the most demanding, heartbreaking, and frustrating of my entire life.

Harry called for us at nine in the morning, and dragged us from one end of the city to the other. We walked and rode up and down countless streets that all began to look alike to me after a while. We followed Harry into old houses and into new ones, where respectable-looking people practiced legal infanticide.

It was always the same. Up the steps, ring the bell, and plaster a smile on your face, pretending to be a young married couple eager to adopt a foundling.

I looked into hundreds of cribs, boxes and even bureau drawers at lost, eager little faces. The impulse to snatch them all and run coursed through me.

By the end of the day, my nerves were strung out halfway to the Continent, and my aching feet could barely carry me up to my hotel room. Yet I couldn't sleep. Pale, wide-eyed faces—some healthy and unaware of their future, others painfully aware—haunted my dreams.

As I lay there in the darkness, I thought of Amabel, distraught and waiting for news of her child, and, in spite of myself, I thought of Mark. His dark, brooding face haunted my dreams as much as the children did. Why? There was nothing between us. If we did find

Peter, I would not return with Colin to Raven's Chase. I would remain here in London.

London. Everything had changed in only a month. Mrs. James was dead, and Harry was as good as dead. If there had been hope for him before, there was none now. He was lost.

I fell asleep, feeling strong arms around me and Mark's insistent mouth on mine.

I broke down on the fourth day.

"It's horrible! Horrible!" I screamed in the middle of a busy London street.

Colin held me in his arms, shielding me from curious stares. "Ssssh. It's all right, Nora."

"Finally got to her," Harry muttered as he hailed a cab.

"I'm sending you back to the hotel, Nora. Now don't argue with me. You either stay in bed, or spend the day shopping or visiting friends. Harry and I will keep looking for Peter, and you can join us tomorrow, if you feel up to it."

"But . . ."

"Don't argue with me, Nora. Why don't you visit your publisher, or some of your father's artist friends?"

Or my father, I thought, as a calmness settled over me.

It was past noon when my cab pulled up before the bright white-washed house that had been my home for so long. For a moment, I couldn't move. I sat there and stared at it through the window, until finally the driver poked his head in.

"You gonna sit there all day, lady?"

I paid him handsomely and stepped down. As the cab rolled off, I stood on the curb, thinking, "You're home, Nora. Home."

I was worried that something was amiss. The house looked inhabited. The crack over the front door had been filled, and the door itself was freshly painted. Perky geraniums grew in the flower boxes which were guarding windows with their drapes thrown open. Perhaps Father had let the house to a friend while he had gone traveling.

I stepped up to the door, knocking once, then twice. No sounds stirred within, no hurrying footsteps, no opening doors. I waited, then tried the latch. It opened freely, as I knew it would, for Ivor Stokes always left the front door open in case any friend happened to wander by. He was a trusting man, my father.

I walked in, and was assailed by small ghosts.

The mahogany table I had loved to kick when I didn't get my way still stood in the foyer, patiently waiting to receive hats or gloves or kicks.

There were gloves on it now, and my heart gave an absurd lurch. Oliver had spoken the truth. My father was in London. He was in this house.

I moved down the hall and into the drawing room. No one was there. But of course! My father would be in his studio, his bright sanctum at the back of the house.

I whirled around and raced back the way I had come. Taking the stairs two at a time, I ran past the upstairs bedrooms toward my goal —a closed door at the end of the hall.

Oh, Nora, do you dare? There was still time to turn away. Instead, I turned the knob and pushed the door open with my fingertips. "Hello, Father."

Ivor Stokes jumped at the sound of my voice. Always a brawny man, he appeared smaller now. The round monkish face was grave, as though the temptations of youth had given up and gone elsewhere. It was outlined by a splendid lion's mane of a beard, streaked with gray. But those laughing eyes that had never lied to me had lost their spark.

"Nora," he said, as though I had just returned from a walk in the park. Then he turned back to his painting. But his hand began to shake so badly that he finally snarled, "Jill, that will be all for today."

I noticed the other occupant of the room for the first time, a willowy girl with an ethereal look who was posing for my father. She watched me with interest as she gracefully crossed the room. Then she stopped at the door and turned to my father. "Will you be requiring anything else, sir?"

"No, Jill. Not today."

And with another curious side-glance at me, she left us alone.

Father wouldn't look at me. He began cleaning his brushes with savage wipes of the turpentine-soaked rags. I walked over to his easel and looked over his shoulder at the painting. Deep disappointment brought tears to my eyes. I said nothing, but began sauntering around the room, picking up a paperweight here and a brush there.

"Have you seen Rossetti lately?" I asked conversationally.

"Poor fool," my father growled. "He hasn't been the same since The Sid died. It's his guilt eating at him, if you ask me. Dante never should have married her in the first place. And that zoo of his!" The leonine head shook pityingly. "You can't go into the place without a monkey jumping out at you or a wombat tripping you up."

"Must smell delightful, too."

A smile hovered about his mouth for just an instant. "Heard you left that treacherous snake. Always knew you'd see reason in the end."

"Oliver's dead," I said quietly.

"Glad to hear it. I'll shed no tears." He finished cleaning his brushes, then said, "Is it that bad?"

"Is what that bad?"

"This painting. You didn't praise it to the skies after you looked at it, so I assume you were trying to spare my feelings."

I gave it a second look. "It's not your best."

"The subject is Keats' *Lamia*."

I squinted at the canvas, which depicted the beautiful youth Lycius confronting the woman-serpent Lamia. I grimaced. "Your colors are vibrant and beautiful, as always, and you haven't lost your touch for applying the paint. But why such a gruesome subject? It may be Keats, but it's appalling. If I were your model—Jill, is it?— I would be incensed to be painted as a serpent. I'm sorry, Father, but you did ask my opinion."

Suddenly he groaned. "I'm so tired of looking back to the past for inspiration. I'm sick unto death of knights and Round Tables and maidens palely loitering."

"Don't let Rossetti or Morris hear you speaking such heresy."

"I know, I know." He was deep in thought now. "The French are doing so many new things. And I met this artist, Nora, by the name of Whistler. . . ."

And Ivor Stokes was off talking about light and shadow. Finally, I had to say, "Is this all we can talk about? After four years, Father, nothing but Rossetti's animals and my dead husband and your painting?"

Ivor Stokes sniffed and turned from me. "We can talk in the library."

I followed him downstairs, to the library. It was only a box, compared to the one at Raven's Chase, and had only two chairs. But as I looked at them, a picture of Mark sitting there, stretching out his lame leg, came unbidden to mind. The image hit me so strongly that I had to walk around the little room, making a pretense of reading the titles on the shelves. Suddenly, I stopped.

There, on a center shelf, were *Leomandre* and *The Green Tree*.

So, our estrangement had cost my father something, too.

"They are very good, Nora, girl," he said.

The tears came then, and I threw myself in his arms. "I missed you so much, Father."

"I know, Nora, girl, I know. I've missed you, too."

We had so much to talk about. Four years of our lives. So I made tea, and we sat in the library until it was nearly nightfall. I was pleased my father had forgiven me. We each reached out, and I felt calm and whole again.

When he began talking of Rome, I could not help but think of Mark Gerrick. "I know someone who met you in Rome," I said.

"Small world. Who?"

"Mark Gerrick."

My father's face glowed. "Gerrick, eh? A fine man. One of the best. Although we didn't meet under the best circumstances."

"I know. You crippled him in a tavern brawl."

His eyes became grave. "I'm not proud of what I did, Nora, girl. I was blind drunk when those Italian sailors came at me. Gerrick tried to help me, but I was so crazy drunk I thought he was one of them. I brought a table down on his leg and crushed his shin."

Oh, my God, I thought in horror. Everything Oliver had told me had been the truth. Getting me down to Raven's Chase had been part of his warped plan of revenge. His words of love had all been lies. Lies.

But my father kept on talking. "Any other man would have become bitter, but not Gerrick. After he was better, he came to see me to find out how I was. He never held it against me that I had crippled him, and that he could never sail again. In fact, we became the best of friends, although I couldn't understand why he would want to be friends with me after what I had done." My father shook his head and looked somewhere beyond me. Then he perked up again. "Why, Mark even bought some of my paintings, and about a year ago, he wrote to tell me he had bought that portrait I had done of you some years ago."

"*The Edge of Experience*," I said.

"That's the one. Nora, are you all right? You look quite ill."

"You're sure Mark Gerrick never bore you any ill will? You're sure he hasn't been planning to hurt you, through me?"

"Nora, girl, your fancies are running away with you. Mark Gerrick would never harm anyone. Why are you asking me such questions?"

"I've been a fool, Father. . . ." And for the next hour, I heard my dry and brittle voice tell my father all about Mark Gerrick, and how Oliver had succeeded at last.

When I finished, Ivor Stokes exploded. "That bastard! May Oliver Woburn rot in hell! Always looking out for himself. Always waiting to turn something to his advantage. I said it before. Good riddance." He stopped his tirade long enough to say gently, "You're in love with Mark, aren't you?"

Agitated, I rose and went to the window. "Me? In love with him?" I sighed. "Nonsense! I don't need Mark or any other man. I have my freedom now. My writing has made me an independent woman, and I refuse to be shackled by a man again. You know yourself, Father, that if I marry I will be expected to remain in my husband's shadow. I'm sorry, but I don't want it."

My father didn't reply for what seemed like an eternity. Finally, he said, "Perhaps you are right. It's very difficult for a man to have a bluestocking for a wife. Your mother was content being my wife though."

"That was Mother," I snapped.

"Tell me, Nora. What sort of future do you envision for yourself as one of London's literary lights? Do you fancy a salon, or will you live alone with a hired companion? You could always take care of me in my declining years, I suppose."

"That's not amusing, Father."

He shrugged. "It's what's going to happen to you if you deny what you feel for Mark."

"I must be getting back to my hotel," I announced. "Colin and I must get an early start in the morning."

Ivor Stokes rose and placed his hand on my shoulder. "Good-bye. Thank you for coming, and please come to see your old father more often."

I smiled, hugged him with all my heart, and left.

The following morning, I arose before sunrise and, wrapped in a thin robe, sat before a window and silently urged the city to come to life so we could search once again. It was one of those cool English mornings, misty around the edges, unpopulated and hushed. In an hour or so, the city would rouse itself, clattering and shouting, but for the time being, its voice was stilled.

Soon, thin white light forced itself down from the sky into the streets and sharply defined each alley, doorway, and cobblestone below me. A solitary street sweeper dressed all in black dragged his broom through the gutter, so that its raspy swish and the beating of my own heart were the day's first sounds. For a few moments, we were the world's only inhabitants.

"Peter, where are you?" I cried silently to the rooftops, as I dug my nails into the windowsill.

Time was running out for all of us.

By the time I finished washing, dressing, and combing my hair, it was time to meet Colin for breakfast. We faced each other silently across a table in the near-empty room. A sleepy old man hobbled over to bring us our coffee.

"You should eat something," Colin said. "A roll, at least, or a sausage."

"This is all I ever eat. What about you?"

He said he wasn't hungry.

We drank the coffee and spoke of inconsequential things—the hotel's uncomfortable beds, the genteel charm of its dining room—until Colin's watch indicated it was time to meet Harry. We finished our coffee and departed.

"We've wasted so much time already," I said as we walked out into the street in search of a cab.

Colin chuckled under his breath. "You can't expect everyone to start their day before sunrise just because you do, Nora."

"I wish they would. I can't stand the waiting."

"I know."

A cab clopping by stopped. We jumped in and gave the driver the address of Mrs. James' house. Since cabbies balked at driving to Harry's street, we had thought it best to meet on neutral territory.

"We'll be successful today," I stated with conviction.

"Why should today be any different from yesterday? Or the day before?" Colin's voice sounded weary.

"I have a feeling. I can't explain it."

"I hope you're right."

We rode on in silence, until finally the cab rolled to a halt. As I looked out the window, Harry detached himself from the spiked fence he had been leaning against and joined us. After greetings were exchanged, Colin asked Harry where we were going today.

"Fairfax Street," he replied. "A friend of Sarella's, a girl who works the Haymarket, heard tell of a farmer who just got some new tenants within the last few days. It may be something, and then again, it may not."

The rookery's vast information network was working for us, and the thought filled me with hope. I had done the right thing, coming to London, seeking Harry's help.

Harry was regarding Colin and me with pity in his eyes. Our cause must have seemed like a lost one to a man who counted daily survival a triumph.

Fairfax Street was a quiet, sedate-looking street, where all the houses turned freshly-painted faces toward the world. What was going on behind these drawn organdy curtains, I wondered, as I shivered in the still-cool air. No doubt the majority of them concealed innocent, hard-working people who went about the daily business of living, while next door, a neighbor packed children together until they died. I shivered again.

"Which house is it?" Colin whispered, as we stepped out of our cab.

"Number sixteen," Harry said.

I wondered aloud if we weren't too early to call. "I'd hate to antagonize anyone because we woke them up."

Colin said, "It's almost ten o'clock. We may as well try. We just can't stand here in the middle of the street." Then he turned to me. "Are you ready, Nora?"

When I nodded, he climbed the stairs and knocked on the door. We waited. Finally, out of the corner of my eye, I saw a white curtain move imperceptibly. A minute later, a gray-haired woman with a soft, motherly face came to the door. From her tidy hair to her clean, freshly-starched apron, she presented a respectable appearance.

"Yes? What may I do for you?" Her voice, however, was anything but motherly.

Colin came to life. He smiled and doffed his hat. "Good morning to you, madam. We apologize for the early intrusion, but"—he lowered his voice conspiratorially—"we've heard you have children for adoption here."

Her eyes narrowed. "I may and I may not. Who says so?"

"We've sworn not to tell," he replied quickly.

The woman just stared, and for one terrible instant, I thought she was going to slam the door in our faces. Then she said, "This is highly irregular, sir."

"If my wife and I waited for a regular method of obtaining a child, we'd never have one." Colin kept smiling.

She refused to yield. "Who sent you?"

It was a bad moment. Colin looked at me, his eyes pleading for help in desperation. Suddenly, Harry stepped forward.

"You came highly recommended from Jumping Josie. She said you were the best. 'Mrs. Greene has prime goods,' Josie herself said to me. And that's why I brought these good people here. To get the best."

The thin lips twitched. "Josie, eh?" Then she laughed. "Aye, Josie's one of the best herself, but in another way from me. Why, she's even supplied me with a lusty piece of merchandise herself."

My knees buckled in relief. I felt like sinking to the ground, but resisted the impulse. How Harry had known what to say eluded me, but I silently thanked Jumping Josie, and wished her a brisk business.

"Well, don't just stand there. Come on in. I'll show you what I got, and you can take your pick," Mrs. Greene said, ushering us in. "For a price," she added.

"My wife and I didn't expect to get a child for nothing," Colin said as we followed her into the house. Harry remained outside.

The house emphasized Mrs. Greene's respectability. The hallway and parlor to the right were spotless, freshly-papered, and cluttered with furniture that, while not new, was neither shabby nor threadbare. Looks could be so deceiving.

We mounted the stairs.

"Can't have any of your own?" she called back over her shoulder.

"No," I replied.

"You poor dearie." She hustled down a narrow hallway and threw open a door to a large, sunny room she affectionately called "my nursery."

There were four polished wood cradles in the room—no boxes or drawers here—and all appeared filled. The room came alive with the soft sounds of baby noises as they rolled restlessly in their cradles.

Suddenly, a curly blond head popped up and a pair of bright blue eyes, Colin's eyes, stared into mine.

"Da!" a high-pitched voice squeaked in joyful recognition.

There could be no mistake. It was Peter.

"Oh, darling, I must have this one!" I cried, rushing forward and sweeping Peter into my arms.

I must not think of the others, I reminded myself, only Peter. Peter is all that matters now.

He laughed and tugged at my hair and squirmed in my arms. The baby was dressed in a coarse gray gown that would have made Amabel burst into tears, but he was clean, at least. After what I had seen these last few days, I supposed I should even thank Mrs. Greene for taking such good care of him.

Out of the corner of my eye, I saw suspicion darken Mrs. Greene's face once again. "He sure took to you mighty quick."

I replied, "That's because he knows we'll be good parents."

Colin, meanwhile, took a sack of gold from his pocket and casually jiggled it. "My wife wants this child. How much?"

Mrs. Greene licked her lips greedily. "The woman who brought him here wasn't sure she wanted him adopted yet."

"Can you tell us her name and where she lives, so we can ask her ourselves?" He fingered the sack. "We'll make it worth your while."

"I don't know . . ."

I spoke from across the room. "Why did she bring the baby here if she didn't want him adopted?"

"I don't ask 'em their reasons," she snapped back.

We stared at each other with animosity, while all around us tiny scraps of humanity fretted and whined.

Finally, Colin said, "We'll pay you for the baby, and then we'll make a deal with his mother. In any case, you won't be responsible."

"All right," the woman agreed. "Wait here."

After Mrs. Greene left, Colin and his son stared at each other for the first time. Colin's face wore a mixture of pride, wonder, and hope at the prospect of immortality.

He held out his arms and said, "Nora, bring my son to me."

"Colin, what are we going to do about these others?" I crossed the room and placed Peter in his father's arms.

"Peter Trelawney," Colin murmured, unable to take his eyes off the baby. "He even has my eyes! Don't you think so, Nora?"

My exasperation and jealousy added a sting to my words. "Colin, we have no time to discuss Peter. We must find out who took him, and then do something for these other poor mites."

He stared at me. "I'm sorry, Nora. You're right, of course. But even if she doesn't tell us who took him, I still have my son and no one is ever going to keep him from me again."

Mrs. Greene returned with a slip of paper, and, after taking almost all of Colin's gold, she turned the paper over to him.

"She called herself Mrs. Cardiff—Mrs. Clara Cardiff. Gave me the most pitiful tale of the laddie here being born without a father, and now she couldn't even care for her little one any more." She forced a smile and attempted to pat the baby's cheek, but Peter recoiled and hid his face in Colin's shoulder.

"Anyway," Mrs. Greene went on with a sniff, "she's a tall, dark woman, very striking. The father must have been fair to get this golden-haired laddie."

A tall, dark woman, and very striking.

I looked at Colin. "Jane Standish," I said.

14

"Why? Why would she do such a thing?" I asked Colin in a dazed voice as our cab raced as fast as it dared toward the Regis Hotel, the address Mrs. Greene had given us. We had thanked Harry, who just bowed, flashed me a bittersweet smile, and melted back into the rookery. I knew we'd never see each other again. He had St. Giles and Sarella, while I had—what? After parting with Harry, Colin and I deposited Peter in the arms of my startled father, clambered back into the cab, and went careening off again to find Clara Cardiff.

"I don't know why," Colin replied. "To get even with Mark, I suppose."

The pieces of the puzzle didn't fit. "That doesn't make sense. Taking Peter would hurt Amabel more than Mark. And how did she kidnap Peter? Someone would surely have seen her."

Colin shrugged. "Nora, don't worry about it. We will find out soon enough."

But I could not help but worry. My image of Jane Standish, a witch prowling the moors that day, came to mind. Jane was capable of vengeance, but to kidnap a child? No, her revenge would be on a grand, tragic scale.

I asked Colin if we should contact the police and let them question Jane.

"After I talk to her first."

We reached the Regis, a modest and unpretentious building, and were told Mrs. Cardiff was in room 210 upstairs.

Colin knocked, while I stepped back out of sight.

"Yes?" a muffled voice I couldn't recognize replied cautiously.

Colin disguised his voice. "Message for Mrs. Cardiff."

When the door opened, he pushed his way in with me not far behind.

I stopped in my tracks when I saw the occupant of the room. It was not Jane Standish.

"You're supposed to be in Surrey," I said irrationally.

"Get out of here!" Marianne Meadows snarled like an animal at bay.

I stared at her in disbelief. "So it was you. You kidnapped Peter."

"I don't know what you're talking about."

"Oh, but you do." Colin closed and locked the door behind him.

"Why did you do it?" I demanded.

She stood there haughtily, in command of herself, hands clasped primly in front of her. Marianne Meadows looked down at me as though I had accused her of dropping a dish. Could nothing break through her iron facade?

"I didn't kidnap anyone. You have no right to come to my room and make these accusations."

Colin gave an exaggerated sigh. "Mrs. Meadows, we have just been to Fairfax Street where we found my son, in a baby farmer's nursery. Yes, Peter is my son. The proprietress was most kind and cooperative. She gave us this address"—he waved the paper under her nose—"and a description that fits you perfectly."

She was cool, this one. "I don't know what you're talking about."

"Oh, but you do. In fact, Mrs. Greene is willing to swear in a court that you brought the baby to her establishment and made provisions for its adoption."

I saw doubt creep into her eyes, then vanish. "You're wasting your time. I admit to nothing."

Colin was growing impatient. His voice hardened as he said, "Mrs. Meadows, if you don't tell us the truth, I am going to become very unpleasant. You have such beautiful hands, Mrs. Meadows." He picked up a pen from the desk and toyed with it. "Such delicate, fine-boned fingers." Effortlessly, he snapped the pen in two, and both Mrs. Meadows and I recoiled at the sickening crack it made.

A look of such fear crept into the woman's face that I almost felt sorry for her. Colin had found the crack in her armor. Mrs. Meadows could not bear the thought of physical pain.

"You wouldn't dare! You can't do this! I'll call the police."

Colin laughed. "Go ahead. Call them. I'm sure they'd be very interested to hear our story also." When she hesitated, he continued with, "If you don't tell us the truth, I'll see you're transported. Do you fancy Australia, Mrs. Meadows? I've been there. It's a rough, brutal country, inhabited by even more brutal men." He let his eyes rove insolently over her body, so that she actually flinched and edged toward the window.

"All right. All right. I'll tell you everything." She collapsed into a nearby chair.

Colin let her cry for a while, then he took out his handkerchief and pressed it into her hand. He had won, but he looked disgusted with himself.

Mrs. Meadows' voice wavered. "This was all Sam's idea from the beginning, and I'll not take the blame alone."

Sam. I knew only one Sam. "Dr. Price? You mean *Dr. Price* had you kidnap Peter?" I'd sooner believe my father had.

Marianne Meadows gulped and nodded. "His name really isn't Price, it's Lawton. Samuel Lawton. He changed it so the Gerricks wouldn't know who he really was."

I turned to Colin excitedly. "Lawton! That was the name of the girl in the Gerrick Bible, the one Sir Charles had listed as Damon's wife. You mean she's Dr. Price's, er, Lawton's daughter?" I recalled the day I had visited his office and saw the portrait of his daughter. "But she died in a boating accident."

"Not an accident," Mrs. Meadows declared bitterly. "Damon Gerrick killed her."

I looked at Colin in shock and disbelief.

"Why don't you start at the beginning, Mrs. Meadows," he suggested.

The woman blew her nose. "Sam was a very successful, talented surgeon here in London. He had a lovely wife and a beautiful daughter."

The photograph on the doctor's desk flashed before my eyes.

"When Lucy was sixteen, she was introduced to Damon Gerrick and began meeting him secretly." Mrs. Meadows closed her eyes as though shutting out a horrible memory. "One spring day, they fished Lucy's body out of the Thames. Sam found a note from her, saying that she was with child—Damon Gerrick's child—and since he had refused to make an honest woman of her, she preferred to take her own life rather than bring any shame on her parents."

I murmured, "How senseless."

"Sam was devastated. Between dealing with his wife's grief and his own, he couldn't even practice his profession. Emily—Mrs. Lawton—was especially bereft because she could have no more children.

"So Sam began making inquiries, and found that Damon Gerrick was a student at Oxford, and the son of a wealthy lord in Devon. Sam wasn't an evil man. He just wanted to see justice done. He arranged to meet Sir Charles in Plymouth to discuss the matter. He told him what his son had done and demanded restitution." The housekeeper's lip curled in contempt. "The bastard just listened to Sam, expressed his regrets that Lucy had died, and said something about young men having their sport. Sport! Do you call a young girl taking her life sport?" She looked beseechingly from Colin to me.

"That's why Sir Charles plucked Damon out of Oxford so suddenly, and sent him to India," I said. I recalled Amabel telling me about Damon's summons to the library, and his blind anger when his father was through with him. And I thought of Sir Charles. His personal sense of justice must have been overwhelming for him to sentence his own son to such hell. "He wanted to punish him for what he had done to Lucy," I murmured softly.

"Punish him?" Mrs. Meadows scoffed. "He just wanted to put his precious son out of Sam's way."

I reminded her that Damon had lost his fiancée and mind out there.

"He deserved to die."

Colin came between us. "Please, ladies. Mrs. Meadows, do continue."

"After Sam returned to London, Emily's health declined. She died of grief a year later. Sam became a bitter and disillusioned man. The law would do nothing. He had lost a wife and child, and the Gerricks went blithely on their way, free to debauch again. So Sam decided to take the law into his own hands." She looked at me. "Can you blame him?"

"Where do you come in?" Colin asked.

"Emily was my older sister, and Lucy my niece. I had been recently widowed when Sam approached me with his plan."

I asked her if he had forced her into becoming a part of his scheme.

She gave a derisive laugh. "Sam didn't have to force me to do anything. I joined him willingly. I loved my sister and her child. People like the Gerricks, with their money and their titles, think they have the right to step on others, to do as they please. They had to be taught a lesson."

"And how would you go about that?" Colin asked.

"Sam heard that a doctor in Sheepstor was giving up his practice. Just about that time, Sir Charles died, so that eliminated the one person who could identify him. Once he got himself set up, he kept his ears open for something for me. Shortly thereafter, he heard that a housekeeper was needed at the Chase."

Mrs. Meadows pressed her fingers to her temples. "Damon was home from India at that time, and I was able to report on his mental state to Sam. Sam began to cultivate Sir Mark's friendship, and was soon entrusted with the family's health, especially Damon's. It was so easy to drug Damon without anyone finding out, so easy to make him think he was crazier than he was."

I could only gape at her. "Then it was drugs that made him go out to the ruins night after night."

"Drugs and me. Sam had discovered some old manuscript at the Chase that told the location of the abbot's secret passage."

I asked her where it was.

"In one of the cells beneath the chapel. You press a stone and the wall swings out. There's a tunnel that leads to the black stone cottage up by the hill."

The black stone cottage that the Gerrick children had used as a playhouse. The same cottage that Amabel and I had ridden by countless times on the way to the moor.

Mrs. Meadows continued. "One day I told Damon that Lucy would be waiting for him at the abbey that night. When he came, there I was, waiting for him and wearing a blond wig. He was sickening. He'd sit there and babble about his great love for Lucy, how he was sorry for what he had done. But it was too late. Too late."

I said, "And when they came after Damon, you fled through the tunnel and back to the house. And between the two of you, you drove Damon Gerrick mad. Then it was very easy for Dr. Price to suggest he be put in Goodehouse, where he'd never get well." Revulsion welled up inside of me.

"Sir Mark was reluctant at first," Mrs. Meadows admitted. "He wanted to keep his brother at the Chase."

"But Dr. Sam kept working on him," Colin cut in. "I'll wager he kept telling him it was for Damon's own good."

Mrs. Meadows nodded. "He also convinced Amabel that it was Mark's idea to have his brother committed, that Mark was envious of her and Damon."

Outrage coursed through me. There needn't have been any discord between Mark and his sister, but because of Dr. Price, those two hated each other.

Suddenly Mrs. Meadows began to tremble. "But I never expected him to kill your husband." She stared at me. "There wasn't to be any killing!"

"Did you say the doctor killed Oliver?"

She jerked her head up and down. "He said he had to. Years ago, your husband was Sam's apprentice. He would have recognized him and given us away. So he had to be killed."

I leaned back in my chair, stunned. So the surgeon Oliver had once been apprenticed to was Samuel Lawton Price. Poor Oliver. My thoughts flew back to the day Oliver had arrived at Raven's Chase, when I had met the doctor on the landing. At the time, I hadn't given any thought to why he had made a hasty retreat to "examine Peter," and had never joined us for luncheon. He had seen and recognized his former student below in the foyer with Mark, and wanted to get away as quickly as possible before Oliver recognized *him*.

"How was that arranged?" Colin was in control again, holding this inquisition together.

The woman cleared her throat. "Sam forged likenesses of their handwriting and sent them both notes, each seemingly from the other, to meet at the ruins at midnight. I had no difficulty slipping the note under Mrs. Woburn's door, and Sam put the note under Woburn's door at the inn. That night, Woburn came to the abbey, looking for his wife. Sam hit him over the head and killed him. He had hoped to get both of you out there. Then you would have been accused of your husband's murder."

"But your plan didn't work," I said triumphantly. "I decided to ignore Oliver's note." Gradually, I could see the fate Dr. Lawton and his sister-in-law had planned for me. If I had gone out to the abbey, I could never have proved I hadn't killed Oliver. And I would have hung for a murder I didn't commit.

"I told Sam to watch out for you. You were dangerous with all your snooping and prying," Mrs. Meadows said.

Dangerous . . . prying and snooping. Those words touched off a responsive chord in my mind, and I recalled the day I had overheard the voices in the library discussing me. Mark hadn't called me dangerous, it had been the doctor and Mrs. Meadows. By the time I came into the library, they had left and Mark had entered.

Nora Woburn, you fool, I chided myself. And all this time, I had believed Mark had wanted to harm me.

Colin spoke. "With Damon out of the way, what were your plans for Amabel and Mark?"

"We planned to take her baby. We weren't going to harm Peter, just give him to a farmer."

"That's tantamount to murder!" I cried.

As Colin shot me a warning glance, Mrs. Meadows said, with astonishing naiveté, "He would have been all right. Someone would have adopted him. That would fix that spoiled little bitch."

She's mad, I said to myself. "But I found the baby-farm letter and spoiled your plans."

"It's regrettable Gerrick saw the stone falling that day at the abbey. We'd have been rid of both of you once and for all."

I was not surprised. "So even that was the doctor's doing." When Marianne Meadows smiled, I said, "Don't tell me. Let me guess. He loosened the stone with the intention of killing Mark eventually, and it was Mark he was aiming for that day. Then Sam ran into the cellars and out through the tunnel before Mark could get up the stairs to search for him." I recalled now how we had met the doctor on our way back to the house. He must have been coming from the black stone cottage.

"You were lucky," she agreed. "But I'll wager you never suspected Sam of poisoning Gerrick."

My hand flew to my mouth.

"I didn't think so," she said with her cool smile. "Sam would put it in Gerrick's wine, and I would wash his glass out later. He only tried it a few times lest Gerrick get suspicious."

I turned to Colin and told him about the night I had found Mark ill from a stomach complaint that he attributed to the recurrence of a tropical disease. "Shortly before we left for Plymouth, Mark kept having dizzy spells."

"So Sam advised him to get away from the Chase," Marianne Meadows said. "It was all part of the plan. Everyone thought I had gone to visit my ailing mother, but in reality I was hiding upstairs at Sam's house. You almost saw me at the window," she said to me, "but I stepped back in time."

"So you were the 'patient' I saw upstairs."

She stifled a little bubble of laughter. "When the three of you left for Plymouth, we waited until the day before you were supposed to come back, so the hue and cry wouldn't be raised. Sam and I went to the Chase, and I hid upstairs in one of the empty rooms. When Nellie's breakfast tray was left outside her door, I slipped the drops into her food. Then, when she was asleep, I took the child and a carriage to Plymouth. That's why no one saw me."

What a perfect, nearly foolproof plan, I thought to myself as we sat there, listening to the housekeeper unravel the whole evil scheme. No one had any reason to believe Mrs. Meadows was anywhere else but visiting her ailing mother. And when she went back to the Chase for the baby, if any of the other servants had seen her, she had merely to explain that she had returned early. As housekeeper, she knew Nellie's schedule, and she was also a familiar face to Peter, who of course would make no sounds when held by someone he knew. While Constable Tibbins scoured the Devon countryside, this woman and her precious charge were chugging toward London.

"Your scheme is over, Mrs. Meadows," Colin said quietly.

"Oh, no," she contradicted him, "not yet. Sam has Mark Gerrick to take care of yet. It's been almost a week since you left Devon. Gerrick is probably dead already."

My father and I sat across from each other on a train charging back to Devonshire. "Mark is dead. Mark is dead," the rails insisted as we sped along.

The hours following Marianne Meadows' confession were the longest I had ever endured. First, she had to be turned over to the police, while Colin and I faced a battery of questions and forms. Next came a mad race to my father's house, and after I hastily told him what had happened, he insisted on accompanying me while Colin made plans to follow later with Peter.

Nightfall slipped over us without warning on the train. I tried to sleep, but finally gave up. My father dozed fitfully, his hat covering his face as he snored in time to the gentle rocking of the train. I twisted my fingers together, knotting them like my thoughts of Mark.

Mark, I love you, I recited over and over in my mind, as though the words could form a shield of armor around him to keep Dr. Lawton at bay. I cursed myself for being so blind. Suddenly I was sobbing silently into my hand.

"Nora, girl," my father admonished me as he shook himself awake. "Tears aren't like you."

"I'm sorry to wake you."

"Worried about Mark, are you?"

I nodded, and cried afresh, while he leaned over and patted my hand. I had never seen his round, jovial face so serious and concerned.

"I've been such a fool, Father. I love Mark so much. I guess I've always loved him, but I was so afraid of being hurt again. Being away from him has made me realize how much I want him, how much I need him." I laughed. "Look at me, prattling on like a romantic schoolgirl. Nora Woburn, who always placed herself above such emotionalism."

"Love is nothing to be ashamed of," my father said.

"I know that now. Only now it may be too late."

"Let's hope that it's not too late."

When we finally reached Sheepstor, it was ten o'clock the next morning. After telling my father where to find Tibbins, I ran to the Headless Horseman and rented the fastest-looking horse they had, a bull headed roan with a wicked rolling eye.

To this day, I don't know how I got to Raven's Chase with all my bones intact. Riding that horse was like flying, and even though I rode astride, fear rode with me from the inn's cobbled courtyard until I pulled the exhausted creature up before the familiar lion's head knocker.

Sliding down in a flurry of skirts, I threw myself at the door, stumbled into the foyer, and started up the stairs.

Suddenly Amabel appeared on the landing. "Nora! What are you doing here? You're supposed to be in London."

"I haven't time to explain. Where is Mark?"

"What I want to know is, where is Colin? He dashed off about the same time you did, and—"

I grabbed her shoulders and shook her. "Amabel, where is Mark?"

"Why, in his study, with Sam."

"Oh, my God!" I flung her off and charged up the rest of the stairs, ignoring her petulant cry of, "Nora! What is going on?"

Please God, let him be alive, I prayed, as I ran down what seemed like miles of corridors. Finally I came to the study door. I burst into the room.

"Nora!" Mark exclaimed, while the doctor rose to his feet.

Before I had time to blink, the doctor lunged, grabbed my arm, and viciously pulled me against him. I felt something hard dig into the small of my back.

"Don't move, Gerrick," he said. "I have a gun sticking into Nora's spine."

"Sam's responsible for everything," I babbled. "Damon's madness, Peter's kidnapping—everything!"

"And I'll kill Nora here if you so much as breathe," he said to Mark, who looked like a wolf about to spring.

Mark's voice was soft and quiet. "You won't get very far, Sam."

"Far enough. Now, I want two fast, fresh horses saddled. I'm taking Nora with me, as a hostage, and if you try to follow me, so help me God, I'll blow her head off."

"He killed Oliver, too," I said. At this news, Mark's face turned white, but his eyes were cold and deadly, and his mouth set in a grim line.

The doctor dug the muzzle deeper into my back until I cried out. "Well, Gerrick? What's it to be?" he said.

Mark walked past us. "I'll get the horses."

"And don't try anything heroic," Dr. Lawton called after him. "Or I'll kill her, I swear."

The doctor, shielding himself with my body, followed Mark. On the way, we met Amabel.

"Mark, what is happening?"

"I'll explain later. Just go to your room. Please, Amabel."

I saw the old spark of rebellion in her flare, but I quelled it with, "Please do as Mark says, Amabel."

She gave me a questioning glance, but did as she was told.

"Splendid," Lawton murmured into my ear. "You're both cooperating beautifully."

Mark's hands clenched into fists at his sides. "If you hurt Nora, I'll kill you myself."

The doctor only laughed as we marched out of the house toward the stables. We had gone halfway when he stopped near some sheltering oak trees.

"All right. We'll wait here for the horses. Remember, Gerrick, no heroics. If anyone asks why you need two horses, tell them you and your sister are going riding. Choose those horses carefully, Gerrick," he added, "or you'll never see Nora alive."

Mark cast a venomous glance at the doctor, then turned toward the stables. He soon disappeared around a bend in the path.

"You're very clever, Nora," Lawton said, without releasing his grip on my arm for an instant. He was a strong man, for one so slight of build. "How did you know I was the one?"

"Colin Trelawney and I went to London to find Peter. I had a wild suspicion that a baby-farm letter I once found had something to do with Peter's disappearance. We found your sister-in-law and the baby in London. She told us everything."

"Very clever." There was a grudging admiration in his voice. "So that's where you two disappeared to all of a sudden. I should have guessed you'd think of that letter. I'm offended that Gerrick didn't take me into his confidence." Then he whistled. "I'm surprised at Marianne. She is such a cool one."

"She never would have told us anything, but Colin was most . . . persuasive. Now the police have her," I said. "So you see, you'll never get away."

"We'll see," was all he said.

We waited in silence. After what seemed like hours, we heard the muffled clopping of hooves, and Mark reappeared leading two sleek, fast-looking horses. My hopes plummeted when I saw that my slow, beloved Guinevere was not one of them.

"Good choice," the doctor said as Mark halted our horses. "I'm pleased to see you left Nora's usual mount behind. All right, Gerrick, now turn around."

Mark hesitated, glanced at me, then reluctantly did as he was told.

Before I could draw another breath, the doctor struck him on the back of the head with the pistol.

"Mark!" I started forward instinctively, as he crashed unconscious to the ground. He lay as still as death. "You've killed him!"

"I dearly hope so."

I tried to break away and go to Mark, but Lawton's cruel fingers bit into my arm as he restrained me.

"If you don't get on that horse, I will kill you, too." He flung me away so that I fell against the horse, causing it to start in alarm.

I struggled to scramble up on the horse always conscious of the deadly pistol trained on my back and Mark's lifeless form sprawled on the ground.

The doctor mounted without ever taking his eyes, or the gun, off me.

"All right. Let's get out of here, and fast."

As I urged my mount into a canter, I glanced back over my shoulder. Mark lay face down, one limp arm flung out. My heart constricted against my ribs. I prayed that someone would find him soon.

We rode onto the moor, but veered south, away from Raven's Chase. Lawton set the pace, a slow canter that would cover ground without tiring our horses. He rode slightly behind me, so he could keep me within range of his gun should I decide to do something foolish.

What was he going to do next? Lawton was a hunted man now. He needed to buy himself time, to put as much distance between himself and Devon as possible.

I kept my eyes straight ahead so I wouldn't have to speak to the man. Since he didn't seem particularly eager to converse with me—

except to bark directions now and then—we rode in silence. Out of the corner of my eye, I saw him glance over his shoulder once or twice to make sure we weren't being followed. Whenever we happened upon a cottage, we skirted it before the inhabitants could come to the door to investigate.

I was oblivious to the stark beauty of Dartmoor today, for I was concentrating on how I was going to save myself. The hopelessness of my situation brought futile tears to my eyes. I didn't want to die, not now, when Mark and I were on the verge of finding each other.

In retrospect, Lawton's plan now seemed so obvious, I berated myself for not suspecting him sooner. I recalled the day I had announced my discovery of Lucy Lawton's name in the Gerrick family Bible. Marianne Meadows had been so startled and shaken she dropped a dish, and the doctor appeared dreadfully pale. I had come so close . . . so close.

After an hour, our horses were lathered and on the verge of exhaustion. "If we don't slow down, they'll be dead," I said.

"All right. We'll walk them for a little while."

"Did you have to hit him?" I cried out suddenly.

The doctor looked across at me. "Of course I had to hit him. He could have gone back to the house or stables, gotten a gun, and shot me. Or followed us. No, Mark Gerrick is better off dead."

"Why did you do all those horrible things?" Although I knew why, I couldn't resist asking.

His mouth hardened into a thin, cruel line, and behind his spectacles, I knew his stare was merciless. "The Gerricks took all that I loved," he said simply and with great feeling. "And they thought their money would ensure that they got away with it. I couldn't let them go unpunished. Justice must be served, if not by the law, then by the people."

I shook my head. "It's all so pointless."

"Is it really? How do you feel about me, for instance? I have tried to kill Mark Gerrick. I may have succeeded, because I hit him very hard. Can you honestly say that you wouldn't shoot me if I gave you this gun? After I killed the man you love?"

When I didn't answer him, he laughed. "You see? Revenge is such a natural emotion."

"But to kill Oliver. . . . What did he ever do to you?"

"Woburn was a lazy, opportunistic fool. He would have done something to spoil my plan if he had recognized me. So, he had to be eliminated. And if I could get rid of you in the process, all well and good." Dr. Lawton stood up in his stirrups and scanned the horizon. "Come. We have a distance to go yet."

The horses, renewed from their walk, sprung to life. They were good mounts, and tireless. I wished they would throw a shoe, or a stirrup leather would break—anything to slow Lawton down.

We didn't stop until he topped a sloping incline. On the horizon, I could see treetops and houses huddled together against the cloudless azure sky. But between us and the village rolled a particularly treacherous stretch of moorland, dotted with clumps of marsh grasses that marked the bogs like signposts. I shivered.

Lawton smiled to himself as he gazed off into the distance, and my terror intensified. Panicky, I glanced around, searching the landscape for someone—a shepherd, farmer, or even a child—who might help me.

Far in the distance behind us, the black silhouette of a horse and rider was etched against the sky for a heartbeat. Then I blinked and they were gone.

Mark? I dared not hope. I turned my attention back to my captor, and hoped he wouldn't notice the surge of excitement that had brought color rushing to my cheeks.

"That's Cornwood," he informed me conversationally. "A train will stop there in a half hour, and I intend to be on it."

"Then you can let me go now," I said. "By the time I find my way back to the Chase, you'll be long gone."

He smiled benevolently as he shook his head. "Ah, Nora. So innocent and trusting as a child. I'm sorry, my dear, but that's not what I had planned for you."

I had to keep him talking, to give the rider time to reach us. "What do you have planned?"

"You don't really want to know that."

"Oh, but I do."

Was the rider getting closer, I wondered?

Lawton suddenly reached out, grabbed my horse's bridle near the bit and began leading it down the hill. I breathed a sigh of relief, for now the horseman was out of sight, hidden by the slope.

We stopped at the base of the hill, and the village, which had been visible from the summit, disappeared. In the bright sunlight, the mire looked innocent and almost inviting, for its surface shimmered with an incandescent glow. The aura enveloped me, numbing my mind and ruining all my hopes.

"I'm afraid this is where we part company, my dear," the doctor said. His voice was almost kind and regretful. "By the time this bog throws up your body, I'll be only a memory in Devonshire."

My fierce will to live suddenly galvanized my protesting limbs. I had no idea how I could save myself, but I resolved to fight for my life.

Acting instinctively, I jabbed my toe into my horse's soft belly, causing the animal to squeal and swing around, jostling Lawton's skittish mount.

"I admire your courage, but your situation is quite hopeless." He aimed the pistol at my heart.

At that moment, the thunder of hoofbeats came rumbling behind us, as a horseman charged down the hill.

"Mark!" I screamed.

It was all I needed. Lawton instinctively turned. As his attention left me for a half second, I swung my arm and felt it strike his face. Then I dug my heels into my horse's ribs and crouched low over his neck. Just as the animal bolted, a shot exploded in my ear. I felt something scorch my arm like a red-hot poker, but I managed to stay in the saddle as I rode toward Mark.

A second shot rang out, and I heard the bullet buzz by my ear like an angry wasp. Odalisque drew up beside me, and Mark, his face livid, shouted, "Get down, Nora!"

I did as I was told, half jumping, half sliding off my horse before the frightened animal could fully stop. As soon as my feet touched solid earth, I flung myself on my stomach and stared up at Mark through tears of relief.

He was holding a pistol, his arm extended as he took aim at the doctor. There was a cold and compassionless glint in his eyes that I prayed I would never see again. I squeezed my eyes shut, waiting for the shot. But it never came.

"Nora," Mark said, his voice strange. "Get up."

I rose to my feet, and saw why the shot had not been fired.

Dr. Lawton was on foot, whimpering with rage as he searched the grasses for something. He was oblivious to our presence as he patted the earth like a blind man, weaving to and fro, bellowing in frustration.

Suddenly he tripped and pitched forward. The earth shivered and half of the man disappeared.

"Gerrick!" Lawton's screaming of Mark's name as he realized he would not even live to hang will haunt my dreams for a lifetime.

Before the sound left the doctor's lips, Mark sent Odalisque charging down the hill, with me running after. But in the few seconds it took to reach the bogside, the mire had closed over Lawton's head, filling his lungs and sucking him down. We heard one final gurgling hiss, and then the surface was calm and composed again.

Mark dismounted and bent down to retrieve something in the grass. When I reached him, I saw what he held: Dr. Lawton's spectacles.

"You must have knocked them off when you hit him." Mark's face was ashen. "Sam was always half blind without them. That's why his shots went wild, thank God."

I shuddered and flung myself into Mark's arms.

"Don't feel too sorry for Sam," he murmured into my hair. "The hangman would've gotten him anyway." Then he held me at arm's length and scowled. "Nora, you've been shot!"

I looked down at my torn sleeve and was surprised to see a growing patch of red. "Oh, so I have. It doesn't hurt, Mark, really."

He examined my arm gently, careful not to hurt me. "You're lucky. The bullet just grazed your arm. Why did you bolt that way?" he growled as he took a clean handkerchief and bound up the wound. "You were right between us. You took ten years off my life."

My teeth began to chatter as my arm suddenly began to throb painfully. "He was getting ready to shoot me and throw me in—down there. I was trying to save myself."

He smiled down at me. "My brave darling."

And he kissed me soundly.

After a while, I reluctantly drew away. "How did you find us? I thought Sam had killed you."

Mark smiled. "This old head is harder than it looks. And anyway, Amabel was at her bedroom window and saw you and Sam riding off without me. She came down to investigate, found me lying in the grove, and revived me. I got Odalisque and began tracking you, hoping Sam wouldn't see me."

He reached for my waist and lifted me onto his horse. Then he swung up behind me, and encircled me with his arms. His lips were hard and demanding as he kissed me.

"Oh, Mark. I've believed such horrible things about you."

When I finished telling him about Oliver's accusation, he was incredulous. "And you've been tormenting yourself all this time, thinking I wanted to kill you?" His arm tightened around me and his voice became curiously tender. "My darling, why didn't you tell me?"

"I was afraid Oliver was telling the truth."

He sighed. "I really can't blame you for not trusting me. I must have seemed like an ogre to you, locking my brother away and tyrannizing my sister."

"Yes, you did," I admitted.

He lifted my chin with his fingers, and his cool gray eyes scanned my face. "I want to show you another Mark Gerrick, but I'm afraid it's going to take a lifetime."

I smiled. "Only a lifetime?"

He nodded. "Marry me, Nora?"

"As soon as we can find a minister to perform the ceremony."

"Golden-eyed witch. As much as I'd like to kiss you again, we have to get back to the Chase. Let's get the horses, and you can tell me all about Sam and Marianne on the way back." He kissed me again. "And you and I have other things to talk about as well."

Mark caught the other two horses, and prepared to lead them back to the Chase. I was loath to leave the shelter of his arms, for my wound had begun to ache again.

On the leisurely ride back, I told him all about London, and how the search for Peter had led Colin and me to Marianne Meadows, who had finally unfolded the whole sad tale of Dr. Samuel Lawton, his beloved daughter, and Damon. I also told him about Sam's plan of revenge, how he and Marianne had lured Damon out to the ruins to hammer away at the last remnants of his sanity.

When I mentioned the abbot's secret passage, Mark whistled in surprise. "The black stone cottage . . . So that's how the abbot got the three crowns out of the abbey. He could get away without being discovered, and he could even hide in the tunnel until King Henry's soldiers left. All the times we played there as children, and we never realized what we were standing on."

Mark flung back his head to stare at the sky. "All Damon's fault. Destroying lives and expecting someone else to pick up the pieces. How tragic. And how senseless. Five lives ruined. Damn his irresponsible behavior!"

I reached up to touch his cheek. "He's paid dearly. And he's not totally to blame."

"True," Mark agreed. "Sweet Mama and her Golden Gerricks, her utterly spoiled and selfish children. I'm glad she's not here to see what unhappy people her favorites have turned into."

I thought of Colin, at this minute on his way to Raven's Chase with his son. "Perhaps Amabel has a chance for happiness now with Colin."

"Yes, but will she take it this time?"

"I think so. I think she's realized you can't live in the past forever.

With Colin and Peter, she can begin to live her own life, whether here or in Australia."

We rode in silence, each caught up in our own thoughts. Finally, Mark said, "I can't believe my father was so callous about Sam's daughter."

"I think Damon's behavior hurt him deeply. We'll never know what passed between your father and Damon unless he tells us someday, but I think that in your father's mind, Damon and Lucy were married as surely as if a ceremony had been performed. That's why he put her name in the Bible. And when Damon came home from India half out of his mind, your father saw it as the Lord's justice."

Mark looked grave. "His health did deteriorate." A wicked gleam crept into his eyes. "And you don't believe I pushed him down the stairs? Peter's old nurse found Father at the foot of the stairs, with me at the top, staring down at his body. I was in shock, of course, but she told everyone who'd listen that I had killed my own father."

"I know."

He stared at me in surprise. "Who told you?"

"Nellie. And I never believed it for an instant."

His arm tightened around me in an appreciative squeeze.

I looked up at him. "Mark, what's to become of Damon? Now that we know he's not really mad?"

"Take him out of Goodehouse as fast as we can and bring him home, to Raven's Chase. It's the least I can do, after all I've done to him. We may have to watch him carefully, but I think we can help him. You won't mind him living with us?"

"Do you even have to ask me such a question?"

He smiled and kissed the top of my head.

Soon, our weary procession filed up a steep hill, and Raven's Chase came into view. Mark halted Odalisque at the top, so we could gaze across the valley.

Home. It looked splendid and shining in the bright afternoon light. There was nothing foreboding about it now. In fact, it looked most inviting. A fierce knot of hope burned in my heart. If I were a gypsy, I would foresee a bright future for the house. Amabel and Colin would marry, and Damon would one day be whole. My father would create masterpieces once again. And Mark and I? I smiled to myself.

Mark said, "You know, Nora, I never suspected Sam for an instant. I trusted him completely. I really believed he had Damon's best interests at heart when he suggested I commit him to Goodehouse. I was ready to believe Dennis Standish was responsible for all the 'accidents.'"

"We all had our blind spots, and the good doctor skillfully played on all our weaknesses. Yours was Dennis, you were Amabel's, and I was so jealous of Jane Standish I couldn't see or think straight."

Mark grinned. "Oh, were you now?"

"Yes. Every time I thought of the two of you in your bedroom—" I caught myself and blushed furiously.

I heard Mark's sharp intake of breath. "Nora, you make it damned hard for a man to keep his head."

"You'll have to," I teased. "At least until we're married. And then you can lose your head to your heart's content, my darling."